STOLEN DAYS

R.K. HIGGINS

Copyright © 2022 by R.K. Higgins

All rights reserved.

No portion of this book may be reproduced in any form without written permission from the publisher or author, except as permitted by U.S. copyright law. This is a work of fiction. Names, characters, businesses, places, events, locals, are all a product of the author's imagination. Any resemblance of the characters within to actual persons, living, or dead is purely coincidental.

I dedicate this book to anyone who has overcome the sting of this thing we call life.

Contents

1. Prologue — 1
2. 1 — 7
3. 2 — 17
4. 3 — 25
5. 4 — 35
6. 5 — 51
7. 6 — 63
8. 7 — 73
9. 8 — 79
10. 9 — 89
11. 10 — 99
12. 11 — 107
13. 12 — 115
14. 13 — 131
15. 14 — 139
16. 15 — 149
17. 16 — 155

18.	17	165
19.	18	175
20.	19	183
21.	20	191
22.	21	197
23.	22	201
24.	23	205
25.	24	209
26.	25	217
27.	26	227
28.	27	231
29.	Epilogue	241

Prologue

As she often did, she watched crowds go about their daily rituals. Lately, she was not amused with the monotony of her existence. She looked down at her watch and saw that yet again, a soul was to be harvested.

On this day, she had been particularly insubordinate in her duties. She'd disregarded all notifications from her death-watch and let those she was to collect go on living for quite a while. She wondered what would become of her, what would become of them. Would there be a punishment for such disobedience? She didn't care.

Celia had grown tired of late, even bored of collecting the dead. She had done it for over a century, and if Lucifer or one of his commanders offered her this "exciting" promotion again, she would have told them to keep it. Instead, Celia sought out an old friend. Someone she hadn't seen in decades...

"Let me get this straight? You missed the last four harvests?"
"Yes."
"Celia! I don't even know what would become of me if I did something like that!"
"I don't really care, Rubella. Haven't you ever looked around at all these mortals and thought — fuck, they live so

decadently. Most of them seem completely unaware of their mortality." Celia looked down from her perch at them. Her gray and dark demonic lips scowled with contempt, and that worried Rubella. Celia continued.

"They experience pleasures they don't deserve. Wouldn't it be nice to experience those pleasures, those mortal senses, just once?"

"Celia, I'm just grateful to have a job on the Earth and not one lingering about in Hell. When did you become so bitter anyway?"

There was silence between the pair for a moment as they stood atop Toronto's CN Tower on a clear late summer's day. They watched the mortals below as though they were their ruling deities.

"Look at them, Rubella, working so hard to attain their next pleasure from life. They don't deserve any of it. If I was among them, I'd take it all in freely, and I'd never take it for granted. When you accepted this position, did you imagine you would live to move only to your next reaping?"

"It's better than working below," answered Rubella.

"Is it, though, really? I don't even have time to think between the amount of people dying in this huge friggin' city. Let alone all the rushing around, trying to harvest their souls."

"Listen, Celia. We've been friends since Lucifer appointed us these posts together. As your friend, I'll cover your few missed reaping's, but you have to get your shit together, girl."

"I *have* gotten it together."

"I don't know about that. I wouldn't call missing the reaping of four souls in a day together, would you? That's a pretty busy day."

Celia looked down on the wondrous living city they called Toronto and smiled. "I know what I want."

"And what is that?"

"I've been watching someone for quite a few months, a man."

"And?"

"He's at death's door. I'm going to experience some form of joy, just once in this so-called existence of servitude."

"I don't like the sound of that, Celia."

Celia smirked. "I do."

Celia eyed her death-watch for the first time in a while. She'd ignored so much without consequence as of late. It was indeed Rubella messaging her, along with a slew of other missed messages.

Celia, I can't cover for you anymore. There are people alive that should have died already, and I can't keep up with it all. Malgore is asking about you... He said he'll find you one way or another. I know he has a soft spot for you, but be careful, Celia.

Rubella

Celia flicked to the next message: *Celia — you know who this is. Meet me tonight in the Distillery District. I will find you no matter the form you materialize in. Don't do anything foolish either; you've already caused me enough trouble.*

Malgore

Celia smiled and walked on into the wintery night over to Toronto's Distillery District. It seemed hilarious to her how she'd shirked her duties for so long. Malgore had seemed firm in tone in his letter, but she wondered just how mad he would be.

Tourists and residents of the Distillery District took in the annual Christmas Market. Golden lights glowed above her; the market was a thing of beauty. Steam from the hot drinks of passing people danced in the night, and Celia was envious; she didn't have mortal taste, touch, or even smell. She walked the red-brick walkways, looking around in wonder. She smiled at a white-haired man with a matching twirled mustache.

He wore a long black overcoat and sat at a bench on the outskirts of the market, alone. She knew it was Malgore. He always materialized in the same form. Over the years it was always a white-haired Englishman in his early sixties, a handsome man of sophistication who seemed to see right through Celia as she drew nearer. He waved her over from afar. Celia passed coffee booths and pretzel stands. Food was something she'd always desired to try. Mortal pleasures taken for granted, she thought, and shook her head.

"Sit, Celia," said Malgore.

"What am I, a lapdog?"

"SIT."

Celia took a seat beside Malgore.

"You know why you're not back down below, cleaning scum from a mortal fear pit?"

"No."

"Because I had Rubella, Netoxia, and Mucidious reap your souls these past months."

"I needed a break, okay? I didn't want to upset Luc..."

"HUSH," interrupted Malgore.

"Why, afraid Luci..."

Malgore waved his hand, and with that Celia's voice was gone.

"Are you going to mention who I think you're going to, or do you want to speak again?"

Celia shook her head regretfully and found her voice restored.

"And yes, I am afraid of what might happen if he found out I couldn't control my own flock."

"I will return to my post," Celia said.

"You're right, you will. Your little vacation is over starting with this pissant tomorrow night. I have no one to cover for you this time, Celia, and after you harvest this last soul — you will come back to me for reassignment."

"Reassignment?"

"No deed goes unpunished. You will be reassigned, and I will go down as a demon of authority who did not tolerate insubordination."

Celia looked down at her death-watch. She smirked faintly at the irony of it all. The very man she'd been watching from afar. It was indeed his time to die — on New Year's Eve.

1

New Year's Eve cheers filled neon-lit streets as Billy Walker buried his sorrows in the corner of an all too familiar tavern.

Sarah, a waitress that knew him only in his recent and darker times, came over. She was a kind soul. She had gotten to know Billy quite well in these past months, and because of that she could read him fairly well. If he kept his head down when she came over, she knew he wanted to be left alone. This evening was one such occasion.

"Another one, Billy?"

His eyes focused on the grain of the old oak table. A subtle nod let Sarah know that yes, he would take another old-fashioned. Sarah gently placed Billy's drink down in front of him. She left to tend to another table, and Billy looked up from his trance just long enough to hear the countdown televised from downtown Toronto. People in the bar blew noisemakers and celebrated, couples kissed, and Billy's eyes glistened; he was reminded of the past he was trying to drown. The last of his drink was sipped away, and he left a tip for Sarah. He looked past the patrons to the polished brass exit doors and shambled out from The Saucy Blokes Tavern, taking out his phone. Billy looked at it. Only a single text from his parents:

Happy New Year sweetie! This next year will turn around for you, we know it!

They were the only ones who hadn't truly forgotten about him in these dark times. It wasn't much help for him, though; they lived across the country, and he was at his breaking point alone. In reflections that he'd drunk to escape, he walked, making fresh tracks on snow-touched sidewalks. Billy slipped his phone back into his pocket. This year had been trampled by disappointments that he could not escape. Accompanying those disappointments had been the decree to drink himself senseless, and at least he'd accomplished that.

Billy had hit thirty last summer, and after his birthday, his life had spiraled downward.

He thought back to the catalyst that began that spiral...

• • • ● ● • ● • • •

"Dr. MacNeilson will see you now," said the secretary at Billy's doctor's office.

Billy took a seat and waited in the worn wooden chair next to his doctor's examination table. He wouldn't need an exam; he'd already been through a slew of those. Today he would find out the results of his blood work. The first thing Billy had noticed was a general lack of energy, but what really had concerned him was the night sweats. He woke up quite often to a cold sweat. It was his fiancée, Tina, who had convinced him after the third night of interrupted sleep to see their doctor.

Dr. MacNeilson was an older and bald man. He usually wore a kind smile, and he was patient as he spoke. A slight East Coast accent lingered in his voice; he was originally from Newfoundland. He sat calmly across from Billy and opened a folder, then he hummed and hawed for a moment and looked up through his silver-rimmed bifocals.

"Billy, how are we feeling today, son?"

"I've been sleeping better lately and changed my diet a little."

It didn't matter what Billy said. He could see the expression on the doctor's face, and he knew it wasn't good. Concern grew in the man's eyes, and his lips revealed a frown that suggested bad news was inevitable.

"It's the white blood cell count, Billy. It's alarmingly low."

Billy stared into his lap and sighed. "Cancer?"

"Yes."

"Fuck."

It was a Monday like any other, except for Billy. It was noon, and he had no appetite for lunch as he sat at his computer, droning on. Lines of code that normally seemed automatic seemed to be a chore for him. He had zoned out so badly that at one point the screen went to sleep. He still remembered looking at his reflection in the darkness of the monitor. Red hair normally combed to the side now messy from his hand holding his forehead. His normally bright blue eyes seemed dim and exhausted. He remembered his counterpart, Angela, walking over to him that day.

"Billy, you look like hell. Are you alright?"

"I'll be fine, Angela. I just need to finish this last line of code," Billy responded.

He wasn't fine at all. His head was a spinning mess, and the simple lines of code he should have finished an hour ago seemed endless. He hadn't told his coworkers at the Bay Street office building about the private battle he'd been fighting. Angela had been his peer for so many years, and by now he knew she could read him too well. Billy had gotten her the job when his friend Doug, with whom he played rec league hockey, told him his wife was looking for a job in network security. Billy could tell she knew something had been going on with him the past while, and today it was manifesting worse than before. Angela sat down beside him.

"Billy, what's going on with you? You haven't been yourself around here lately. Even Doug has noticed you haven't hit the ice in over a month."

Billy sighed. He was a private person, even with those who were close to him. He knew there was no use in trying to hide it from Angela or Doug anymore.

"It's cancer. Doctor said it's spread like a wildfire."

Billy had never seen Angela cry before, but her eyes welled up, and she hugged him. When they separated, it was Billy that handed Angela a tissue. He wasn't going to relive the diagnosis; he'd come to terms with it already. There was silence between them for a minute. Billy thought perhaps Angela didn't know what to say, but then she spoke.

"I can finish this. Just go home for me, please... Go home and be with Tina."

Billy wasn't the type of person not to finish something he'd started, but on this day, he had no problem with it. He popped a few pills, took a swig from the water cooler to wash them down, and left. He remembered the elevator ride down when he'd decided that he'd been working far too hard lately for someone fighting this illness in secret.

Now, on his drunken New Year's walk, he remembered how he'd fought the battle alone for the most part. In his self-reflection, he realized that had been a weakness, not a strength.

Billy thought back to that day again when he came home from work early. He'd opened the white door to their condo. His fiancée, Tina, was home for some reason that day, and he was surprised. They had been fighting lately. Fighting about Billy's cancer. He'd been an asshole about it. He'd been so distant with Tina, and he knew it. She had told him last week that the stress of it all was piling up too much, and she didn't know if she could take anymore.

Billy took off his shoes and noticed something odd as he stood in the front entrance. Another sizable pair of runners were beside his own. He was confused for a moment.

He heard rhythmic music coming from their bedroom and walked slowly toward the slightly open door. Through the crack he stared infidelity in the face. Tina, in a reverse cowgirl, slid carelessly, repetitiously, over another man's member.

Billy's illness didn't really matter in the heat of this moment. The glorious and familiar feeling of adrenaline coursed through him again. Much like in one of his rec-league hockey games, it took over, and he reacted accordingly, kicking open the bedroom door.

"Motherfucker!" Billy yelled. Tina leapt off to the side between their queen-size bed and the wall. The man, who Billy had immediately sized up and recognized as the building's delivery man, stood erect, amongst other things. He put his hands in front of himself. "Take it easy," he said, but underneath those words was a smug grin. The man backed up to reach for his uniform splayed across the bedroom floor.

Blinding rage took over after that, and the rest was a blur of red and mayhem in Billy's mind. Billy did remember Tina in her blue silk house coat trying to pull him off the deliveryman.

Now, as Billy walked drunkenly in the streets, he kept thinking back to how that scumbag used to say hello to him when they passed in the building. All the while, he'd been eyeing Tina and had pounced at the first hint of vulnerability. For that, he made the man's face a bruised mess. That afternoon still flashed through Billy's mind. No matter the amount of booze he'd consumed this evening, there was no drowning the memory. Pride had taken over that day when he'd seen it all. Billy still remembered the stinging in his fists from that day. As much as he tried to forget it, he lived with pain and regret.

A brief incarceration had led him to the loss of his programming and network security job. It also had showed him who his real friends were. One by one, they turned their backs on him, and from that a way to kill the pain was born.

As it turned out, though, spending your time drinking was an expensive habit. Now unzipped, Billy stood in the dimness of a midnight alley and pissed away the last of his twenty. He was truly piss-poor. He wandered down the freshly snowed sidewalks of Toronto, passing a few tiddly New Year's well-wishers. In his shambling, he'd ignored their greetings. He had only one thing on his mind at the moment — well, two things. He had no one in his life who loved him, and he was going to end it all tonight. It was the sting of heartache he carried with him as he lumbered through snow in the Toronto winter night. He drew nearer to his destination and thought again about what had gotten him to this exact point...

Drinking alone tonight, on the brink of a new year, he'd realized that dying on his terms was the best choice he had. He wouldn't be a burden in his last days, immobilized in a dependent existence at the hands of a caretaker or nurse. No, he was going to find a way out on his own. His feet dragged as he made his way to a park he and Tina had frequented on walks.

He didn't care for those memories. As he brushed past the pretty, snow-hugged trees, still wrapped with holiday cheer, the bulbs flickered. Oddly, they flickered. Then, one by one, even the street lights dimmed as he walked by. He didn't think much of the electrical disturbance; instead, he found himself where he'd planned to be. Billy was at a bridge. He leaned against steel handrails and looked ahead. They were the very guardrails he use to stand at in thought and contemplation during better days. He looked up to the stars, and for the first time in a while, he prayed.

Billy had been a Catholic all his life, but through the drudgery of existence, he'd somehow set aside his faith. It had lived in the back of his mind for so long. Now, it was at the helm. He prayed with his eyes to the stars, "Forgive me for all of this, the past and the future. My misery is too great to heal this broken heart, and this is all I know to do."

Here, he felt, was the perfect spot to say goodbye. If he wasn't killed by the passing train that came in the night, he'd be killed by the impact of the fall.

Intently he listened and intently he waited. First came the distinct sound of a chug in the distance accompanied by box cars clacking along tracks. He peered down at evergreens along the tracks as the lights of opportunity shone through and captivated his pupils.

A deep breath in. His left foot lifted, resting on the first steel rail of the three-rung railing. It wouldn't be long now. A quiet contentment filled him as he realized it was all ending. With the train's fast approach, he wouldn't know what hit him. Soon, there would be peace. He smiled, closing his eyes, thinking of nothingness. A tear trickled down his left cheek as his grasp closed around the railing.

"That end will be more traumatic for the conductor than it will for you, Billy," he heard a feminine voice say.

"What?" he said, opening his eyes.

"I said, what you intend to do is selfish. That poor conductor will never be able to work again."

"The fuck you know about selfish!" Billy slurred as he was caught off guard.

"Oh, by now I think I know a little."

Billy gripped the railing tighter; he was doing this. The train was seconds out, and he didn't care what this woman in the shadows had to say. His mind was on the swift lights of death's approach.

The woman had different plans. She started to count. "Ten!" she belted out, approaching from the shadows.

Stunned, he looked at her, wide-eyed.

"Nine!" she blasted and moved closer.

"Eight!"

"Seven!"

"Six!"

"Five!" She was almost within arm's reach of him. As she got to three, Billy shook in fear.

"Who are you! How do you know my name!" he demanded.

Her soft, cold hand guided Billy away from the railing. "In your heart, Billy, you've already done this. You already ended your life; I can feel it. I too have a choice to make, and I think you can help me."

Billy tried to sober his thoughts. He looked into the eyes of the woman. They seemed to swirl about like stars in the Milky Way. He thought it was the booze. "Who...who are you?" he fumbled.

"I have brought you from the brink. You would have been my last harvest."

"What?"

"I am here for you Billy. I collect the dead."

Billy laughed. "You're crazy!" he said, stumbling down the concrete pathway away from the bridge. He mumbled, mocking her, "I'm death. *Hah!*"

He laughed again and continued on his way, thinking about the encounter. Fairy tales, he told himself; like Santa Claus in the damn sky. Why would death stop a death? He chuckled again, stumbling about.

In the moonlit night of the new year, death had come for him, even if he didn't want to believe it. Somehow, she stood in front of him again. He hadn't taken in her features much before, just her mesmerizing eyes. Her long, dark gray wool overcoat with hood had kept her concealed. She pulled it back and let her dark, wavy, shoulder-length locks out. She was young, twenties perhaps.

Her eyes met his again. "I'm not an omnipresent Santa Claus, Billy," she said with a smirk. "More of a reaper of the dead. I can't catch you all as you die. Ten in a week is reasonable, I suppose. There are plenty of us around to do the work."

"I don't have time for crazy, okay? Thanks for stoppin' me and that's all, I guess..."

"No Billy, that's not all." She stepped closer. "I will be back to take you away in a few months."

"Fuck off!" Billy snapped back.

The girl looked up at the moon, her skin shimmering in the moonlight. Slowly, her features shifted from pleasing to something more frightening.

Her plump red lips and those hypnotizing eyes were absent now as Billy watched. The supernatural glow of an ancient skull with empty eye sockets rapidly palpitated his heart.

"Your time is up, Billy, and I propose we try something... Different. I can help you stay in this place."

"How?" Billy squeaked as her false youth and feminine beauty returned.

"I will bind myself to you. And you will steal time. You will steal days, weeks, and months from the lives of those that walk among us, and together we will live."

"I'm listening."

"I will give you my scythe. With it you will take time for us, and together we will have...fun, sound good? I mean, it has to be better than what you were planning..."

Billy thought for a moment. As best as his drunken state would allow, he said, "And what if I refuse?"

"You say no — you die. If that happens, then I'll be taken to a place I'd rather not be. Lets call it head office. If this works, then I won't have to worry about being taken back by the Grim Collectors, and you don't have to worry about your illness. So, do we have a deal?"

Billy walked over to a nearby bench and sat down. "How much extra time can I get?" he slurred.

"I don't know. Likely, more than you've got now, that much is certain. All you need to know is that I like being here and I intend to stay."

"Alright."

"Then we have a deal!"

"Yeah, a deal," Billy slurred again.

Astonishingly, the reaper flicked her wrist and held a scythe that materialized in an aura of smoke and vapor. "Open your palm," she commanded.

Billy reached out. With a grin, she pierced his right palm with the tip of her scythe blade. Like the crescent moon above them, it glowed. How it burned as it touched Billy's hand. He cursed as blood pooled in his palm. Then, quickly, it cauterized, and the mark of a black scythe was left. "You see that mark?"

"Yeah."

"You know what that means?"

"No?"

The reaper girl laughed. "It means you're my bitch."

"*What?*"

"Relax, Billy. It means my timeline is fused with your mortality. As you take time from people, days will be added to your life. In turn, I will stay here, with you. Now go home to your shit-hole apartment, Billy. It's going to be a big day for you tomorrow."

As she walked into the darkness of the surrounding foliage, Billy hollered, "How will I know where to find you!"

With her piece said, she was gone as mysteriously as she came, and Billy wasn't sure if any of it had even really happened.

2

The tickle of something on Billy's cheek woke him from his drooling slumber. He swatted at himself and opened a blurred eye. Another damn cockroach flew across the room. He'd blown through so much of his money in these last days that he knew he didn't have enough left for rent. He hadn't cared. Up until today, an exit plan had been in place. The truth of the matter was that after he was released on bail, he'd had *those thoughts.* Last night, after his obnoxious tavern exit, he thought it was going to happen.

What the hell did happen exactly? He sat up and found he was still a bit queasy from last night. Billy grabbed a blue sports drink from the fridge and took a couple extra-strength pills for his nausea and headache. The bed creaked as he sat back down and rocked gently, wrapped in a blanket at its edge. He would will away the nausea, as he had many times before. Slowly, he leaned back onto the bed and closed his eyes. Moments later, as he had calmed his stomach, someone rapped on the door, disturbing his brief peace. *Slam! Slam! Slam!*

"WHAT!" he responded.

"Where is your rent! You are a useless tenant, just like the roaches!"

"You'll get it Mr. Kowalski. Give me 'til the end of the week!"

"Bullshit, it was due weeks ago!"

"You'll get your money. Fuck!" Billy yelled again.

The truth was, the rent wasn't even worth the place, but in this crowded city, and with his past, that was what he'd found. There were roaches and even bedbugs in some units. Drug addicts passed out occasionally in the stairwells. Billy hated it, but after his release, he hadn't exactly bounced back.

Mr. Kowalski was a prick who worked for an even bigger prick, Devlin Gainsmore. Gainsmore owned so many properties in this city, you'd be hard pressed not to pass one on a drive through. Billy had heard in working near Gainsmore's office building on Bay Street that the word was crooked foreign investors cleaned their money through Gainsmore. They apparently didn't give a shit how he returned their money, even if it was through a slum like the building Billy was in. Kowalski only cared about collecting the rent from the four slum properties he oversaw. If a problem arose, it was always quickly cast aside by Devlin, who gave even less of a shit about these properties. The irony was Billy remembered that when he had coded for a major financial institution, he'd been a fly on the wall during a meeting between his employers and Devlin Gainsmore.

Billy remembered the man ignoring them with his face buried in his laptop. He was the perfect simile for a marshmallow, all of 5'5" with an accent Billy couldn't pinpoint and a strawberry nose rumored to be from years of alcohol abuse.

Billy remembered peering over his computer when he'd heard voices rise. Devlin had spoken so arrogantly to Billy's employers that day.

He'd turned his laptop around and started playing a porn movie disrespectfully as they tried to speak to him. Billy remembered he'd said, "You think I care what you have to say to me? Get the fucking transfer done, or I'll sue."

Billy never did hear what exactly that was all about, but he'd made assumptions. At the end of the day, he'd just cared about keeping firewalls up and systems running smoothly. All he wanted now was to drink away his last days. He rubbed his right hand and immediately was reminded of last night. He remembered an attractive little brunette talking him out of his permanent solution.

Then he remembered the skull in the moonlight. He looked down at his right palm, nothing. He smiled. He'd never been so drunk that he blacked out and imagined something like that. How he'd gotten home last night, he did not know.

Billy stood up, stripping off the clothes he'd worn out last night and then crashed in. He had a moment of solace when hot water hit his skin. He thought about last night and wished that it had been real. A second chance at life, perhaps, he thought. As he scrubbed his nether regions, Billy saw a shadow in his peripheral vision.

Then a voice. "I'm glad you feel that way, because your landlord is the first asshole that we're going to rip time from."

Startled, Billy dropped the soap. "*Fuck!*"

"Relax. Hey, Billy, you think I look better in purple or cherry red?"

When Billy peered out from behind the curtain, it was indeed the brunette from last night. She had put on a royal shade of purple lipstick while taking in her beauty in the bathroom mirror.

"How'd you get in here? Get the fuck out of here!"

"C'mon, Billy. Do we really have to go through this again?"

"That's' it. I'm calling the cops," Billy threatened with his soaked face peering out from the shower curtain.

"Hah, not like that you're not."

Angrily, the taps were turned off and Billy protested, "Gimme some fuckin' privacy, will you!"

"Why? Ashamed of something?"

He cursed under his breath and reached for a towel while the petite brunette jumped up and sat on his bathroom counter. She smirked. "I've seen bigger, but not bad, Billy."

He walked out furiously from the bathroom, toweling off in his bedroom rather hastily. Billy stepped into his boxers and jeans and slid on a t-shirt from his bedroom floor.

The brunette knocked gently at his bedroom door. He looked down at his right palm, feeling a tingle, the black scythe mark — it was real. This time, it glowed softly. A yellow light around the mark's edges highlighted it.

"Come in then," Billy said, mesmerized by the mark.

The girl entered, standing in his bedroom doorway for the moment. "You made a deal with me, remember? We are tied together; I need you and you me."

Billy remembered. He agreed to steal time, days, even weeks more from people. *Can I really steal people's days?* he thought as he looked at the mark again. "What am I supposed to do now?"

The brunette smiled. "You want to live?"

"Yes."

"Your landlord is on another reaper's radar. Soon, I think he is going to die. He's not a healthy man, so what is a few weeks? A second chance at life for the mere theft of a few days that he doesn't need. Yes, you can do it, Billy."

"*What?* You can read my thoughts?" Billy wondered exactly how she knew what he was thinking.

"Yes."

"Swell." Billy shook his head. "And how did you get in here?"

"I walked through the door."

"It was locked!"

"Right, that's why I walked *through* the door — dumbass," she said, putting her hand through the dresser in his room.

"A second ago, you were putting lipstick on in the bathroom," Billy questioned. He was a little puzzled and even freaked out. The girl could tell.

"If I desire to, I can materialize."

"Must be nice. Wish I could zip around through shit all day."

"It isn't as amazing as you might think. So here is what we'll do. We are going to test my theory, okay?"

"And what is that?"

"When I marked you with my scythe, I didn't know what would happen entirely. You could have died, but you didn't have anything to lose at that point."

"Gee, thanks." Billy thought about it; she had a point. He had literally been teetering on the edge when she found him.

"So, anyway, I wasn't sure if the scythe would kill you or what. I did have a theory, though, and it turns out that I was right. To reap a soul, we always dig into the chest through the heart. I just cut you ever so gently on the palm, and look what happened! I willed you to have my scythe!"

"So, you're saying you took a gamble? You had no idea what would happen to me?"

"Yeah, fun, right!"

Billy shook his head. He'd found out what happens after death. He would have been collected by a bubbly, air-headed valley girl reaper.

Now he'd been branded as her "bitch," as she'd put it, and he'd somehow, drunkenly, placed his trust in her. Billy ran his palm down his face.

"Do you have a plan, or am I going back to that bridge tonight?"

"Don't worry, Billy, I'm not going back to head office. I so have a plan! Try summoning the scythe in your hand."

"How?"

"Visualize it, feel the wood."

"Feel the wood?"

"Yeah, feel that hard shaft in your hand, Billy," she said, grinning.

Billy shook his head. "Are you kidding me?"

"What? The shaft, Billy, the shaft. Caress it in your palm."

Billy concentrated, closing his eyes and imagining how the wooden shaft of the scythe felt. He remembered its glow in her hands last night. To his astonishment, the feeling of old, twisting wood grasped in his hands was there when his eyes opened. The shimmering crescent moon blade and twisted wooden shaft. Billy couldn't help but feel a grin creep up, and his new accomplice saw it.

"Ah-ha! Bad ass! Am I right?"

"Yeah. You're damn right," agreed Billy, smiling at the shimmering weapon.

"Now whatcha gonna do with your big stick, Billy?" she said, biting her lip while she slid off the sink counter and winked at him.

Billy took in the beauty of the blade. Its natural moonlit glow held his gaze. He thought about the reaper's question, then he answered, "I'm going to live."

"You're right — you are." The reaper girl smirked then crossed her fishnet-covered legs and sat down in a small navy-blue armchair across from Billy.

"How does it work? How do I use this?"

"Normally I'd say stab someone in the chest with it. This is not what we are trying to do, though, not this time, anyway. I'd say let's just tap people on the back a bit."

"Okay?"

"No one can see me or the scythe, understand? Not unless I will them to. So, don't worry about holding the thing. Easiest thing to do, I would say, is wait until you're behind someone. Just like I saw it do last night with you, the scythe will likely feel their life force — it will glow more and more. We'll do a three-count for our first drain and see where that gets us time-wise. Sound good?"

"It sounds simple enough."

"So, we will test it on your landlord. What's that doughboy's name again?"

"Mr. Kowalski? I don't think he will talk to me unless I have his rent. Besides, I don't even know where he is."

"He's on the third floor, collecting rent from the lady above you. All you need to do is get close and let the scythe do its work."

Billy smiled. "I don't even know your name. How can I even trust you, and how can you trust me? I mean, this all seems surreal."

"It's Celia, and like I said, Billy, we need each other. I couldn't just let you jump into that train last night."

"So, what, you collect the dead and now you wanna help one. Why the change of heart?"

"I saw you there all helpless and felt terrible for you... Besides, I don't want to go back below for reassignment. I don't enjoy that. I like people, and up here I get to keep up on the latest fashions." She smacked her lips together with a different shade of color.

"Seriously? The latest fashions?"

"What? You have a problem with a girl who likes to look nice? Maybe that's why you're single, Billy."

"I don't have a problem with it."

"Relax, I'm just messing with you. When you're ready, I think we have some time to steal," Celia said with a flirtatious wink.

Billy grabbed his thick black hoodie from a hook beside his apartment door. He looked over at Celia, leaning in his bedroom doorway, and she nodded.

"Do as I said and all will be well. I'm going to wait here so I won't be seen."

"Seen by who?"

"Not who, Billy, but what. Don't worry, they don't bother with the living; you'll be fine."

Billy nodded, and he was off.

One, two, flights up and he was already winded. He had felt a decline of his strength recently, and it was becoming clear his diagnosis was catching up with him.

When he opened the door to the dingy stained hallway, he saw Mr. Kowalski angrily talking with his neighbor. As the door shut, Kowalski took notice of Billy.

"My rent! You've come to give the rent?"

"No, I don't have it yet. I've come to tell you I can ge..."

The tanned, portly man burst past Billy with an elbow, interrupting his words. "Fuck off then. You keep it up with the rent, you can go sleep under the bridges with the meth addicts."

Kowalski's back was turned, and now was the time. Billy's heart raced. He thought of the wooden shaft and the mesmerizing moonlit blade, but he hesitated. Then, just like that, before he knew what had happened, he felt a thrusting motion. The scythe seemed so weightless in his hands. He hadn't realized it would sink in with such ease; he hadn't even tried to move it. There in the third-floor hallway, Billy watched his landlord fall on his knees. His body slammed down against the piss-riddled carpeting he'd been asked to replace by the tenants months ago. Billy stood in shock for a moment. His landlord's fat carcass had flopped down, sprawled out in front of him. Billy gasped, and Celia's head popped through the closed fire door at the end of the hallway. She was wide-eyed, with hot pink lipstick on now.

"What did you do, Billy! *FUCK!* I said tap him on the back!"

"I...he..."

The sound of his neighbor Ms. Bonstein's door creaking open startled him. Rather than walk, Celia drifted over to Billy, hovering by him for the moment in her ethereal form. She spoke quickly, looking him in the eyes. "Mr. Kowalski has suffered a heart attack. Call an ambulance. *SAY IT NOW BILLY.*" she firmly commanded.

Billy was breathing heavily, but he gathered himself. He turned to Ms. Bonstein in her worn burgundy housecoat and repeated Celia's words verbatim. The old lady didn't rush. She shuffled back inside her unit with pink velvet slippers on. Then, moments later, she emerged with her cordless phone in hand. Calmly, she asked for an ambulance.

3

Police and paramedics flooded the three-story walk-up's hallway. Billy stood back with Celia in wait. He'd done it: he'd killed his miserable landlord. The paramedics' defibrillators bounced the landlord's man tits defiantly against death.

"Can they save him?"

"Don't talk, Billy. If they see you talking out loud to no one, they'll think you're crazy. No, they can't save him. Once a reaper digs their scythe in, that's it."

"But I'm not a reaper?" Billy thought, knowing Celia could hear still.

Celia looked curiously at him. "You've got a point. You're not a reaper, but you do have a reaper's scythe."

In that moment, Mr. Kowalski crept up from his body. Now that he stood translucent with a dull shimmer, he looked around, somewhat confused. "C'mon, Billy, you don't want to see this, believe me."

Celia led Billy back to the end of the hallway, and together they descended the stairs. Billy's curiosity got the best of him, though. He paused, looking back through the slit glass window of the hallway fire door while Celia still looked away. A darkness filled the hallway, flowing through with the whistling screams and growls of some thing or things. The lights flickered, but the paramedics didn't see a thing. It was only Billy and his out-of-body landlord that seemed to notice. Mr. Kowalski saw Billy and screamed with eyes of terror, witnessing arachnid-faced gargoyle-like creatures grabbing at his legs. Like translucent shadows, they shifted about frightfully. Their parallel rows of red eyes pierced Billy. He counted six as they sent shivers through his soul. It was all cut short when Celia grabbed his arm after she'd materialized in the stairwell. Sharply, she pulled him away.

"Come on, I said."

"What was that?"

"We need to chat about it. I'll explain in your flat. Now come on."

The pair went down one level and quickly were back in his apartment.

Billy sat at the edge of his bed as Celia paced back and forth somewhat nervously.

"Will you sit down? You're making me fucking nervous!" Billy shouted.

Celia flopped down in a huff on the blue armchair she'd sat at earlier. "You really messed things up, you know that?"

"Me! You gave me the damn scythe! Up until this morning, I thought this might have been shit I imagined on a drunken walk!"

"I saved your damn life!"

"You may as well not have!"

"Dammit, Billy."

Billy took in a tense breath. "How could I see those, those, things... And I just killed a man! What does this mean for me, for us?"

Celia looked strangely at Billy for a moment. He thought he saw her smile for just a second, but when he looked again, she frowned.

"Means the Grim Collectors will be out for me now. You saw those things because of your connection to me with that blade. We'll just have to be more careful now."

"The Grim Collectors?"

"Yeah. The ones who drag me back to Hell after my last reaping or when you make a mistake."

"I thought you said you went somewhere else?"

"I went to Hell, Billy! I'm gonna get dragged down there, and who knows what might happen. They might even punish me for sparing your life. You have no idea how bad it is down there."

"Like how bad are we talking then? They always called it the lake of fire in church..." Billy was genuinely curious as he still sat on the edge of his bed.

"There is a lake of fire... If you're lucky, or you could get eaten by a giant fucking cyclops toad! Only to be shit out and eaten again! All because of a mistake like this!"

"*Cyclops toad?*"

"I can't do it Billy! I can't go back there!"

"Hold on, hold on. What can we do about this? You said it, I need you, you need me. We are in this mess together now. That much is clear."

There was a few silent moments between them before Celia spoke again. "When the Grim Collectors come. I'll just have to hide somewhere."

Billy sat silently for a moment. He didn't do drugs, he hadn't even drunk much until his separation from Tina. If he'd somehow seen this was going to be his new year last night, he'd have thought he dropped acid. Then he thought, surely, he would have dived off that bridge if he caught a glimpse of all this. He gathered his thoughts and continued...

"So, tell me where are you going to hide when this Grim Collector shit goes down..."

"I, I don't know, Billy. They just swirl about like alpha predators and appear so quickly to devour you, then they spit you out at Hell's burning gates."

"What else happens when you're down there?"

"Could be anything, even eternal punishment. I didn't do well at this job, Billy, and now that I gave my scythe to a mortal,

I'm probably doomed." Celia's lips trembled as she tried to hold in tears. "I'm an idiot." She shrugged hopelessly.

Billy sighed, stood up, and walked over, placing a hand on Celia's shoulder.

"Why did you do it? I mean give your scythe to me?"

"You were on my radar." Celia held out her wrist, and a square digital watch could be seen. "When I saw you, you looked so desperate and sad, I felt bad for you. Billy looked at the digital watch. It read: *Billy Walker – six months left.*

"Six months left?"

"What?" Celia looked down at the watch. "You had no time because you were suppose to die on that bridge..."

Both surprised, they looked at one another and blurted out in unison, "*It worked!*"

"I'll be damned," said Billy.

"Hah, not today you won't," laughed Celia.

"What is that, anyway?" Billy asked, pointing to Celia's black watch.

"What, the death-watch? Standard issue for reapers, just like the scythe."

Celia's watch beeped in a sad, slow rhythm. Celia took a look at it then showed it to Billy. It read: *Report for reassignment – Harbourfront – Midnight.*

"So what? Lets say you never report, then what?"

"They'll put a hit on me. Not just Grim Collectors, but Dreadlings, Billy. They'll be all in."

"Dreadlings?"

"Those shadowy little bastards you saw pull your landlord down south just now."

"And what if you report?"

"Then it's fire and brimstone. Maybe just a job down in Hell, and they won't punish me if I'm lucky."

"I have an idea." Billy grinned and summoned the scythe. He looked at the glimmering moonlit blade. "We'll meet this Grim Collector, and when we do, we'll surprise it."

"You don't understand. They have senses we can't comprehend. They aren't mortal; they are mindless devouring beasts. If you're planning on using that thing against one, you can forget it. I saw a reaper try to fight back once. It was messy."

"What happened?"

"I've only ever seen one. It was after my training was complete, when I was to do my first reaping. A man had died in a traffic accident. My teacher told me he would show me one last time how to reap because I was nervous. The man had been hit in the face by a flying tire that went right through his windshield. The thing was complete with the rim still inside. The driver of the truck hauling that load in the flatbed never tied it down. Then, *BAM!* Right through the other guy's windshield."

"That's a terrible way to die."

"I watched as my teacher pulled the soul from the victim's body with his scythe. Moments after, Dreadlings dragged that car accident victim away. Then my teacher suffered the same fate. He tried to slash at the black mass with his scythe, but it sucked him in like a devouring black hole and blew the scythe from his hands. After he was gone, I picked up his blade and carried on with his duties. From the clear blue sky overhead, the darkness of the Grim Collector had come whipping down on him. It was like... It was like a swirling mass of serpents and darkness. When it reached him, he faded into it, sinking into the ground like an eerie black puddle. I was petrified, I can't take that." Celia sniffled and carried on, "I don't deserve it. I mean, I'm not perfect, I know, but I can't be swallowed by darkness and taken down to Hell again, you know?"

"After seeing those damn Dreadlings, I don't think I could picture something worse, really."

"They are so much worse, Billy," Celia went on.

"You said your teacher took a swing at the thing? He never hit it, though?"

"No."

"Then we don't know what this thing will do if we lay into one. Do the Collectors attack mortals?"

"The Dreadlings take away sinners' souls when we remove them from their bodies. The Grim Collectors, well, they collect reapers."

"So, there is an orderly way about it all."

"They don't attack the living, but those Dreadlings will go after anything dead. That includes me."

"What a fucking mess, Celia…"

"Calm down, Billy."

"I'm trying to remain calm, but if you'd said, 'Hey take this scythe and steal some time to keep living. Oh, but by the way, creatures will chase us and chaos will fucking follow,' well, I might have just jumped into the damn train."

"Look, we can work this out. We have each other now."

"How, how will we work this out, Celia?"

"Maybe we can overpower these creatures somehow."

"You ever see anything overpower one of these Grim Collectors?"

"Yes, once."

"What was it?" Billy asked with a raised brow.

"An angel. It looked like a man in blinding golden armor. He wielded a sword like fire that burned through the Dreadlings so easily."

"And what caused this fight?"

"The Dreadlings had tried to drag away a little boy. I remember the angel almost coming from nowhere with a burst of light. Then, with a booming voice of authority, I'll never forget what it said: 'The child is innocent,' and then it slaughtered the Dreadlings."

"Well, shit, Celia, we aren't exactly angels, are we…"

"No. We are far from angels," she replied.

"Wow," Billy said sarcastically.

He then stood up and walked over to his fridge, grabbing the only drink left in there, a beer. Then he sat down while he flicked the white and blue cap off the wall and into a waste basket. He smirked at his remarkable accuracy.

"You're feeling better after taking that time, though, aren't you?"

"Yeah, but I feel a little guilty about it." Billy sipped the beer and continued, "I honestly didn't mean for it to happen like that. It sank in without me doing anything, it seemed. It felt like I hadn't even moved the scythe when it happened."

"It's my fault. I just told you to take it. I didn't train you with it. Then I sent you on your way while I tried on lipstick. I'm so stupid." Celia buried her head in her hands. "I ruin everything."

Billy stood up from the edge of his bed walked over again to put his hand on Celia's shoulder. "You did stop me on that bridge, so you haven't ruined everything. I'm sorry for what I said. I wouldn't have been better off in front of that train."

"I guess that's worth something." Celia looked up with a faint smile.

Billy grabbed his black hoodie and put it on again. Then he slid on a black baseball cap, closed his apartment door, and followed Celia into the hallway. In the drab, rusted stairwells of his dingy building, Celia and Billy moved past a woman rocking and hugging herself. Billy was use to it. Living in this place meant tweakers hiding from the cold to get high. Before he reached for the fire escape door, Celia stopped him.

"Wait." She looked down at her death-watch. An hourglass with barely any sand left appeared.

"She has maybe a month, Billy. This woman is going to take her last injection in February. Death-watch says she'll kill a family on her way out of this world." Celia covered the watch face as if to hide it from Billy, but he paid no mind.

"What do you say to that, Billy?"

Billy hesitated. He needed that time, but how did they really know this addict was going to take out a family with her?

"How does she do it then? I mean take out a family?"

"She drives high."

Billy flicked out his right hand. The rough wood and moonlit blade materialized from a dusty haze. He stepped in closer. Still, the woman was tucked inside her cigarette-burned hoodie, hiding from the world. She continued to comfort herself with rhythmic metronome-like motions. Overhead, the glowing scythe dangled. Gently, with Celia's instruction, Billy let the blade hover over the woman's back until it glowed wildly. It was only for three seconds, but it seemed longer. Billy felt strange again, like he was not in control of the blade at all. He felt better physically, but inside he felt an unease about it all.

Celia looked at Billy as he pulled away and the scythe vanished. "You going to be alright?"

"Yeah, I just... I don't know about all this."

"C'mon, we'll talk about it outside."

The stairwell fire door slammed shut behind them with the tweaker still in a catatonic state, and Celia looked at her death-watch once more.

"There, now she has a day. How long did you hold the scythe to her for?"

"I did a three-count."

"So, we know you can count to three and take a month. Any more and she might have died right then and there."

"Don't I have to dig in to kill someone?"

"I had to dig in to pull out the soul out of a mortal, but not to kill one."

"I see," replied Billy.

Celia walked through the three-story pothole-riddled parking lot with Billy. Together they passed many a questionable crowd. Billy was accustomed to it, and Celia didn't give a damn. He glanced over at her, realizing she was sizing people up constantly. He didn't have to read her mind to know that she was on a mission and not hiding it. All of this time stealing business seemed like the clear path to Billy. Live by theft and try to forget life as a depressed man of desperation. Billy's clarity was better today than yesterday, though. Watching

Celia size people up seemed questionable, but he was indeed alive because of it. Urgently, she watched her death-watch, examining the time left of everyone they passed.

"I've got eight months now, you said it yourself. Can't we just enjoy the day and look for more time in a little while?" Billy questioned.

Celia looked over at him oddly. "Let's get you a few years before we think about taking a vacation, 'kay?"

"I mean, I feel fine for now. Is that not enough for the day? We can start fresh in the morning and just enjoy the day, no?"

"Ah, look at this one. This guy has fifty years left. The watch says he was a rapist, Billy. Says he has committed that sin at least three times. You think someone like that deserves fifty years?"

"Hold on a second, hold on a second," Billy said, somewhat irritated. "You telling me that watch reads off the sins of the people you are looking at?"

"Damn right it does. Now, do you really think that asshole deserves to go on another fifty years?"

Billy sneered at the troubled man who roamed freely around his neighborhood. "I see your point, and I would agree. He doesn't deserve the time he has."

"Then what are you going to do about it, Billy?"

Billy flicked his hand out and held the moonlit scythe at his side. The man in his crosshairs stood asking for a light from an acquaintance, and Billy walked right up beside them.

"Either of you spare a smoke?" Billy asked, even though he did not in fact smoke. The young man did spare a cigarette. They all stood around, shrouded in the disgusting manifestations of their addictions, and Billy let the scythe do its work. It was true, he didn't care for smoking, but the convenience of the lie was taking away the days of a certified scumbag — or so he thought. It wasn't long before the man Celia had labeled a rapist walked away, but the damage was done. Billy walked off and flicked the barely burned cigarette to the ground.

"What did we get for our efforts?"

Celia looked at Billy and then her death-watch. "Says three years!" She smiled devilishly.

"Not bad for thirty-six seconds, I guess. I feel like we should rid the world of that guy and follow him."

"Not just yet. All that matters right now is that it's working and your body is healing," Celia said with a grin.

4

Billy walked the familiar Toronto streets with Celia by his side, breathing in crisp winter air. He couldn't believe how much better he felt in this new year. The guilt of what he was doing seemed to drift from his mind as he laughed with Celia. Knowing who he was taking time from justified it, he told himself in that moment.

Celia had materialized now, for Billy's sake. They walked into downtown Toronto's Dundas Square side by side. Billy looked at her amber eyes, and she smiled up at him. For the first time in a while, he felt a peace that had been absent since his messy separation from Tina. The bustling of tourists and shoppers flowed out from everywhere around the square. To their left was the Eaton Centre, a sprawling shopping mall. A news reporter was asking passersby about their resolutions for the new year. Billy and Celia walked by together, and as Billy tried to dodge the question, she somehow managed to catch him, despite it. Seeing as Celia had materialized in her little 5'3" frame compared to his 6'2", Billy realized they probably looked like the perfect cute couple to prod with resolution questions. The reporter began, and Billy reluctantly accepted.

"You two make a cute couple. A new year, and a new relationship perhaps?" she asked.

Billy smiled at Celia. "Something like that."

"And what is your resolution for this new year, if you don't mind me asking?" the reporter said, looking at Billy.

Billy looked at Celia and smirked. "To truly live, I guess."

Celia smirked mischievously as well. Then the reporter asked Celia the same question. She gave the same response, "To truly live."

"That's a great answer." The reporter gently smiled. "I hope you two enjoy this new year together."

Billy thanked the reporter and left the square, wading through crowds with Celia until they reached a crowded four-way stop.

"Okay, Billy, the goal now is for you to learn to use the scythe subtly so you don't look like a complete psychopath."

"What? I thought I did pretty good the last time holding it."

"Yeah, it wasn't bad. Remember, people can't see any of this, unless of course they're dead. All they can see is you waving your empty hands around, so keep your movements subtle. That scythe is not of this realm."

"Right, but they see you just fine."

"That's because I materialized, duh…"

"Can you do *anything* when you materialize?"

"Like, what do you mean?"

"Never mind." Billy dismissed his question, too embarrassed to elaborate on it.

Celia smirked because she knew what he was curious about, but she didn't answer. The jealously she had for the mortal experience was due in part to touch, taste, and even smell, all things that were absent even when she materialized, because she was not human.

"There, across the street. The bum on that sewer grate, taking in the heat. A sad existence if I ever saw one, Billy. Watch says it's not long before he dies of pneumonia."

As Billy eyed the man, a luxury car pulled to the curb in front of them both just as they had almost finished crossing. A man in a dark gray suit stepped out to the sidewalk with a cigar burning the last of its embers in his hand. Carelessly, he flicked it at the homeless man with a grin. The bearded homeless man shrugged it off without a hint of self-worth.

"Let the homeless man live the last of his life, Celia," Billy mumbled.

"No, Billy. C'mon, that's not what we need here. This is easy pickings. We should play it safe."

Billy already had the scythe in hand. Casually, he held it by his side and walked after the man in the dark gray suit. As Billy found himself walking angrily, he also found his thoughts and his justifications about all of this changing. His mind seemed to listen to the hiss of the scythe, and that hiss seemed to speak to him, even control him on an unconscious level.

He doesn't deserve his time; you're right, take his days Billy Walker.

This guy is asking for this, Billy told himself.

Celia smirked, watching Billy catch up to his target. The man impatiently waited at another crosswalk. She wasn't going to stop Billy. The truth was, she didn't care where the days came from, just as long as they kept coming.

"Let his days be ours Billy Walker," she hissed quietly.

Catching up, Billy let the scythe extend. Subtly, it dangled mere inches behind the man at the crosswalk. Billy was careful not to let anyone else touch it. It was a five-second count when the signal to walk came again.

"How much time does the prick have left then?"

"He still has decades; you took five months off him."

"He won't miss them."

Celia smiled, looking up at Billy's much taller frame. "Here, a present for you."

"What?" Billy looked surprised as Celia handed him the asshole's wallet.

"How did you..."

"When you've been around as long as I have, you pick up a few tricks." Celia grinned in a devilish, flirtatious way.

She had swept into his life like wild winds over the calm of Toronto's harbor front. He took in those sparkling amber eyes that reminded him of Tina. As much as he didn't want to think about it, he thought perhaps he was catching feelings for this bubble-headed valley girl reaper. What he was to make of that, he did not know. Together they walked back around Dundas Square, quietly, happily, for a little while, until Celia broke the silence.

"So just a recap about the time theft thing, 'kay? I know you're trying to be subtle about it. I know you kept your hand down at your side back there, but I'm serious. What if he stopped or you tripped, and you touched someone else? We can't have another landlord incident and have Hell-beasts appear, right? That could fuck up the plan."

"I'll be careful," Billy responded, mesmerized by Celia's amber eyes again.

"The good and the bad, they both have their most-wanted lists. I don't want to make that list for insubordination. We keep a low profile, and we'll both be safe in this world."

"Yeah, I get it."

Billy's thoughts drifted back to Celia's concerns and those beasts he'd seen earlier. "What about tonight then? You said forget about trying to use the scythe on the Grim Collector thing. Either way you lay it down, you said the thing is coming tonight, whether we like it or not. You have a plan?"

"You're not gonna like it, but it'll have to do."

"What is it?"

"We'll talk about it somewhere nice and quiet. You know anywhere?"

"Yeah, I know a few places."

"Keep them in mind." Celia continued, "This city is ours now, Billy Walker. We can take time as we please, from the right people, of course. Just say the word, and I'll tell you what the death-watch says about them."

Together they walked by eye-catching holiday storefront windows adorned with shimmering decorations and lights.

Billy stopped for a moment to take in one display. He saw his reflection in the window and actually paid attention to it for the first time since he'd remembered. He looked healthy, his cheeks were full, his red hair had the glow of health he recalled. He looked handsome. He was actually starting to enjoy spending time with her. Perhaps it was the lonely days of the prior year spent sulking about lost love. He still gulped with the pain of a broken heart every time he thought about Tina, but Celia was slowly helping him forget.

Celia came to a crossing and stepped into the street. Billy's hand slipped, brushing against hers, and he noticed her smile. He could not believe how strikingly similar she looked to Tina in her features. Perhaps that was why he felt so comfortable with her. They stumbled upon an alley, and in it, Celia spied another quiet target. It was a derelict man huddled in the shadows. His thick forest-green overcoat protected him from the elements. He huddled for warmth, not even looking up as Celia and Billy approached. Billy flicked his wrist, and the scythe materialized. Billy heard the hiss again. This time he swore it was similar to Celia's voice, but it sounded darker, more sinister in tone. The voice echoed in Billy's mind between his own thoughts: "An easy target Billy. He doesn't deserve his days; he doesn't deserve *our* days."

Before Billy could close in, the homeless man stood up so quickly that he fumbled back in surprise.

Wide-eyed, Celia grabbed Billy by the hand.

"Not this one. C'mon, Billy, let's go."

Billy listened, and together they departed quickly. The scythe exploded into dust, disappearing from his grasp. He swore that homeless man saw it. As Celia tried to direct him away, Billy couldn't help himself and looked back. The gray-bearded man, perhaps in his fifties, looked at him — even *through* him, it seemed. In the pit of his stomach, Billy knew something was not right. In that man's eyes Billy could feel that what he was doing was wrong. For the first time in a while, he thought about himself. Mostly about the way he was acting.

This was not him. Perspective seemed to hit so fast now, much like the train he sought on New Year's Eve was meant to. What had he let himself become. The control he'd lost, the way he use to be before his life went down in flames. He would never have stolen days from people — even from the worst people.

Celia clutched Billy's hand hard and pulled him back into reality. "Let's go, now!"

Surprised again, Billy fumbled and scurried away with her. "What, what was that?"

"A schizophrenic maybe, I don't know. I thought he might hurt you. Our goal is to truly live, you said it yourself. You're no good dead."

"I guess, yeah..."

As they rushed down the alley, Billy didn't respond. He had clarity again, at least for the moment. He knew he did not want to carry on with this. Something in the pit of his stomach told him not to tell her. Something told him he needed to accept his fate. He didn't know how to tell her that he couldn't keep doing this. He couldn't steal the time of other people; it wasn't in him.

Celia walked across a snowy, untouched church parking lot with Billy close by, until they stopped by a cross out front of Church of the Redeemer Jesus Christ. She took Billy by the hand and touched the scythe marking on the inside of his palm. Celia grinned at the irony of her evil deeds in the lot of a church that had no use for her.

Billy's mark tingled, and Celia looked deep into his blue eyes while she traced it with her index finger. She was cold to the touch, like winter itself. As she touched him and their eyes met, his thoughts grew cloudy and distant.

"So, you were about to take me someplace quiet, you said? Someplace we could sit and talk about your future, *our* future. Maybe take me to one of those places you had in mind earlier?"

Billy put his hand to his forehead in confusion. "I was, I uh..."

"Oh, c'mon, silly, you said you were hungry."

"Yeah, I guess I am, actually."

There was silence between them as Billy felt like he'd forgotten something, something important. He felt blank, yet he still went along with Celia's request, and they walked toward the Japanese restaurant that Billy now had in mind.

"You still have that man's wallet I gave you?"

Billy smiled and clutched the rude businessman's wallet that Celia had taken earlier.

"Hopefully you like ramen? And if you aren't a fan, I guess it doesn't matter, because it's on this guy's dime anyway," Billy said, holding the man's ID then tossing it in the snow.

Celia shrugged. "This isn't a normal body. When I materialize, I can't eat food."

"Sucks to be you, eh?"

Celia stared at Billy resentfully for a second, then, seeing his reaction, she realized hers and quickly smiled flirtatiously.

"It was a joke, Celia."

"Hehe, I know."

As they walked along the Chinatown streets, Billy strained to remember something that he felt he was missing. Still, he felt so hazy as he walked, it was no matter. Celia was quite a distraction when she wanted to be.

"So, you know anyone here, Billy? Anyone you want to impress? Anyone you want to make jealous?"

"What?"

"Yeah," Celia said with a playful hop in her snow-crunched steps. "It doesn't have to be all business all the time, you know. Come here, follow me, Mr. Walker."

Billy curiously followed Celia down a narrow side street and into a quiet little alley, where she looked around suspiciously. When she knew she was safe, she waved her hand from her head to her toes and completely changed her wardrobe.

Billy's eye widened as he took in her surprising curves. Purple lipstick, shimmering amber bedroom eyes, and a revealing purple dress taunted his eyes. A faux-fur coat rested nicely on Celia's frame.

"Damn."

"Damn right," she said with a grin.

"This place is sort of a hole in the wall. You're dressed a little formal."

"Say no more then." Celia waved her hand again and toned down the style with skin-tight jeans and a similar low-cut purple top.

"Now, let's go sit and talk about our next move."

Celia looked over at Billy with a faint smile as they walked along. He felt strange and still cloudy. He felt something important coming back to him. Like it had been missing somehow, but it was fighting to come back. All he could remember was Dundas Square and then he was here in Chinatown. As he took in the familiar storefronts and beautiful sweeping rooftops, he felt something that important return. It was certain in his heart that he couldn't steal time from people, no matter how unfit Celia said they were. The truth was, he didn't want to tell her this was not going to work out. He was indeed afraid to die, but he was not this person.

Celia smirked. "Maybe after you eat, we will spend the rest of this jerk's cash on something fun?"

Billy smiled reluctantly and hid the uncertainty. "Sounds fun."

The snow of the day had swiftly turned to a gray, slushy mess in the streets of Chinatown. Each block flowed with sounds of transportation and people hustling to their destinations. Red and white streetcars stopped by a traffic island lined with decorative golden dragons scaling huge red wooden pillars. Billy walked past an eatery with hanging ducks in the window. The steam from something delicious cooking inside blinded the windows. He felt a growl in his stomach. Thoughts of his mortality were still there, but not daunting for a change. He was in this moment accepting his fate. He had made peace with his decision. At dinner, he would tell Celia he couldn't follow through with their plan, and he would live out his remaining days.

"Here it is."

"This is the place?"

"I know outside it looks like I said, a bit of a hole in the wall, but give it a chance. They've got tea infused eggs in there, and their sake is pretty tasty too."

Celia smiled. "Sake, eh? Maybe someday I'll get to try their food."

"Right, the food thing. You can't eat. What else can't you do in that body?"

"I have sight and sound. The mortal senses are taste, touch, and smell."

"Bummer."

Celia raised an eyebrow. "Yeah, it is..."

They stepped into the ornately decorated restaurant outfitted with Shogi screens and a giant red and white rising sun fan above the bar. They were seated by a young waitress that recognized Billy from when he'd frequented the place with Tina.

"Haven't seen you here in a while. How've you been?" she asked.

"I've been well, thanks," Billy lied.

"You look well," she said with a smile and took Billy's order of appetizers.

Celia looked at the menu. "Hmm. This place is nice, you're right. We'll take this bottle of sake, please."

The waitress nodded and left to tend to another table.

"Hold on...bottle?" Billy questioned.

Celia gazed at Billy from across the table with those shimmering amber eyes again. "You want to truly live, I thought." She giggled, and it wasn't long before cups of sake were flowing at the table. He drank them one after the other, falling into Celia's trap. He thought he needed that liquid courage to disappoint this supernatural girl. He found the familiar warmth of the alcohol take hold, and he smiled at her from across the table.

"Listen, Celia, I've got to be honest with you."

As if Celia knew what Billy's next words were, she leaned forward suggestively. His eyes were led to her alluring curves. "I think you owe me at least one favor for saving your life, don't you, Billy Walker?"

"I–I suppose that is reasonable."

"Help me dodge this Grim Collector, and then we can do whatever you want. We've got one thing going for us: we know where it's going to be."

"You sure?"

"Yeah, my death-watch tells me where I should report to for collection and reassignment. Perhaps there is a way I can dodge collection. I think I have a plan."

Billy was stressed and nervous. He took another few swigs of sake, and when he'd built up enough courage, he asked, "What's the plan?"

But the waitress interrupted with Billy's order of fresh rolls, and Celia waited. He was half in the bag, and his appetizers had only just arrived. He smiled and thanked her then looked back to Celia.

"I'll need to hide somewhere. These Grim Collectors, they hunt like beasts. They have no eyes. I think they have some kind of tracking sense for celestial beings, like a homing sense of smell almost."

Billy sat and listened for the moment. He'd gained a few more years courtesy of Celia. The least he could do was to hear her out and help her before he told her it was over.

"So how do we trick this thing?"

"I'll go to the bathroom, then I'll shift forms. When I come out, we'll try something."

Billy looked nervous. "Celia, what are you talking about here?"

"*Possession.*"

Billy felt the liquid courage of the alcohol rising up inside. Maybe it was the alcohol dampening all reason, maybe it was the D-cups that Celia kept showcasing on the other side of the table. Billy took another sip of sake and told himself, *What the hell, she helped you.*

"Is it safe?" he said and hesitated. Then he drunkenly leaned in, like he was telling her a big secret and whispered, "I mean, this possession thing."

"Totally," Celia said, leaning forward suggestively again. Then she told Billy exactly what she knew he needed to hear as she read his intoxicated thoughts. "You've got yourself a few more years now. You want to call it a day and live that short time, that's fine. Just do me this one favor."

Billy rubbed his chin and sat in contemplation for a minute. *Fuck*, he thought. Somehow, she knew he couldn't go on with this. "Yeah, I'll help you," he said, feeling obligated. "Let's do this before I change my mind then."

"It's the least you can do for the sacrifice I made to save your life, isn't it, Billy?"

Billy rubbed his forehead. "Just give me some kind of warning before you do this. I mean, don't just jump in and take me for a test drive, okay?"

"Hopefully that won't be what it's like. We'll work together. I'll hide in you, and when the Grim Collector is gone and I'm in the clear, I'll go in peace."

Celia got up from the table and disappeared into the bathroom. She was glad he'd accepted, because without his guard down, she wasn't possessing him.

Billy waited. The fresh rolls were just as good as he remembered them. Several other items he'd ordered came to the table. He'd seen about a thousand in cash in the wallet Celia had stolen. With the stress of trying to back away from this supernatural deal he'd gotten himself into, he'd amassed a bill of over two hundred dollars. Billy was stressed. He didn't have the heart to steal time from people; it wasn't in him.

"What a mistake," he mumbled and took another sip of sake. He let his mind wander to better days, times when he and Tina would spend their weekends volunteering. That was how they met — volunteering at an animal shelter.

Billy remembered his first words to her as he struck up the courage to speak to her that first weekend.

"Hey, are you looking for some companionship?"

Tina answered awkwardly, "Um..."

Billy interrupted, "Er, no, I mean a dog; are you looking for a dog companion?"

That was the first time he'd seen her laugh. That sparkling white moonbeam and the way her eyes followed suit, smiling along.

"Honestly, I don't really have the time for a dog. Ten hours alone in an apartment during the week seems unfair."

"You're like me, then; you come to get your fill on the weekends."

Tina smiled again. "Yeah, it's good exercise for me and for them."

"So, no time for a companion, but what about for a date? Do you ever have time for that kind of thing?"

"Maybe," she said flirtatiously.

Billy still loved her. He wasn't kidding himself. He reached for his sake, drinking the last of it, when he felt an odd tingle, like a gentle electric pulse fizzling into his body. Then a dizziness in his head, but not from the alcohol. His mouth involuntarily shot a misty cloud of sake across the room, like it was a foreign contaminant, and he heard Celia's voice in his mind. "Sorry," she said.

Speedily rushing to his aid, the waitress questioned, "Are you okay?"

"My apologies, I swallowed the wrong way," Billy choked out. "I'm okay."

What an odd new sensation, Billy thought. He knew Celia was there; he could feel her feminine energy take hold. The evening had come around faster than anticipated. It seemed now like he was buried inside himself. Like the vehicle was moving, but he wasn't in the driver's seat. The sake shots had become the entire bottle before he'd known it.

"Oh my gosh, this miso soup is to die for." Billy heard Celia speak to him inside his mind as he slurped it up.

"Whad I tell yah," he slurred as the soup was put down. He heard Celia laugh.

"So, it worked! I can't believe I did it!"

"Yeah, yeah just try to keep it down in there; my head is spinning."

"It will only be temporary, Billy, I promise. There's just one problem."

"What's it?" Billy replied, slurring out loudly.

The waitress looked over at him oddly.

"Billy, think, don't speak, okay?"

"Right," he thought.

"Anyway, I don't know that I can get back inside if I leave right now. So I'll have to stay until this is all sorted out, okay?"

"Whatever," Billy replied.

"Good, because that wasn't the easiest thing to do."

Billy found himself drinking even more shots of sake, and he found himself less and less aware of the evening's events. He saw a second lavish blue bottle of empty sake that he didn't remember ordering.

"Good," he heard Celia say with a wicked laugh. Her voice echoed in his mind. Billy kept hearing, "Another, another." Before he knew it, a slew of little empty blue sake bottles lined the table. He wasn't in the driver's seat even a little now; Celia was.

Chinatown was lit up so wonderfully in the night, and Billy watched his body go through motions that he wasn't commanding. Time had passed so quickly for him. He was so drunk that when he pissed in a nearby alley, all he remembered was Celia saying, "Wee!" Then he saw her write the same remark in yellow cursive throughout the snow. It wasn't long before they had made it down to the Toronto Harbor front as planned. Somehow, Celia had killed quite a bit of time. Beyond himself, Billy watched like a movie as his drunken body was commanded. She'd caught a cab and taken him somehow to a white suspension bridge over the Harbor front waters. There they leaned against a rail in the night, watching, waiting together.

"Reminiscent of the first time we met. Isn't it, Billy?"

He was so drunk, he couldn't have responded even if he'd wanted to. In Billy's body, Celia smiled, taking in the winter beauty of everything Toronto had to offer. She was truly living just as she'd wanted. The food and the drinks at that restaurant — Billy had been right, it was delicious. Celia recalled the last thing she tasted at the Japanese restaurant when she'd hopped inside Billy. She had known food would be incredible, and she had already decreed that she would taste more and experience more of a mortal's life. Even that piss in the alley had been a wondrous orgasmic relief.

Celia took in all the bystanders in from the view of that bridge. She thought about mortality. She realized then that the old expression, *stop and smell the roses*, was something all too often forgotten. She told herself that unlike Billy Walker and the vast majority of mortals around her, she was going to stop; she was going to smell the roses, and the coffee, and the food-scent-laced sweet air of the night. It should have been hers. Never again would she allow Billy to take it for granted.

The half moon glistened over the calm winter water, and the clear sky brought a peculiar calm upon the landscape.

"You in there, Billy?" Celia questioned. She heard no response.

My, how that sake did him in beautifully, she thought. She knew her timing had to be perfect. The whirling strands of darkness and whistling screams of her plan appeared overhead. This was it. The lie she'd told Billy to fear was closing in all around him. Celia had summoned one of her own portals that she traveled with, and she was going to use it to take Billy for a ride, like she'd planned all along.

She materialized the scythe in Billy's hand. Then she plunged it into his own heart. Billy's expression said it all as his own soul was torn from within his flesh. He was bound to that scythe, and now that he was pulled from his body, he was bound no more. He stood on that bridge, wide-eyed beside his possessed shell, looking at himself in shock.

"No! Celia, No!"

Before he knew what happened, he saw his body smiling at his soul with a twisted grin of joy, and he was devoured by darkness. The horrific swirling black mass that Celia had called a Grim Collector was but a portal of Celia's own design.

Now it encompassed Billy and devoured him. The cold, ethereal puddle wrapped around Billy's soul. There was nothing alive about it. It was not a beast; it was not a monster. It was, though, the end of Billy Walker's mortality. Billy fought so hard that his hand was seen pushing out from the whirling black mass. Down, away from this realm he was pulled, despite his attempts to resist. The darkness and Billy himself disappeared into the bridge floor, and with him gone, Celia's worries disappeared. She was free. Free to live the mortal vacation she'd planned for a while. All that remained now was Celia's scythe on that lonely harbourfront bridge.

She picked it up triumphantly as the beauty of a gentle snowfall started. Then she sang one of her favorite songs, "Girls Just Wanna Have Fun," strolling happily into the night with scythe in hand.

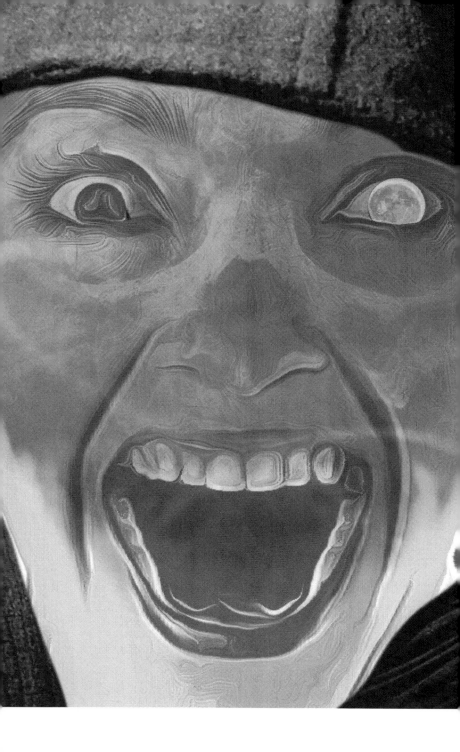

5

Each newfound step was met with renewed excitement. She had done it. Billy only had one more month to live, and he would have wasted it entirely. What use would it have been for him to throw it away? No, thought Celia, He didn't deserve the time he'd had anyway. Billy's days were wasted drinking alone, wallowing in self-pity over his ex. He hadn't even changed much once he'd gained more time. Instead, he gave in to his addictions and wallowed on about his ex-fiancée Tina. Celia shuddered at the thought of such an existence. She had ideas. She wanted more time in this body, and that was what she would get, thanks to her scythe.

It hadn't been easy orchestrating Billy's demise, playing the ditsy girl and finding the right form to cause him to lower his guard completely. Celia wasn't even really a brunette; she'd shifted to a closer resemblance to Billy's ex fiancée when she'd shown herself to him. There was something to be said about familiarity. Something comforting about it on an unconscious level, and Celia had played in that. When she had studied Billy from afar, she made sure to take on the look of comfort and familiarity, subtly, just enough. That was one thing she would miss, being able to materialize in a feminine body; it was, after all, her natural demonic form in Hell. The makeup, the hairstyles, the clothes, she was a demon, yes, but she liked having fun. It was too risky now for her to step out of Billy's body, even for a second. For one, the body needs an energy source to live, and she was it. If she stepped out, the body was dead, and she was vulnerable. Vulnerable to Dreadlings that could indeed see her and report her to someone in higher authority. She would stay in the hidden safety of Billy's body and enjoy these new senses.

The now calm Toronto Harbourfront neighborhood brought ease and joy to Celia. She'd left the bridge, optimistically looking to track down the other half of her master plan. Celia felt Billy's wrists. The odd sensation of such large wrists was unfamiliar. There on Billy's left wrist materialized her death-watch. *Excellent*, she thought.

The Toronto streets still sparkled with fluorescent lights and pedestrian activity. It excited Celia. She passed a little grocery shop attached to the bottom floor of a mocha-colored brick condominium building. Traveling slowly on foot compared with the way she used to levitate around when she hadn't materialized would be different, but she didn't mind. Celia was going to enjoy her new mortal experience. Being intangible for the most part and materializing with only sight and sound when she was a reaper had left her jealous of the living.

Now she would gain more time for herself and take time away from those that wasted it. She had a sense of entitlement that she indeed deserved this vacation from her duties as a reaper. She didn't feel guilty about the loophole she'd found in abusing her scythe's powers. Not in the least. Now, just as she'd planned, she would find Billy's ex, on whom she'd also kept a close eye. She knew that somewhere around this neighborhood, she and a group of her girlfriends were out on the town, partying. Celia had unapologetically been spying on Tina when not watching Billy. She knew a couple of things about Tina, but most importantly she knew Tina still loved Billy and regretted her infidelity.

The winter nightscape of Toronto's bustling downtown kept no one from enjoying the offerings of the nightlife. Celia walked several blocks, heading to the club she knew Tina would be attending with her girlfriends. All the while, she took in her new senses. She even stopped at a street meat vendor. When the wafting of oily, glistening hotdogs hit her virgin nostrils, she knew she had to taste the damn things.

"One foot-long."

Celia was so enticed by the sizzling meat that she didn't bother with condiments when the vendor handed it to her. Instead, she just took a huge bite, looked at the vendor, and said, "Oh, fuck, that's good."

He looked confused that some guy put nothing on his hotdog but ate it like something profound had hit his taste buds. Celia walked on, eating the rest of the street meat in her travels. She saw the club Tina was supposedly at a few more blocks up. Then, with her last bite, she had caught up to a group of women at a crosswalk. It was clear they had enjoyed an evening full of cocktails, by the sounds of their speech. Cackles and talk of male celebrities entertained them while cars passed. Celia listened intently as they talked of who they would ride and who they would "let slide," as one woman phrased it. One of the women mentioned a celebrity that Celia didn't recognize and then said, "Ride or let slide?"

"Girl, he's so short, I bet he isn't even equipped for all this," one responded, gesturing to her booty.

"You never know, I had this guy once, 5'5", but downtown, wow! He was so deep, I had to tell him to literally back his ass up. He kept hitting my IUD. I get it, you're big!" She laughed.

The women's drunken cackles filled the night air again as they began to cross the street. Celia sped up a little and was about to pass one of them on the right side when she heard Billy's name spoken.

"Billy!"

Celia turned casually with a faint smile. There, stepping drunkenly to the crosswalk's end, was indeed Billy's ex, Tina.

Celia thought about what to say. She remembered the condo Tina had shared with Billy was not far. Things were moving in her favor. She wouldn't need to go to the club, by the looks of it. Her twisted plan would fall into place; she just had to be careful now. Celia knew she would have to endure some unpleasant things for a while, but who knew how much time she could get out of it?

"Tina, it's so good to see you," Celia said.

The flock of Tina's friends moved on, heading under the Gardiner Expressway underpass. Tina waved them on, saying she'd catch up, but Celia knew where this was headed. Celia stared into Tina's heavy and drunk lustful bedroom eyes. *My, how I perfected her look to entice Billy*, Celia thought. She couldn't believe the tramp was even attempting to talk to Billy now.

"It's good to see you too, Billy. Listen, I'm so sorry."

Celia stopped Tina from apologizing, "The past is in the past, isn't it?"

Tina giggled. "You look so good!" Tina fell against Celia's new body and placed her hands on Billy's chest like no fight had ever happened between them.

"Yeah, the doctors said I'm in the clear, indefinitely."

"Really! Like, for good?"

"For good I think, yes. I've felt healthy and strong lately."

Tina stepped back and twirled her now highlighted brunette locks with her index finger. Although Celia's telepathy was gone while in this mortal shell, she didn't need it to know what was on Tina's mind.

"You should come back to the condo for a drink. Seriously, we can catch up."

Celia flagged down a taxi for them both. Like Billy would have done, she held the taxi door open for Tina. There was no hesitation from Tina as her hands glided down Billy's shoulders and clutched his biceps. She leaned in. On the inside, Celia was filled with discomfort and contempt for Tina, but the well-played charade of attraction left Tina craving more.

Black leather seats ruffled as Tina's tiny frame leaned in to Billy's. Celia had never kissed a girl before, but apparently she was good at it. Celia indeed wanted to steal more mortal time for her new body, and this little act was going to cost Tina a lot of it.

The taxi driver paid no mind to the pair in the back. Through Tina's lustful lips against Billy's mouth, Celia somehow called out Front Street and Church.

It was true, Celia had kept her eyes on Billy since his terminal diagnosis. Cancer was supposed to leave him alone and hospitalized. Even though she assumed where Billy was now, Celia felt she'd spared him something he didn't need. Now, somehow, with Tina all over her, Celia spied a look at the sands of Tina's lifespan in the hourglass on her death-watch. Tina only had another ten years. Celia thought about trying to switch bodies and steal Tina's. Then she thought the better of it. She was lucky she'd pulled it off on Billy. Tina would likely not be as accepting of the supernatural. One slice of her hand to make the bond with body and scythe and Tina would probably run screaming. Celia smiled as she pictured that.

Tina thought the smile was for her. "You like kissing me again, Billy?" She spoke lustfully. Tina's desperation for Billy's body was getting embarrassing, thought Celia. Tina's seatbelt had been voluntarily removed, and she pounced on Celia's lap now. Her hips grinded rhythmically and obnoxiously against Celia's newly discovered crotch. The feeling of blood rushing to unfamiliar territory was surprisingly pleasing, despite her disdain for this woman.

Finally, the taxi driver spoke up, looking angrily in the rear-view mirror. "Hey!" Ignored by Tina for a second, he yelled it louder now. *"HEY!* I'm not gonna get my license gone for this bullshit! Out, out of my fucking taxi!"

Then he cursed in French under his breath. "*T'es une reclure de bidet.*"

Tina laughed wildly and inappropriately, as she often did in embarrassing times. Celia dropped a twenty from the stolen wallet for the driver's trouble. It was no matter. They were let out on Front Street, and from there it was only a couple of blocks to the condo Billy and Tina once shared. The dance into the lobby was a sexually driven blur of Tina's hungering hands grasping Billy's denim bulge. Celia was mildly amused. She had been curious what the experience of it all was like for a mortal man, or even for a mortal woman. She felt dominant, powerful in her new flesh as she let Tina explore.

Celia hit the button for the ninth floor, and Tina, correcting her, hitting the tenth.

"Right."

"Hasn't been that long, Billy," Tina whispered.

They fumbled down the hall, not far, and Celia quickly found herself in the very room where Billy's life had taken a downturn. Oddly, she smiled.

"What's so funny?" Tina questioned playfully.

What's so funny is your life is about to take the same downturn as Billy's, in the same room, thought Celia. "Oh, nothing. Just a lot of good times in these four walls."

"Lets make some more." Tina reached for Celia's jeans, pulling them and the boxers underneath down with force. The foreign sensations of what came next, Celia never imagined. Quickly, she found out why Tina had Billy wrapped around her finger, but Celia wouldn't fall for these same tricks. She let Tina carry on for a moment and then pushed her playfully onto the bed.

Tina laughed and then sat up, lifting her top off, slowly, seductively. She bit her lower lip and undid her scarlet lace bra, tossing it to the floor while staring hungrily at Celia at the bed's edge. Tina's flirtatious nipple play did nothing for Celia; in fact, all she could think of again was how much she'd nailed the look of Tina physically. She'd lured Billy in so easily with her curvy figure and girlish flirtations. The stories of pity from a cruel afterlife to play on Billy's empathies. Celia thought of her victory and the new sensations of mortality; she was going to enjoy these stolen days.

Tina leaned back against the bed's chestnut headboard. "You miss these?" she said, hugging her breasts together and fingering her cleavage. Celia looked over Tina's body again, trying to hide her disdain for the woman still. Tina didn't deserve her life. Regardless of if Tina deserved her time or not, Celia was a demon, and she didn't give a damn. She'd worked so hard to earn this vacation, this freedom, and now she would ensure her own pursuits for pleasure were met. Celia would endure this chore for more mortal fun and gain. She thought about how there could be no pleasure derived from fucking a person she couldn't even stand. Perhaps it was the fact that she had to model herself after Tina. Perhaps it was that she had to act bubbly to lure in Billy, she didn't know why exactly she scorned Tina so much, but the opinion was there.

Celia flicked off the lights and locked lips with Tina at the bed's edge. She let her pull her in close, climbing on the bed. Celia pictured kissing someone else, someone whose lips she'd rather have tasted, although Tina's tasted like cherry. My how Celia did like the taste of this cherry lip-gloss.

Tina didn't waste any time, wrapping her legs around Billy's hips to let Celia ease inside. Slowly, warmly inside. Tina shook as Celia eased deeper. It was clear that she desperately still wanted Billy. It was more than that, though; Celia could feel it. The emotion, the eye contact, it was not just lust, as Celia had originally thought.

"I missed you, Billy Walker," Tina said, locking her brown eyes with his — now Celia's baby blues. Celia grew more uncomfortable with each thrust, not physically, but emotionally. Tina was looking for it, she was looking for the acknowledgement of a love that still remained. Celia was a natural liar and a demon. She knew true love was exactly that — true, and she also knew enough that feigned love could never hold up. With ease Celia pulled out and motioned at Tina to bend over the bed. Thankfully for Celia, Tina was game. She could not reciprocate a love that was not true, and now she would be more careful and even more guarded to try to fool Tina into letting her guard down. She could not afford not to have Tina fall for Billy again. She was too close — so close now to her goal.

Celia's thrusts and motions hastened; she had to admit it, the harder she pounded Tina, the more she started to enjoy it. She wondered just how hard Tina could take it and decided in the moment that the frustrations of having to fuck her would be the driving force in the situation. From then on, the utter loathing she had for Tina was manifested in Billy's member deep at work.

Tina's fingers had now made their way between her legs. She screamed, "Punish me, Billy, I'm coming!" Celia thrust, faster, harder, and deeper until Tina shook and bit a pillow she'd grabbed in the midst of passion.

After that, Celia didn't know if it was the drink, the centuries of watching people at play, or a natural ability that had served her so well. She'd somehow lulled Tina into a sex coma. Celia smiled and thought, *not bad*. Only twenty minutes work, and now she'd literally reap her reward.

Celia sat quietly at the bed's edge. She summoned her scythe and took care not to make noise. Tina's face was buried in the down pillow Billy had bought her. It was easy now just to let the scythe dangle over her. How much time could she take, though? She looked at her death-watch as the sands of time in Tina's hourglass shifted. Months turned to a year, and finally a decade was shaved off. Better to go for the gusto, thought Celia. Tina had only ten years and one week left — much to Celia's disappointment. For now, that was all the time she would need, though, she supposed. Every speck of time minus a week was taken from Tina, and for the next week Celia would work her way back into Tina's life. When Tina was gone, well, home sweet home, as they say. Celia lay there, facing the ceiling, feeling accomplished. She thought about the stupidity Billy had put up with through the time that she'd watched him and Tina.

Tina and Billy had been two very successful people. Tina was a popular realtor who came off as quite good at what she did.

In Tina's spare time outside of work, Celia could see that her inner airhead was often released. That was when she thought about how to lure in Billy. Celia had observed it while looking for a way out of her reaping duties. Tina was the type that had a duel life, thought Celia. The perfect successful professional appearance, but in her personal life she'd made poor choices like cheating on Billy when he'd needed her the most.

One thing Celia noticed about Tina, which she respected, was she had been good at getting what she wanted or convincing people that something was right for them. Billy had let her have almost everything in their split. He'd been a pushover. Then she laughed, because all she had to do was look a little bit like Tina and act the part, and he'd been a pushover a second time.

Celia looked at Tina breathing in so deeply. In a strange way, she felt she had avenged Billy by taking Tina's time. The world had sorted itself out, she thought. She believed Tina was getting what she deserved in exactly the way it was meant to happen. In her delusions, Celia thought she was indeed the right one to hand out the punishment.

Sunday morning came, and Celia had slept only an hour. She would have to get use to shutting her mind down for sleep — it was strange to her. The incredible sensations of taste and touch were certainly welcome, but her new dependency on sleep was not. Celia wondered about Billy. There was certainly nothing special about him. She smirked, thinking about where in Hell might he have ended up. She could not refrain from that smirk turning to a grin as she thought of the many possible ways he would suffer. *He deserves it. They all deserve it*, she told herself.

Tina rolled over, putting her hands all over Billy's body.

"You were fantastic. I don't know what's gotten into you, Billy Walker. You were so aggressive, so different," she whispered, digging her nails subtly against Celia's chest.

"I guess maybe I have a new appreciation for life."

Celia let Tina climb on top of her, and together, unbeknownst to Tina, they began her last week of mortal life on Earth.

From her time as an ethereal spectator, Celia remembered where most everything was inside the condo. She had watched Tina and Billy together for a little while after his diagnosis. She took down a copper-colored frying pan from the overhead rack then lit the stove, placing the pan on the burner. Celia would make French toast. Not because she wanted to make Tina's last days enjoyable but because Celia had always wanted to try French toast. Decades of watching these mortals eat the most wondrous foods left her angry that she didn't know what half of it even smelled like. First, she let butter melt. Shimmering, glistening, coating the pan. She took a piece of brioche bread and couldn't help herself dipping it in the melted butter and taking a bite. "Good God," she said. Then she looked unapologetically up to the ceiling. Tina walked over and placed her hands on Celia's broad shoulders, then she leaned in close.

"Why don't we put on some tunes, like old times."

Celia smirked, "Sure, how about something from the eighties. Oh, I know, how about... 'The Final Countdown'?"

"Seriously, Billy? You once said the eighties were the worst era in music, remember?"

"I know, but that song. It really hits home for me right now."

"I don't know what has gotten into you Billy Walker, *but I like it*."

Celia's devilish smirk remained as Tina played the song over a large Bluetooth speaker. Then she carried on dipping brioche bread into a mixture of egg and cinnamon and breathed in each new scent with excitement.

6

Billy was confused. He was enveloped in a cold darkness that he could not fight. Heat rose up as the darkness around him exploded away into a thousand little shadowy serpents and slithered off. Now he could see his destination. Such heat, such burning heat stung his body from everywhere. Melancholy, hopeless faces walked hesitantly in single file to the edge of a yellow brimstone cliff. A man-like figure in a torn black- and scarlet-tipped cloak stood by the rocky edge of a pit. His cloak wisped and flowed as though it caught powerful winds from the below. Billy heard the same question asked as each person came reluctantly to him. "Are, you, guilty..."

The terrified looks on their faces before their leap off the brimstone cliff drove fear into Billy's heart. Celia had screwed him. How stupid he felt now falling for her flirtations. Her seductive words and those light amber eyes, just like Tina's. *Dammit.*

One, two, three people all jumping off into the brimstone pit seemingly on their own. Billy was four people away from his turn. Nerves and unease set in as each person before him jumped. He thought he might vomit from the crippling anxiety of it all, then it was time.

The hooded figure lifted his head slowly and questioned Billy menacingly, "Are — you — guilty."

His baritone tore at Billy's ears and echoed into the pit below. Billy looked at the revealed face. It was like a mirror, and in it Billy's tired, defeated, reflection stared back. Unlike those before him, Billy was not going to submit. He didn't answer yes; instead, he said his peace.

"Look, man. I don't belong here!"

The figure asked the same tired question, louder this time, despite Billy's answer. "ARE YOU GUILTY."

"No, I'm not fucking guilty, okay! Some reaper named Celia steals my body and lies. She manipulates me into helping her hide from something that was a lie! And then she casts me alive down here!"

The mirror faded, and behind it was a void of nothingness.

"Looks like you're telling the truth... That is a problem... Well, nothing we can do about that now. It's down the pit of despair with you!"

Before Billy could respond, the being's mirrored face had rematerialized, and one lengthy skeleton index finger pointed at him. With a flick, Billy was cast through the air into the pit of despair. The last thing Billy saw flying through darkness was his own shock reflected at him through the mirror man's face.

Endlessly, he soared down the pit. Alone, he spiraled out of control until the light above shrank so thin. It was the size of a pin's head, and eventually it was gone.

Billy had pieced it all together. He knew where he was going. Celia had screwed him when she'd branded him with her scythe. Long after the light had disappeared and it seemed to him that he would be falling for eternity, strange sounds began to rise up through the pit. Perpetual darkness and the sounds of hissing. The burning smells of decay and sulphur. Billy surmised that several earth hours had likely passed, and he still hadn't reached the bottom. He said to himself, *if this is eternity, then I'm not interested*, and began diving in an attempt to reach the end faster. No matter the flying poses he struck, no matter the efforts he made, they were useless. The damn pit went on forever.

Darkness and the smells of rot with burning fire would be his only reminder that he was not alone as he sailed through nothingness. It wasn't until he felt utter despair that nothing would ever change that he noticed something tiny start to appear below. Although the light from above had long since disappeared, below a new light grew with each panicked second.

"Oh, fuck... *Oh, FUCK*!" Billy hollered.

He tried the Superman and shot a fist to the sky; he flapped his arms like an idiot; he tried everything. He realized quickly that impact was inevitable. Billy hit the yellow brimstone ground terribly hard. He lay there writhing in pain, his body on fire and his bones crushed. Yet moments later, he stood. Still, the constant sting of the burning heat around him set in. Black brick pillars and clichéd flaming gates waited ahead for Billy. He was in Hell.

Billy stepped closer to the gates. His feet now bare, he noticed his clothes had also disintegrated. A simple loincloth kept his tally-whacker from flapping about. He looked at his tired body covered in black ash. At Hell's gates, he saw them biting at the burning orange bars, those damn Dreadlings that had taken away his landlord earlier. Some clawed, others licked with burning tongues and chewed at the flaming gates. Multitudes of blood-red arachnid eyes followed Billy's movements, some glowing through darkness, some exposed by the brightness of hellfire. Billy reluctantly closed the gap toward the gates. The squealing sounds of moving, grinding metal tore across the yellow stone landscape as he approached. Then, noise from beyond, the screams of people. Billy was terrified.

"*WAIIIIIIT!*" a voice from behind him hollered. Billy turned to see an old man in thick-rimmed black glasses approaching at his best pace. He was adorned in a light-emitting formal white suit. Dreadlings poured out of the gates, leaping on all clawed fours at Billy as the man approached.

"Back! Back!" commanded the old man. His clothes emitted pulses of holy light with each step closer. Dreadlings exploded into translucent black smoke and ash as he walked forward. The ash rained down around them. "I come with authority, you heathen creatures!" the old man yelled.

Billy stared in shock at the little old man. He didn't look threatening, with his hunched shoulders and kind face. He had a welcoming accent Billy could not pinpoint.

The grinding sounds of something big moving slowly across the brimstone landscape caused Billy to turn around. From behind the gates, a grotesque and giant half man, half slug dragged himself toward Billy's new defender. He left a mucous discharge in his wake, and his skin was a green slimy glow.

"Don't make me pull it out, vile demon!" said the old man.

The slug man groaned. He towered over Billy and his rescuer. His neon-green antennae lit the darkness as he leaned down and spoke with slime spilling out his mouth. "*What do you want?*"

"I want due process. Don't act like you don't know this man doesn't belong here! One of your people stole his body. These documents prove it." The old man held out a dossier full of pictures and papers about Celia. Billy was surprised. Then the old man flicked his hand, and they vanished.

The muscled slug man folded his arms in disapproval. Towering over them, he leaned in. Puss, maggots, and disturbing fluids oozed from sores in his green, glowing flesh. "This man is here because he is guilty. He will come with me."

"You're really going to make me do this?" questioned the old man, pulling out a holy book with a multitude of various religious symbols on the cover from the world's many religions. "I'll flip it open and read you some righteous truth! I'll do it!" As the old man said it, pages even unopened started to glow.

The slug man growled and mumbled something as he turned away.

"That's right, schlep away!" cried out the old man.

The slug man dragged himself away through Hell's gates once more.

"Listen, boy, don't get caught behind those gates. Stay out here in this wasteland, but don't get caught behind those gates, understand?"

Billy nodded.

"Good, because if you get stuck in there, it'll take twice as long to get you out. Now, take this." The old man handed Billy the righteous book. "I'll be back for you as soon as I can. I had to make sure it was actually you, but now that I know it is, I'll be back with what I need to get you out of here. Until then, shalom!"

As the old man walked away with purpose, seemingly toward nothing, Billy asked, "Who can release me from here?"

"He has many names; some are written within," replied the old man, pointing to the leather-bound book in Billy's hands.

"Can't I come with you now, please!"

"Somewhere along the line, they marked you. If you try to leave this realm right now, all they'll need to do is snap a damn finger, and you'll be brought right back."

When Billy opened the book, the pages emitted a blinding light, and he could not read them. He felt such divine power with the book open in his hands. He looked up once again for the old man. He was gone.

The old man had left with such urgency that Billy still had a whirlwind of questions in his mind, and no one to answer them. Most importantly, he asked himself just how exactly how he was going to stay safe. He could see them now, clearer than ever before. The brightness of the flames beyond beamed off their scaly black bodies. Here, they were not the shifting, shadowy figures Billy had seen in the living realm.

Billy shuddered as he felt the Dreadlings' bloody red eyes on him. Their little muscled forms revealed a strength to pierce and climb stone with clawed fingertips. Billy walked backward toward a small brimstone boulder formation. He sat leaning against it, never taking his eyes from the dozens that watched him. Despite the watchful little predators eyeing him, Billy noticed the lack of time in this place. He knew time had passed, but he didn't know how much. This coupled with the fact that sleep seemed to be a release no one was allowed here made each moment seem like days. Closing his eyes and escaping was so welcome, and if he could have done it and made those creatures disappear, he would have. Thoughts of the wasted last days of his life tortured him. Tears rolled down his cheeks. There were many people he never got to say goodbye to. The bitterness of his breakup with Tina had made him a bit of a recluse and, regrettably, a slave to alcohol in his last days. He ruminated over why he had been saved at the Gates of Hell and then, like lighting, the thought of his prayer on that bridge came back to him. He had called out for forgiveness to his Lord Jesus. He looked at the strange book again. The cross of Christ, the Jewish star of David, the Dharma of Buddhism and Hinduism, all aglow. So many symbols of the world's religions, all aglow. Billy opened the holy book. Light beyond comprehension leaked from it, and the only words he saw through the light said: *Billy Walker, saved by faith in his Lord.*

He turned the pages of the book and smiled. He saw a memory; it was him at mass, in his twenties. He had been a man of faith, unwavering faith, actually. As life invariably pulled at the threads of his patience, he knew his faith had waned. Now, though, as he held that book, he knew there was hope. As he turned page after page, he could see the good people of the world. People of every faith, praying for one another. Muslim, Hindu, Buddhist and the like, all of good intent toward one another. The shimmering book seemed so thin to the touch, yet the pages seemed endless as he turned them. Each thought and question he had about existence and why he had been spared seemed to come to light. He saw good things he'd done with his life. Some deeds were so simple, he never thought twice about them. He saw himself standing beside a homeless man, waiting in the Toronto subway system...

Billy remembered; a new clarity washed over his thoughts. He continued to watch as the events unfolded in motion through each page. He saw the exact moment his heart beat with white light. Beside his image in the book, the words *Billy Walker, man of good intent* appeared. He had given the homeless man his lunch that day. He rarely carried cash, but he remembered he'd given the man his thermos filled with soup and the sandwich Tina had made him.

Countless other small actions had piled up in this book of life. Billy clutched it closely, tightly to his chest, but as he did, a dreadful fear from beyond become audible...

The startling sound of inhuman screams above brought a downpour of ash upon him. He looked up. Light emitting from the book he held so tightly had burst Dreadlings into ash above him. Those bastards had gotten behind him somehow. They leapt and crawled down the brimstone boulder behind him.

Billy tried to stand his ground. He even held open the book and let the light within shine through the darkness. For a while, it worked. Dozens of the creatures burst to embers and ash as the books light cut through their being.

The terrible truth for Billy, though, was that those that attacked him from above had merely been a diversion for those that came from behind. Billy had gotten himself turned around in fear. He had not paid mind to the dozens of Dreadlings that poured out from the open gates in the distance. First, the searing pain of claws on his wrist, then they pierced into his sides. Still, he clutched the book the old man had given him, shining it at any Dreadling who came near. Tirelessly they sacrificed themselves, piling on one another to pin his arms down.

It was then that their overwhelming efforts knocked the leather-bound book to the ground, and it closed. As it fell against the brimstone ground, Billy knew he was damned. Dreadlings dragged him away with claws painfully sunk in. Yet all he could do was watch the book shine in the distance and writhe in defiant protest.

"*Scriii!*"

The deafening sounds of triumphant Dreadlings parading him through Hell's Gates had Billy's heart racing. Despite being jostled about atop the claws of the horde, he saw people in black iron cages. Some were fat, some thin, all hopeless. The cages' steel flowed down to one single red-hot spike underneath that wedged into the burning ground below.

"I don't belong here!" Billy cried out.

Black centipedes with burning red feelers crawled along through the fire and the darkness, ones that were as big as Billy and some bigger than any animal he'd seen on Earth. The fires that burned gave flashes and glimpses of beasts that lurked to cause misery. Billy was dropped by the Dreadlings at the hands of the slug man who'd come for him the first time. His grotesque appearance was already stained in Billy's mind from before, but he still tried to look away. The demon leaned over him. The ends of his neon-green antennae lit up the darkness around Billy again.

"No one escapes their destiny," he said, putting one meaty, vile hand over Billy's mouth, and with that, Billy felt his voice leave him.

Dangling by one of his ankles, Billy flailed about in the slug man's clutches. The cuts in his sides from the Dreadlings were gone, but the pain wasn't.

Twisted and towering stained iron torches lined a winding path that spiraled down to levels below. The slug man looked down at Billy dangling in his right hand and grinned. "You will be a fine meal for Theodore, but he likes his meat *seasoned*."

With his free hand, the slug man pried Billy's mouth open. Then, the wriggling of maggots filled Billy's mouth, and he felt them cascading down to his innards. The slug man threw Billy with such force that he coughed up maggots from within as he hit the ground and rolled onto his back.

Billy hadn't even been able to get to his feet before a glimpse of horror from the mouth of a cavern shocked him even further. No longer shrouded in the shadows, a thirty-foot cyclops toad crept out. It was indeed Theodore. Celia had not been joking when she'd told Billy about the beast. With his voice gone and his insides wriggling with parasites, he did not think of revenge. There was no point. Defeated, Billy felt the warmth of Theodore's lightning-fast tongue lift him off the ground, and then he was inside the mouth of suffering.

7

The sickening flex of the toad's muscles pushing Billy down led him to drop into its scorching stomach acids. Splashing against Billy's skin, the acids left no mark, but the sting and shock of the pain almost paralyzed him. He tried to stay afloat and sank as he lost the fight. Below him, digestive sounds and gurgling inside the beast's belly gave Billy a sense of urgency and panic. He kicked hard and treaded up through digestive juices. Shooting up with a giant gasp, Billy noticed another person inside the beast.

"First time in here, then, is it young chap?" said the voice of an Englishman. Billy turned to see a white-haired older man. All Billy could really see was the Englishman's head as he bobbed about. His appearance suggested he was in his early sixties but in good shape. He wore a white, neatly trimmed mustache that twirled about in a circle on either side. "Can you speak, young man?"

Billy shook his head.

"Ah, they took your voice. Well, I can do enough talking for the pair of us. My friends call me Malgore. Well, they did when I had friends. I suppose you're wondering things like, will I be digested and is this truly it for me?"

Billy nodded.

"Well, you can't kill what is already dead now, can you, young fellow? Let me tell you, I've been in here a few times now. You get use to it." The Englishman paused as they continued to tread about in Theodore's stomach. "You'll only experience the pain of it all. I've been in this creature's belly I'd say a month by human time. Let me tell you something, though: this damn creature is a constipated abomination! You get flushed down there and you'll be squished in its rectum for an unprecedented amount of time."

Billy's eyes grew wide as the Englishman continued treading acid.

"There's certainly room for two to dwell in the beast's belly comfortably, I suppose."

The Englishman laughed and carried on, "I wish it was a joke, my lad, but I once was in a conga line of ladies and gentlemen that the beast couldn't pass. Ended up some bloke's fat head had the toad all bunged up." The Englishman looked at Billy with surprise for a moment. "Oh, here we go!" he proclaimed.

Like a waterpark wave-pool, Theodore's stomach acids swished about wildly. Billy quickly resorted to a swimming technique he remembered from his youth. He assumed the position of the dead man's float. His arms and chest relaxed as he rode the waves and bobbed about with the beast's motions. Once in a while, he poked his head up for perspective and carried on. The waves from Theodore's movements seemed never-ending, though. Billy had no idea how long he could hold out like this.

He looked across to his counterpart. The old Englishman was riding the waves like a true champion. He'd even managed a wink midstride as he caught Billy's gaze. *Just what in hell is going on?* thought Billy. He was struggling to keep away from the toad's digestive tract, and here was this man doing the breaststroke with a smile.

"Looks like the beast has settled, young chap."

As fluids settled and Billy clung to a rotted ulcer on the creature's stomach wall, he watched the Englishman look up at its esophagus.

"Ah, new arrivals."

Not one, but two people splashed their way down. A young man with a nice tan complexion in his twenties and a plump brunette with an hourglass figure treaded inside the beast's belly alongside them.

"Ah, we meet again," said the Englishman to them both.

The young man spoke first, looking at Billy. "Never seen you before. I'll tell you something about this gringo over here, though. Don't drop your guard because of his charm, okay? It's everyone for themselves in this fucking thing..."

Billy looked over to the Englishman. Between his devilish grin and the glint in his eyes, he knew the young man spoke the truth.

The young man stared down the Englishman with anger and flared nostrils. Then he yelled. "I'm not spending a month in this thing's ass again!"

"Indeed," the Englishman said, smiling. "We have a problem then, because you see, I'd rather not either."

There in Theodore's ulcer-ridden belly, they stared each other down. The toad's acid had long since dissolved the loincloths that once covered them all. Still, the acid stung against Billy's flesh, but like the Englishman had said, it was pain without visible consequence. Billy looked at all of them treading about, separated by only a few meters. When the brunette made eye contact with Billy, he tried to tell her something. He took his right hand and ran it vertically up his throat, mimicking an explosion like he'd thrown up.

She acknowledged him with a subtle nod, which Billy conceived as understanding. After that, peace was quickly lost and the Englishman disclosed his true nature, lunging toward the other young man.

Billy pounded fist after fist against one of Theodore's ulcers while the Englishman fought for space with his young rival. All the while, sickening wails of a thirty-foot cyclops toad with indigestion were heard even from the inside.

Again and again, Billy struck, kneeling, clinging against the ulcer. The beast stirred wildly, hopping about in anger, and finally Billy lost his footing. Chaotic, acidic, waves immersed him again. Billy took in a mouthful of the creature's acids in a panic after his fall.

How terribly his eyes stung and insides burned. Billy spied the Englishman, who now dunked his rival in Theodore's stomach acid whilst holding him in a headlock. Billy ignored their fight and looked elsewhere. He saw from the other side of the beast the woman do a flying kick to the Englishman's head as an acidic wave swept her toward him. It was all happening too fast when Billy saw light shine down from above.

Theodore's mouth had opened, and he was in fact going to vomit, thanks to Billy punching that ulcer and the ridiculous commotion inside. Billy was the first to shoot up an acidic geyser from underneath him. Behind him, the woman was launched quickly up the toad's esophagus. Still the other two fought below. Powerful muscles pushed them up and wedged Billy and the woman together in the pulsing throat of Theodore for a moment. Billy's face awkwardly pushed against the soft, comforting breasts of his fellow escapee as she slid up to him. Although Billy could not speak, he didn't know that he would have apologized for it regardless. Awkward as it may have been, far worse had happened as of late, and a supple set of dirty pillows to the face was the least of his worries.

Theodore convulsed and shook his wretched head. The woman was shot out first, passing by Billy violently. Then Billy shot out onto the hard and rocky floor of what he thought might be the beast's dwelling. Finally, the battling Englishman and his young opponent slid out of Theodore with less effort. All of them lay against the brimstone cave floor, panting.

The Englishman rolled onto his back and looked up first. There was a dim light from fire outside the cave. In the flickering light, it was clear Theodore had recovered from his episode. With a grimacing cycloptic stare, the toad looked down at its four escaped snacks.

"It's wise to run!" cried the Englishman as he sprang up and passed Billy with what seemed like the sprint of an Olympian.

Billy jumped to his feet. His heels kicked up debris from the cave floor, and he passed the Englishman, running faster than he'd ever gone before. Billy's only mistake was looking over his shoulder in paranoia as Theodore hopped menacingly after his fleeing food. The toad's frightening cycloptic eye caught Billy's. Red veins pulsing, a yellow, revolting iris froze Billy in place. His heart sank with utter horror. He was victim to the toad's paralyzing stare.

The Englishman passed him. "Sorry, old bean!" he quipped. "Better you than me!" Billy felt the Englishman's heel smack down by his ankle, and he fell onto his back. The woman apologized as she ran by, bouncing to the side, away from Theodore's darting tongue.

Billy stood up and tried to run again, but it was too late. The toad had retracted his tongue like a slingshot, and it found its target this time. The warm stickiness of Theodore's tongue clung to Billy's bare back. He tried stretching, resisting to get to freedom. The cave had been within sight for Billy, but the toad's hunger would be satisfied. Billy was lifted up high, and, helplessly, he was swallowed hole.

The familiar slide down and sudden drop left Billy in a state of defeat and depression. Battling for ground to cling to or a giant ulcer clutch was a failure this time.

The squeeze of Theodore's digestive tract had trapped Billy's foot and now was pulling him down for a repulsive ride.

An overwhelming stench soaked into Billy's nostrils as he was wedged into a conga line of misery. Billy's feet touched what seemed like someone's face. Wrapped in a cocoon of flexing viscera, neither he nor the person in front of him could see one another. Now he understood why the Englishman had been obsessed with staying in Theodore's stomach. Mere seconds had passed, and already Billy knew how quickly madness would set in. The toad's small intestine was an organic, claustrophobic nightmare.

8

The groundwork for Celia's lies had been laid through years of Billy's puppy-dog love for Tina. The reentry into Tina's life was happening, and Celia's desire for a vacation filled with mortal pleasure and luxuries was so close. The thought of Tina's blissful ignorance in her final days of deception brought Celia a twisted sort of pleasure.

Last night, they celebrated their reunion with Tina's parents. They had always loved Billy, so the news of so-called familiarity and stability in Tina's life again was welcomed with open arms. Now, according to Celia's death-watch, there were mere hours left before Tina was destined to meet her eternal end. The little grains of sand left trickling down the hourglass one by one as she looked at the death-watch represented a new freedom. Celia smirked as she watched those few grains of time fall.

Celia walked over and took a seat, resting her elbows atop the white quartz breakfast bar countertop. The condo's breakfast bar was a fine spot to gaze out upon the cold world while sipping orange juice. She'd lied to Tina last night. She'd excited her with speculations of a new job in programming and network security that paid twice what Billy use to make. She smirked, picturing Tina's reaction. Biding her time was easy now with so little left. She dazzled and charmed Tina every day of the week with lies and sex. Tonight, she would end the deception.

"If you could do anything you wanted but you only had until tonight, what would it be?"

Tina stepped into the kitchen from their bathroom. She had been straightening her hair and was only half done.

"I don't know? That's a strange question. I suppose I'd come home early from work and do that thing we did last night again, then I'd catch an early dinner. Why do you ask?"

"No reason." Celia grinned. "Why not come home early, and I'll take you to that pasta house you love so much tonight?"

"I'd love to, Billy, but I have so many properties to tour and... Well, you know what? Yeah, I'll see if I can hold off on one or two." Tina carried on happily preening for the day ahead and then said goodbye with a kiss. Celia grinned devilishly as the door closed behind Tina and then sat in the comfort of the condo alone.

She had some work to do before Tina's crescendo took place this evening. She needed to head back to Billy's disgusting apartment for a couple things. One was his ID. Billy often carried his phone and his debit card and nothing else. Celia would need his other particulars. The stolen grand she'd taken had already dwindled down to a hundred. She would look to see if Billy had anything of value left at the place before moving permanently into the condo. Celia threw on a pair of jeans, took a look in the bathroom mirror, brushed Billy's teeth, and headed out the door.

A few streetcars later, Celia hopped out at Billy's old place. She dangled the carabiner Billy kept his keys on between her fingers, then twirled it around anxiously. The usual derelict crowd populated the filthy stairwells of Billy's three-story.

One held her head in her lap while the other stepped down from the stairs and asked Celia for a light. The young man was already high, Celia could tell. He aimed for a bump and tried to spark one last flame from the spent lighter he held.

When it didn't work again, he shook with anger, throwing it to the floor. He looked at Celia furiously. "I said gimme your FUCKING lighter!"

"I don't have a lighter," Celia said firmly while the addict stepped even closer, blocking her path.

"What fucking good are you then!" the young addict screamed and scratched at his sore-covered face.

Celia smiled. She contemplated pulling out her scythe and driving it into the young man's heart. She wondered what effect it might have now that she was in a mortal shell. She knew it would kill him, but would another reaper have to harvest the soul? Above her now, the sound of the fire exit door bursting opening diverted everyone's attention.

A rather short, fat, and completely bald man with an olive complexion stood above them, escorted by two police officers.

"Those are the ones, always in my fucking building. You fucking troglodytes don't even pay rent here. Get the fuck out!"

Celia recognized the man. It was in fact Devlin Gainsmore himself. He'd finally come to sort out the slum that was this building, likely because he couldn't get a new landlord on such short notice. Police seized drugs and drug paraphernalia from the two junkies and let Celia pass by. At the stairwell's upper entrance, Devlin Gainsmore sneered at Celia. There was something strange about the man, something different, sensed Celia. Billy was much taller than Gainsmore, and being in his body, Celia physically looked down on Gainsmore as she squeezed by his belly. A certain unease, one that she hadn't felt in a while, stirred inside her. She ignored it and walked the hallway to Billy's old apartment.

As she touched the scum-encrusted knob to Billy's unit, she concluded he was a defeated man long before her. She would never put up with these living conditions. The wooden door was chipped away from someone trying to break in, the peephole was broken, and the hallway carpet was threadbare from foot traffic. Celia swept through Billy's old bedroom, finding his wallet and some new clothes. Then, with only a backpack to fill, she would leave this dump forever. Celia peered through the cracked peephole to the hallway. Police were still talking with Devlin Gainsmore. She eavesdropped...

"What's going to go on with these squatters then? They'll be out and overdosing again, getting revived in my building by the end of the week, correct?"

Gainsmore grew angry as he carried on. "I'm gonna pay for their shit life choices and they'll be back leaving needles and literal shit on the damn floor again. And you people will be too busy to give a damn, won't you..."

The older more seasoned officer responded, "We can see about the possession and trespass charges and go from there."

The pair of officers walked both cuffed addicts outside, with Gainsmore not far behind. Celia rushed over to the bedroom window to watch them leave. Her unease grew watching Devlin waddle about after the police. When she focused and looked out the window, it was clear why that unease had stirred inside her. The portly businessman held a moonlit blade in hand, much like Celia's but with red runic symbols pulsing on the blade's sides.

"Fuck," said Celia. She was shocked. Devlin Gainsmore was indeed a reaper, or perhaps had been at one time much like her. He had to be more powerful, considering those symbols on the blade. She tried to decipher them, but he was too far away, and they were too small.

Just what the hell is he going to do with that scythe? thought Celia. Then she saw.

Devlin barely moved, but the scythe seemed to stretch out and around a police officer's back. With the officers turned away, Devlin thrust his ethereal blade into each junkie, one after the other. Pinpoint accuracy left the two addicts dropping to the ground with vicious convulsions mere feet from the police cruisers.

Celia listened.

"Get the naloxone!" one officer cried out.

The other radioed for an ambulance. Celia leaned back, taking it all in from above. *An otherworldly end*, she told herself, *and mortal measures are fruitless.*

Celia remained hidden yet curious from the window as Devlin tore the junkies from their mortal shells. The junkies stood over themselves in confusion while police administered naloxone and waited for paramedics. Devlin subtly waved his scythe, and Celia saw just exactly what the runic symbols meant. He was indeed a demon of higher power and rank. The runes burst to a brighter blood-red color. It was with his cursed blade that Celia saw he controlled Hell's Dreadlings.

Like trained hounds catching a hunter's prize, the Dreadlings grabbed the souls of Devlin's victims, dragging them into a swirling black portal. Just like the portal she'd used on Billy, this one burst into a thousand tiny shadowy serpents and then sank into the ground. Their souls had disappeared, screaming.

Celia smirked. She'd always enjoyed the screams of the mortals when Dreadlings clawed them. She was pleasantly surprised by what she had just seen. She knew she was a lower-level demon when it came to the hierarchy of Hell. She had lived that way for a century. Seeing this new power excited her on a primal level. With power like that, she guessed Devlin was certainly still Lucifer's servant, though. Quickly, she weighed the pros and cons of such a state. She told herself that this new freedom was better than any power with the chains of servitude attached.

Five Dreadlings pounced back to their master and sat by Devlin's side like the evil little arachnid-gargoyles they were. Still a little mesmerized by the events, Celia had moved forward and closer to the uncovered window. She watched intently. One of the Dreadlings sniffed the air, and so blindingly and inhumanly fast, it looked up to the window. She swore it looked directly at her with its crimson predatory eyes. Celia dropped down to her knees in a panic. The stinging as she hit the bedroom floor made her gasp. She shook in fear. Had the little beast seen right through her new mortal charade? Did it know her true nature?

Celia was in undiscovered territory. The thought of consequences for her actions was frightening. Hell did not tolerate disobedience, Lucifer did not tolerate disobedience, and Celia knew she was the definition of that these days.

She grabbed Billy's ID and the backpack filled with a few personal belongings, then she fled. It wasn't until she was two blocks over that she stopped to catch her breath and look back. Billy's body was not in its best shape. He was naturally built like a brick, but it was clear he lacked cardio. Celia peered over to the parking lot from behind a nearby bus shelter. Devlin, with scythe still in hand, subtly stamped the shaft against the ground, and the remaining Dreadlings burst to dust. She watched the heavy man wobble into a Rolls-Royce and disappear into the streets of Toronto.

Hell had let Devlin Gainsmore get away with murder, so why couldn't she? Celia had wondered about the way of it all; she questioned it now. After seeing Devlin command Hell's lowest demons in that parking lot, Celia thought about things. The paranoia of the beast looking through not only that window but also perhaps her mortal disguise was troubling. Celia's mind drifted back to her other obligations. My how she wished she could pierce Tina's heart when she got back to the condo instead of spending another second with her. Tina's annoying lust for Billy's body could certainly be avoided with a blade to the heart, thought Celia with a chuckle.

She descended a series of speckled granite stairs below the cold Toronto streets. She pushed open steel turnstile gates to the subway system as she threw in a token. Devlin Gainsmore and the Dreadlings were still a frightening afterthought. She walked to the back of a busy car, looking for a place to sit with what she had seen still swirling about her mind. She stood for the moment holding a support rail and felt a familiar unease, just like when she had first met Gainsmore in that stairwell. Celia looked around the car: a youth buried in her phone wearing earbuds, a man reading a book, a woman staring into nothingness and, yet Celia felt something more. When the car doors closed and it drifted down the track, she shrugged off the feeling. She struck it up to the paranoia of seeing a Dreadling controlled by someone. She never knew the beasts could be controlled like that, not here, not on Earth.

Celia's railcar embraced the darkness of a tunnel and passed an opposing car. The whirling rush of wind from their passing was when Celia's paranoia took over again, this time entirely. She flicked her wrist out of fear and summoned her moonlit blade. In the darkness she didn't care how she looked. She held the scythe with a death grip so firmly, it made Billy's hands shake. All the passengers who rode with her paid no mind to Celia's steadfast posture. It wasn't until she saw the conjoining car twist and align straight again that her paranoia became more than just that. The Dreadling she'd feared had seen her was here, and with it were two more. Their arachnid eyes did see right through her mortal shell, and perhaps they were her to punish her. It all happened so fast that she was not sure who struck first. Celia felt the pain of a mortal as a Dreadling sank its shadowy claw into her. What utter disdain she had for this part of the human condition, she told herself. Celia cleaved the head off the Dreadling that had sank its claws into her leg. Black ash and orange cinder burned away as it died, but her scythe kept moving. It made short work of them, to her surprise. In the same swoop, another of the three met its ashen end as Celia cut it in two. Finally, the last of the three hissed and flicked its dripping tar like tongue at her.

"Shadowy little fucker," she quipped.

Its little quadruped frame leapt about supernaturally from above the car to the floor. Celia caught it in the abdomen as its claw was inches from her left eye. When the last embers of evil dissolved in that car, Celia looked at her scythe in hand and saw something peculiar. Three red runes just like Gainsmore's scythe now branded into her blade. Celia looked around the car at the passengers. Odd looks from all three didn't worry her. She knew they saw nothing supernatural. What they had seem was an insane man tossing his empty hands about at nothing, and for them it must have been another commute in the subway system.

Celia sat at last in one of the red subway seats lined with velvet fabric. She drifted away, thinking, panicking about those three beasts. Where there was one there was more, and where there were three, there was perhaps an army. She could not kill off an army, and she knew it. She would need to pay close attention to her surroundings now and be ready to wield her blade at any moment.

Rumblings of forgotten hunger crept up, pulling her back to her new mortal reality. She was questioning her choices now. Her new mortality was supposed to be fun, but being detected and followed about the city by Hell-beasts was not supposed to be part of it.

Subway doors slid open, and new riders disregarded their mortality through all consuming smartphones as they sat down. Celia thought back to killing Tina before they went out for dinner. Then, while taking in the faces of these strangers, Celia decided there was greater entertainment for her in letting nature take its course. She was not so impatient that she couldn't wait until after Tina paid for her meal to see her last mortal moments unfold.

Red and white accents of passing subway cars blurred while opposing headlights gleamed through the tunnels again. Celia lost her thoughts in it all and dreamed back to before she was a reaper. The days of old, when she was a simple demon, punishing mortal sin rather than collecting the sinners. She was not a complete liar when she'd spoken to Billy about Hell. A grin crept up from memories past. My, how she'd fed so many tortured souls to that cyclops toad, Theodore. She laughed loudly and got some awkward stares again, but she didn't give a damn. Thinking about Theodore, she missed the vile toad. Celia wondered how the repulsive beast was. She hoped the new caretaker remembered that Theodore liked his meat seasoned.

9

Celia took a quick look at her death-watch. There was so much time for the reaping in this subway car. If she knew she could steal a whole lifetime without consequence, she would have. There were unfortunately things she feared now. The truth was, she didn't know what would or could happen to her now. Thieving a mortal's body was proving to have complications. She knew the other side had their own collectors of the dead, or the "good ones," as some called them. Celia wasn't as concerned with the other side, really, not as much as she was with Devlin Gainsmore and his Dreadlings. She knew angels didn't hunt reapers. No, Celia was afraid of what would happen if Gainsmore's little Dreadlings came back again in greater numbers. She sat pondering in the train. She thought Gainsmore was meant to kill her for her disobedience, she thought more Dreadlings were certain to come for her, and she thought there was only one thing left for her. The only thing left for her to be truly safe. She had to kill Devlin Gainsmore.

Celia exited the subway at Union Station and walked the few blocks over to Tina's condo. It was time to pursue her master plan. Caution would be her ally. She would take things slowly, and when all was said and done, the freedom to pursue mortal pleasures without consequence would be her reward. As she rode the elevator up to Tina's condo, she reviewed her plan in her mind. Give Tina her last romp, her last meal, and her final surprise.

Decades of mortal observations had given Celia perspective over their behavior. The average argument between couples was about cleanliness and household chores. This afternoon Celia took every precaution to make sure Tina would be in a good mood once home. Dishes, bed, carpets, countertops, everything was perfect. The time of waiting was at hand.

If there was one thing she didn't mind about Tina, it was her taste in alcohol. A blender of daiquiri that Celia had mixed sat on the quartz kitchen countertop. She poured one for herself and stepped out to the enclosed condo balcony. The view of Toronto's harborfront was magical to her. This city would be her playground soon. Little mortals, so small from above, went about their days, taking for granted the marvels of Celia's favorite new senses, taste and touch. She sipped the sweet cocktail and drifted back to the short time spent with her teacher.

She'd lied to Billy about that. Her scythe had been awarded to her upon completion of her training. She remembered using her instructor's scythe for her first reaping. She hadn't completely lied to Billy about that incident. It had certainly been a man who died in a car wreck. The same way she'd told Billy. A tire had crashed through his windshield, killing him instantly. Her teacher had then awarded her his old scythe and vanished into a swirling black portal of his own design, going back to Hell for reassignment. Celia had taken over his duties after centuries of service. She took another sweet sip and wondered how her instructor, or anyone for that matter, resisted the temptation to take a little mortal vacation, like she had. Perhaps her teacher hadn't pieced together how, or perhaps he hadn't cared. Two things were certain to Celia at this point: this daiquiri was remarkable, and mortal pleasures were not to be taken for granted.

9

The sound of the condo door opening drew Celia away from her daydreams. Tina was home.

"Billy, wow! I see you were busy."

"Made you a daiquiri. I thought we could start there?"

Tina smiled flirtatiously. "You thought right."

"How was your day?"

"Argh, don't get me started. When I rescheduled the one showing, you would have thought I'd ruined their lives."

"Well, they should have been more understanding. You had more important things to do."

"More important *things*, Billy?" Tina said lustfully.

Not even a minute home, and she was ready to mount Billy. One last inconvenience, one last price to pay, thought Celia. The blender of daiquiri didn't last long between them. Celia's disdain for Tina's personality was drowned in rum. She looked at Tina in her work attire. Black skirt, high heels, hair done perfectly with blonde highlights. Tina was indeed an attractive woman by society's ridiculous standards, thought Celia. Celia was a feminine demon and absolutely found the male form more attractive, but the alcohol had caught up with her now. Perhaps this last thrill for Tina could be enjoyed by both parties, she told herself. Up until now, Celia had gone through the motions to keep Tina hooked and take her money. Now, since Tina was here and had mere hours left, there was nothing to lose.

"If I was willing to do anything for you, what would you ask of me?" Celia asked playfully.

"Hmm, I like were this is going."

"I thought you might."

"Come with me," responded Tina.

Celia followed Tina into the bedroom. A black lace thong slid slowly down both stocking-covered legs and was set gently to the floor. Tina gestured Celia closer, curling her index finger. Then, when she was close enough, she pulled her in and kissed her. Celia didn't mind; the sensations were growing on her. She imagined other things and other people. It wasn't long before pillows hit the floor and Tina slid atop Celia. Those drinks had certainly hit the spot, and so did Celia as Tina moaned, "Don't stop, Billy."

She let Celia finish, and she seemed to as well, but underneath it all, Celia could tell Tina had held back a little. Another hidden desire, perhaps? Tina climbed off, still looking hot and bothered. She bit her bottom lip and laughed flirtatiously. Lustful bedroom eyes gazed over, and then she came out with it.

"Now I'll tell you what I want, Billy," she said, rolling off the bed. She stood at the edge and leaned back in, kissing then biting Celia's bottom lip. When she released it, she said, "I want to cum in public, and I want you in control."

"*What?*"

"Remember, Billy?"

Tina pulled out a red lace pair of underwear from her top nightstand drawer. "Still remember that time?"

Celia didn't remember. In fact, she had no idea, but still she played along. "How could I forget."

"That time in the movie theater..."

"Yes, it was amazing," lied Celia.

"This time we'll do it in the restaurant."

Celia knew Tina was a little wild sexually, but she didn't realize just how uninhibited the woman truly was until that moment. Who the hell had a special pair of underwear for fucking in public? As Tina went to another dresser drawer, it was revealed exactly what was so special about this particular pair. Tina pulled out a shiny silver bullet and placed it inside a pocket at the crotch of the panties. She took out a little remote control and tossed it to Celia. Celia smiled; she was going to enjoy this. By very little effort on her part, Tina would be satisfied, and she wouldn't have to touch her ever again. Things were working out wonderfully.

Tina slipped on the red lacey underwear.

Celia looked down at the little black remote. "Are the batteries good?" she questioned, clicking the mid-level speed button.

Tina replied, *"They're good... They're g–good."*

Celia set foot into the hallway first, and Tina locked the condo. She leaned in, kissing Celia in the empty elevator as the doors closed. Through passionate lips she whispered, "After the restaurant, I'll take you home and return the favor."

Not likely. You might not even make it to the restaurant, she thought, looking subtly down at her death-watch in the elevator mirror. Spotlessly polished elevator doors opened, and the pair walked past the building's security guard, who wished them a good night. Tina smiled and wished the guard the same.

Toronto's winter air hit hard, but no one seemed to care. The city thrummed with sounds of its people at play as they found their next destination. Tina held Celia's hand as they strolled the few blocks over to her favorite eatery. They neared a crosswalk, and Celia pressed the button for the light to change. An obnoxiously driven orange SUV just about ran up on the sidewalk as Tina stepped forward to walk.

For a moment, Celia thought it may have been the end for Tina. Quickly, she was disappointed when the SUV squealed its tires and corrected. Celia watched the vehicle park in a commercial parking lot across from their restaurant.

"You alright?" Celia asked Tina convincingly, though she didn't care.

"A little shaken."

"Too much power for the little man, I guess. Don't worry about it; let's just enjoy the evening," Celia said, smiling and taking Tina's hand. She held it hand with such sincerity. Inside her, the contempt for the gesture was well veiled.

Flowing out from an expensive hotel across the street, tourists crossed the two-way road at a moment of calm. There was always a line-up to get into this place. A crowd had gathered outside its brass-decked entrance. On this day, Celia had called in a reservation. They walked up to the reception counter and gave their names. A slender young man in glasses took two menus in hand and led them to their table. The quaint eatery with its stained glass and dimmed mood lighting was to Tina the best place to eat in the city. Celia had asked specifically for a more private table before knowing exactly how kinky Tina truly was — she was thankful for that request now. Their waiter seated them in an old replica train caboose with open windows looking down on the rest of the restaurant. Celia looked across the two-seat table at Tina.

"Will this do?"

There were, after all, two other couples seated a little farther down.

"It's perfect, Billy." Tina smiled back warmly.

Celia could tell from watching Tine fidgeting while she sat in suspense that this wouldn't just be fun for her alone.

A tray of bread and whipped garlic butter arrived. Celia thought about pressing Tina's buttons. Then, after Tina ordered herself a Bellini, Celia began.

Tina's subtle jump brought a smirk to Celia's face. Celia enjoyed being in control so much that it seemed like the waiter was back instantly. She'd always enjoyed control over people, no matter if it was pleasure of pain, it seemed. With the Bellini set down by the waiter in front of Tina, Celia eased off for the moment.

"And have we decided on our order?" questioned the waiter.

"A minute still?" Celia said, and Tina nodded in agreement. Seductively, Tina sipped from her straw, watching, waiting, for the tempo under the table to increase, and my how it did. Celia looked subtly down at the remote and pressed Tina's buttons literally. The little silver bullet hummed quietly enough that only they heard, and Celia let it cascade back down to an easy rhythm.

Somewhere between glances across the table and sips of her colorful drink, Tina decided on her order. It hadn't been hard. She ordered her usual dish of spaghetti with a spicy marinara sauce. Celia, on the other hand, was pleased with the irony of ordering angel hair pasta.

Time passed quickly for them both as each was entertained in their own way. Celia was enjoying herself a little to much with the remote. Tina moved her fingers over the stem of her Bellini glass, up and down its length in anticipation of a change in speed.

Playfully yet sadistically on Celia's part, the pulses were increased from across the table. She'd hit some wild setting with the symbol of a rising and falling mountain. Tina mouthed, "Stop," and whispered, "I want to enjoy this for a little while."

Celia smirked and decided she would allow it. Things slowed down — just a little. She looked subtly at her death-watch as their food arrived. She smirked at the hourglass reading. Barely even a grain was left for Tina. Their eyes met in what Tina thought was a moment of passion, but for Celia it was evil satisfaction.

"Anything else you will need at the moment?" questioned the waiter.

"We're fine," Celia replied.

Celia let Tina have a couple of uninterrupted bites. On the third, Celia hit a button that had rising spikes, then she leaned back entertained. Tina grasped the wood table, and her fork slipped, bouncing off her plate. Devilishly, Celia smirked slowing the remote again. Each time Tina went for her fork, Celia did a little burst. A sip of her Bellini, a rise of the naughty little motor below. A taste of her pasta, a taste of swelling pleasure.

Then, for a moment, it all stopped. Tina slowly put her cocktail glass down. Celia had let her put it down and started again to ease her into it. From the look in Tina's eyes, Celia knew she was completely, entirely, under her rhythmic spell. Now was her undoing.

The silver bullet in Tina's kinky panties was being driven slowly to its peak.

Flushed cheeks and the fight to make her convulsions subtle drew no attention. It wasn't until what followed Tina's crescendo that heads truly turned. Tina's fluttering eyes rolled further back, and then her convulsions eased. Her white-knuckled grip loosened from the wooden table, and shockingly, her face dove into her plate of spaghetti. After it hit with a sickening thud, panic erupted around the restaurant. The people at the other two tables in that decorative train caboose sprang up quickly. Someone, a random woman, jumped up to their aid. Their table looked like a murder scene thanks to the marinara massacre of Tina's pasta. Little red speckles were spattered about Celia's cheeks.

Celia hollered for help so sincerely, she almost fooled herself. The concerned lover was being played wonderfully as she stood by Tina's unconscious side. Inside her was a joy that could hardly be contained, but she fought the smile. Tina was gone, and my how Celia was going to have fun.

Waiters ran over. One started life-saving motions, and Celia stood back as if in shock. Celia knew they would take Tina away in an ambulance. Somewhere along the way, another reaper, one that still obeyed their duties, would separate soul from body and end things permanently for Tina. Paramedics burst into the historic stained-glass eatery.

Celia watched them try to save Tina all the way into the back of the ambulance. She heard one paramedic say to the other, "It looks like a heart attack."

Deep inside, she laughed. *Mortals*, she thought, a*lways trying to defy death. I am death*. She smirked as the ambulance pulled away with siren blaring.

The traumatized restaurant manager came out. "I can drive you to the hospital. Do you need a ride?" he stammered.

Celia turned to face the young man. "Yes," she said with counterfeit sorrow.

The awkward ride over was thankfully not long and came to a stop outside the hospital's emergency entrance doors. Celia walked to the front desk.

"Billy Walker, here for Tina Abdilla."

"Room 306," replied a nurse.

Celia took her time after that. She even grabbed a snack from a nearby vending machine. Mint chocolate candies tickled her taste buds, and she found more exciting and foreign new tastes.

"Fuck," Celia mumbled through sticky lips, "these things are…"

Then, at the end of the hall, room 306 caught her eye. Celia savored her mint chocolate candies a bit longer; she'd coincidentally found a swell spot to observe Tina's room at a distance.

She watched and popped more candies into her mouth. *Any time now*, she told herself, looking at the now empty hourglass that had represented Tina's mortal timeline. Celia waited impatiently. There were, to her surprise and disappointment, no Dreadlings. There was no tortured screaming of Tina's soul, and the familiar gnarled fingertips and evil red eyes of Hell's gargoyles were absent. Instead, a man in a shimmering white suit stood beside Tina's bed.

Seeing that made her bitter. She didn't know how, she didn't know why, but somewhere along the line, Tina had apparently done something right. Celia didn't know if it was repentance or kindness of heart that had made a difference, and she didn't give a damn.

Celia watched, finishing her candies, and threw the empty box at a nearby waste can. She heard the distinct time of death pronounced. A doctor had called Tina's end. Celia smiled as she was joined in the hallway by the man in the shimmering white suit. He guided Tina through the wall, kindly, gently, holding her hand. Tina was adorned in a glowing white gown and stepped with him toward a beautiful white portal of divine light. *Sickening*, thought Celia. Before they went through, Tina caught Celia looking at her down the hall. Celia leaned against the gray plastic hallway railing and smirked back at her.

Celia knew now that Tina was in the ethereal realm, and she was seeing her real form. Celia flicked her hand, summoning and commanding her glowing moonlit blade. Then she grinned and took in Tina's flabbergasted expression. Celia winked, blew her a kiss, and waved goodbye forever. Tina, still shocked and confused, stepped into the light with the kind man as her guide.

"And all that was yours is mine," said Celia as she turned around and walked away.

10

Life was something of a dreamy vacation for Celia now. These new mortal sensations were indeed all that she'd wanted and more. She'd played her role consoling Tina's parents at her "unexpected" funeral. Now, Celia was reaping the fruits of her so-called labor. She lived like a queen in this condo. Cinnamon candles, Enya on Tina's vinyl record player while sitting in the enormous soaker tub. Bubble bath oils touching and tingling her new skin. She did wish she had possessed a female, but beggars could not be choosers she told herself. "If only Billy could see himself now," she said, laughing while covered in aromatic bubbles. Billy's body was sufficient, though, and being a male was a small price to pay for all that was new and wonderful in this mortal shell. It certainly wouldn't stop her from enjoying herself. She sank into deep relaxation, her eyes shut and her head rested on an inflatable pillow. Eucalyptus and hints of sweet-scented candles filled the bathroom, and for just a moment she almost forgot that Devlin Gainsmore and his little beasts knew about her.

Celia thought about time. Billy's body had a little over ten years, around thirteen now. She'd certainly be taking more at the first chance she had. She leaned over the side of the tub and grabbed Tina's tablet from the bathroom counter.

Celia opened several browser tabs and went to work. First, she wanted to find out exactly what building Devlin Gainsmore ran his real-estate empire from. It was better to keep an eye out for his beasts at their source than for them to find her first. Second, she wanted to find a place were she could enjoy herself and steal more time.

Celia identified an office building on Bay Street after googling the man. Gainsmore Holdings Limited was on the top floor of one of the many skyscrapers around that block. She would watch that building every chance she had in the coming days. Perhaps she could take the fat man by surprise. His beasts had seen her, and now she suspected the joys of her pleasure-driven mortality would be in danger again soon enough.

Tonight, was a different matter. It would be her chance to rip a whole lifetime away from someone. The idea of only having to find one more victim to drain time from was satisfying for Celia. She scrolled through restaurant ads and other attractions in the city. Then something different caught her attention. She spied an advertisement for a male strip club in a forum about the city's nightlife, and it was just too irresistible for her. She got out of the tub and pulled the drain, then stopped to look at Billy's frame. His youthful appearance had certainly returned. She could tell what Tina had seen in him. The broad shoulders, the wide, firm chest, the scruffy beard and styled red hair; he was an attractive man in his own right. Celia quickly came to the conclusion that if she was to live in this body and please herself, she would be doing things her way. She would go to the Steel Stallion for business and for pleasure tonight.

First, she would see about getting her new body trimmed up proper. Things seemed foreign to Celia as far as grooming a man went. The upkeep of a male body seemed much easier, she concluded, but having a barber take care of everything would certainly be more convenient. Celia remembered seeing a red and white barber pole a little way down from the condo. She put on Billy's jeans and his leather jacket then set out for a cut.

The brisk winter air didn't bother Celia as she took in a refreshing deep breath of it. She had reaped souls in different districts over the decades.

Toronto was such fun, she concluded. The perfect city to dabble in possession and then take a vacation from her duties. With a skip in her step, she began her walk to the barber shop. She passed a couple laughing together and looked at her death-watch –– loads of time for the taking. She passed a young girl with a lifetime ahead of her. None of it felt right to her. She didn't like creeping about to steal time; she liked the simplicity and subtlety of privacy and distraction. She liked it when her prey was comfortable and vulnerable; it was her favorite time to strike. Outside of a corner store, Celia watched two men argue about something.

One yelled, "Go fuck yourself. It was an accident." The other threw a right-cross and landed it nicely to his chin. The attacker left, angrily storming away from the storefront, and Celia smiled.

She stepped up to the unconscious victim. "How's things," she asked sarcastically. "That good, eh?" She crouched down beside him.

Celia looked at her death-watch: five years left. *He doesn't need all that time*, she told herself. She rested her hand on the man's shoulder and shifted him into the recovery position as though she was helping, all the while dangling her moonlit blade above him. She smiled. The sands of time in her death-watch had fallen completely from above. Sirens came screaming from around the street corner, and the store manager came out still with his cell phone in hand. First one, then two officers were on scene and out of their vehicles. Celia backed up and gave them room.

"Did you put him like this in the recovery position?" questioned an officer as the other tried to check on the man.

"Yes," Celia replied.

"Did you see what happened?"

"A man hit him," Celia replied.

"He's got no pulse," cried out the other officer, who was kneeling by the victim.

"Ambulance is on the way," replied the first officer. The other officer began chest compressions.

Celia backed up some more. She whistled quietly to herself as her back turned and she rounded the street corner. She stepped up to some spotless glass doors and into the barber shop. To her surprise, she was welcomed by name.

"Billy boy! I haven't seen you in like, what, six months! I thought maybe you didn't need me anymore," quipped a muscled man in a black V-neck shirt as he cut a young man's hair. "Take a seat, Billy, it won't be too long."

Dammit, thought Celia. She should have gone somewhere farther away for a haircut. It was no matter. General chit-chat and awkward conversations aside, she would get through.

Oh, wonderful, there's a name tag on this jackass, thought Celia as she responded, "Hey, thanks, Chuck."

When the barber called Celia over, she pulled out Billy's old phone and showed a picture she'd found online of the style she wanted to the barber.

"Damn, Billy, you trying harder for Tina these days? Sure, we can do a new style. She'll likely appreciate it."

Fuck, thought Celia, *this guy knew Tina too.* It was no matter. She thought of a sure-fire way to shut him up and end the awkward small talk. "Tina died. I lost her, Chuck."

The world's most silent trim and haircut followed. Celia had to suppress so much laughter as Chuck the barber fumbled out a real, heartfelt condolence. By the time the cut was done, Tina could see that Billy's image pulled off this new haircut quite nicely. A faux-hawk and symmetrical trimmed, stubbly beard had turned Billy Walker into a total stunner. Celia wasn't done, though; she wanted to complete her new look. A nearby overly priced clothier offered the perfect navy-blue suit. She smiled at her ginger reflection. Never before had Billy Walker looked so damn good.

She'd turned him into a man of sophistication. The perfect image to attract attention at a nightclub. Celia would flaunt cash and see who took the bait. Then, like the viper hidden deep in a tree's greenery, she would strike.

The slushy streets outside the condo were cold and uninviting. Celia wasted no time in catching a cab driver's attention. It was only a few blocks up Church Street to the Steel Stallion, but Celia didn't care; she was not about to hoof it. The line for entry was packed with a broad range of people. Celia was certainly not the only well-dressed one of the lot. There were several groups of women, some in ridiculously short skirts for the weather. They huddled among friends for warmth who also had shown no foresight in the warmth of their attire. Celia supposed they'd sacrificed warmth for the hopes of attention from whoever they were seeking. The line shifted sluggishly, and Celia grew impatient. She looked at her death-watch and lined it up with an obnoxiously dressed loud young man in front of her. His years were plenty; fifty, in fact. It was just what the doctor ordered. The subtle flick of her hand brought about her weapon of choice from the ether. When she inched closer, the bouncer let the young man in purple skin-tight pants in, then he stepped in front of Celia. Saved by the bouncer. Celia smiled at the jacked doorman. He was as tall as he was wide, it seemed, a veritable tank. It was fine, thought Celia. She would catch the young man inside. A couple of flirtatious women that knew the bouncer managed to sneak ahead of Celia, but moments later she was in.

The pulsing vibrations of muffled bass drops leaked into the front lobby. Celia checked her coat and stepped through polished brass doors. Smoke machines, strobe lights, and stage lights created an atmosphere of excitement. A bachelorette party lined the horseshoe-shaped seating area in front of the stage, making cat-calls and cheers as a larger-than-life stripper hit the stage. Amused, Celia took a seat at a vacant table a row back but with a direct view of the stage. She watched contently as gold chains and baggy clothes were peeled away rhythmically.

When the first song ended, he disappeared from the stage for a moment. The second song, "How Many Licks," started pounding courtesy of the DJ, and the dancer burst on stage wearing almost nothing. While the ripped dancer played to the crowed, he scanned the patrons for potential clients. Celia caught his eyes and pulled a wad of bills from her suit jacket pocket while he was looking. He smiled and then invited one of the girls from the front-row bachelorette party onstage. A modest loincloth separated his manhood from the blushing twenty-something girl.

He sat her down on a prop chair and let the thin cotton barrier bounce suggestively inches from her face. The stripper leaned in and whispered something in the girl's ear, and she nodded then stood up. Celia watched, and when the bass hit hard, the dancer turned her upside down with ease to simulate a sixty-nine. The bachelorette party went wild, and the dancer couldn't hide his smile. He winked at Celia while still holding the girl upside down.

The DJ came over the speakers as the stripper's time on stage came to an end, and Celia waited. She knew he'd be out to offer a private dance soon enough. Seeing her first Stallion, as they called them at the club, Celia had completely forgotten about the flashy young man with fifty years for the taking in the lineup out front. She saw him walking to one of the many private booths with another attractive dancer, but out of the corner of her eye she noticed the dancer she'd had her eye on walking over.

"The name's Benson, did you enjoy that?" he questioned.

"Very much," answered Celia.

"Well, how about a private one then, just for you?"

"How about it," Celia repeated, and the pair passed through smoke and lights to a more secluded room.

Purple velvet curtains closed, and Celia sat in a cozy booth surrounded by curved mirrors. Tanned flesh and strong arms excited the demoness inside Billy's body. Celia was curious now as the stripper continued his seductive motions. He seemed to be enjoying himself as much as she was. She looked him in the eyes and came out with it. "Are you gay, or are you good at your job..."

He smiled. "I'm whatever you want me to be."

"Good answer," replied Celia, placing a wad of cash on the nearby table as he continued dancing and closing the gap between them. In the heat of it all, when the stripper bounced and grinded suggestively against Celia's swelling bulge, she took note of her death-watch reading. This man had thirty-two years left. Celia quickly made up her mind. From the smoky atmosphere, a wooden shaft and blade materialized. She would drain him as he pleased her. All but a year was taken from him by the time the lap dance ended. Celia was happy with that. Now, she wouldn't worry about time, but she still had worries. Paranoid thoughts of losing all she'd gained thanks to Devlin Gainsmore and his little gargoyles floated to the forefront of her mind again.

She had so many questions about how he controlled the Dreadlings and what he was doing with power like that in a mortal shell. Celia was quickly snapped back into the moment by the stripper.

"So, another dance then? Or do you wanna buy me a drink?"

Celia smirked. "Here." She tossed three hundred on the table. "What will you do for that?"

"Woah, that's a lot of cash. I don't know what you think I can do for that..."

"What can you do then?"

"I can take you upstairs? We can do bottle service? I'll dance for you more?" The stripper was out of ideas.

"But nothing else?" questioned Celia.

The stripper shrugged playfully, and Celia tossed a grand on the table. His eyes grew wide.

"Looks like you're my last dance tonight, or we can go somewhere now if you want..."

Celia grinned. That was the answer she was looking for. For the most part, her sexual encounters had been done through the invasion of mortal dreams before she was a reaper. Tonight, mortal touch was hers, and unlike her experiences with Tina, lust and attraction would rule this occasion. She waited by the coat check for the object of her desire. Not only had she taken his time, but now she would use him as she pleased.

11

The morning came, and with it the prior evening's delights were a blurred memory of alcohol and pleasure. Celia tossed soft cotton sheets off and sighed happily. If Billy could see himself now. She laughed wildly and stepped nude out of bed. Scattered about the room was her new navy-blue suit and proof of her wild ambitions last night. Sometime after the stripper had left, around 4:00 a.m., she'd passed out. Celia looked to the clock on her nightstand. It was a quarter past two in the afternoon. She'd slept so long, and still she felt like garbage. This was the mortal experience, or so she thought. Live for pleasures like booze and late-night sex, then pay the price of exhaustion the next day. She stepped out of bed groggy and dehydrated and went to the fridge. One sad-looking, almost empty orange juice carton and a jar of organic peanut-butter stared her in the face. With Tina gone, Celia had not done much other than enjoy herself.

As she huddled in a blanket at the edge of the dark gray living room couch, Celia thought about the paradox of mortal existence: die slowly but try to find meaning before your end. Be dependent on food, but if you enjoy too much of it, pay a price with your health. Somewhere along the line, try to enjoy yourself, but don't go overboard; you could end up huddled on a couch, rocking back and forth, dehydrated and nauseous. Celia looked to the bathroom cupboard and washed down some pills with the last of the orange juice. Then she put Billy's tired and abused body back together with an aroma-filled steaming bath.

Despite the price she had paid for a night of fun, she thought about her days as of late. Things were coming together quite nicely. The condo was hers, and her years were plentiful. What she wanted now was to know she was safe. She needed to know those damn Dreadlings of Devlin Gainsmore's were not coming back. She needed to know they could not come back.

Devlin was indeed a demon with the authority to spread chaos about the land. Once she was ready, Celia would spend the day observing Gainsmore at his Bay Street office. There was a café across the street that she'd googled, on the bottom floor of another office building. The view from there would be perfect. She would sit and watch for the man's gaudy Rolls-Royce. Once that pulled up, she would remember the time of its arrival. Then, meticulously and monotonously, she'd repeat the process every day until she knew she was safe. If he or his Dreadlings truly knew what she was, they'd sniff her out. She could not stand the thought of living her life in paranoia. Worse for her was the thought of being Hell-bound again. If she was in trouble, she did not want to face the consequences.

Celia sipped a sugar-filled cappuccino and devised a plan. She'd never heard of such a thing, but my how she smiled at the thought. Celia wondered what would happen if she killed a demon above her rank in the hierarchy. She would wield such power if that scythe of his was hers, and she would still enjoy a little time off in this mortal shell.

Why wasn't it possible? She thought of the portly Gainsmore, who somehow had orchestrated a comfortable mortal life yet was the commander of a small legion of Dreadling demons. Envy of that power swelled in Celia's black heart, and a lust for power bloomed.

She would be careful. Failure was a ticket to the depths of destruction. A layer of Hell reserved for the worst filth humanity had to offer. They'd probably strip her of her demonic birthright and treat her like the condemned mortals. At this point, Celia was sure she was so deep in the shit from stealing a body that she wasn't afraid to get more on her shoes. The thought of still reaping for decades was worse for her than if she'd taken this time off.

April brought about missed sunlight and the blossoming of new life through Toronto. The pleasant sounds of songbirds in the trees calmed even Celia. Mild winds rolled through busy streets and swept the harborfront waters. Sweet smells of baked goods teased Celia from the café off Bay Street. She walked toward it for the second time since she'd watched Gainsmore's building last week. Her nerves were on high. This was to be the day she would execute her plan. She was going to murder Devlin Gainsmore, the sedentary demon of lavish gluttony.

She surmised that she would take him by surprise, possibly bumping into him when he went to his Rolls-Royce and let him die in the streets. Then, as he faded, she would steal that mighty scythe and with it control Hell's Dreadlings. Celia watched and happily sipped her cappuccino from the luxury of her café table. At 2:55 in the afternoon, she looked at her death-watch, took her last sip, and walked out the double glass doors. At 2:57 she was waiting in the wings for Gainsmore. At 2:59, his blue and white Rolls-Royce came to a quiet stop out front of the glistening sun-kissed office building. Celia was ready. She could see the fat smug prick on his way to destruction. The man avoided the turnstile doors as he stepped out from the building's nearby push door instead. He was within reach as Celia flicked her wrist, summoning her scythe from the ether. Celia's scythe was right on course to pierce through the rounded back of Devlin Gainsmore. In her mind's eye, she could feel the blade going through his black suit jacket and deep into his ethereal being, but there was a problem. Despite his size, this man, this demon moved not at all like a sedentary individual.

His supernatural blade clashed with otherworldly power against Celia's, and his baritone voice plunged fear into her. *Do you think I don't know everything that goes on in this fucking city!*

The words never came out from the man's mouth, but they certainly echoed like screams through Celia's mind. As that scythe of hers was stopped by Gainsmore, Celia was shocked. Looking at her with his dark blade clashed violently against hers, he spoke aloud this time.

"Get in the fucking car."

Celia lowered herself in and snapped her scythe back to nothingness. How could she have been so foolish? Inside she was shaking. A demon with authority like Gainsmore's undoubtedly knew what went on in the city. He'd likely been watching her sit in that café and plan his destruction since her first moment there. *Fuck, I'm dumb*, Celia thought.

"You're damn right about that," Gainsmore responded, hearing her thoughts.

The bitter silence wasn't lifted until Celia spoke. "Where are you taking me?"

Gainsmore looked at her. "You'll see."

The heart of Toronto disappeared as they passed the old red-brick and cobblestone distillery district. They ended up on a nearby expressway. Gainsmore's driver seemed to drive for quite some time and twenty minutes later finally pulled up to an empty warehouse property with boarded wooden windows and graffiti. On the aged brick, high up was a billboard: *Gainsmore Properties and Holdings.*

"Get out," he commanded.

Celia was first to slide out of the Rolls. Behind her was Gainsmore, who instructed his driver to wait.

For an overweight man that appeared to be in his early sixties, Gainsmore moved incredibly fast. The delights of this realm may have kept him satisfied, but the demon inside him still commanded the abused body. On a digital pin-pad, Gainsmore typed in a lengthy password. Steel doors clicked, and he held one open while menacingly directing Celia into the building. She stepped in as a few tired fluorescent lights flickered on. A steel industrial fan spun high above, annoyingly and rhythmically. Gainsmore stood in the empty center of the warehouse. Celia looked at him, wondering if this was it. Would she go down fighting in the privacy of one of his vacant properties? Faster than Celia had ever seen, Gainsmore had his dark scythe in hand. It's over, she thought. Billy's mortal heart felt like it was in her mouth, and she became familiar with real mortal fear watching Gainsmore. He didn't go for her, though; instead he stamped the scythe's shaft against the concrete floor. Thwack, again and again. With each shaking thud to the ground, a Dreadling appeared, and the bloated man's expression grew more poisonous. Through gritted teeth and dripping sweat, he'd summoned a small army in under a minute. Perhaps a hundred Dreadlings were snarling and snapping at Celia, awaiting his commands. Hundreds of glowing red eyes watched her row by row as she stood shaking in Billy's body.

"Tell me, how are you going to kill me and take my scythe now? That was your plan wasn't it?"

"Yes."

"So, you think you can take my scythe now?"

"No."

"A shit plan indeed then."

Celia said nothing. She stood ready to run or summon her scythe. She didn't even know if she could kill one Dreadling again, let alone a hundred with her blade.

"So, you fucking survived the test then," Gainsmore announced. "I thought surely they would have torn you out of that shell and marched you down to Hell."

Celia thought back to the three Dreadlings that had attacked her on the subway. Was it really a test, and what kind of test?

"Have you seen a Dreadling born? Do you know what they truly are?"

"No."

Gainsmore smiled. "They are fear itself born from the tortured mortals below. Why do you think souls are sought after? The other side has their soldiers for the fight, and so do we."

"The fight?"

Gainsmore continued, "I'll make it simple for you. I collect sinners before they have a chance at redemption, and you're going to do the same thing whether you want to or not. You've been a naughty girl, Celia. Lucifer told me to unleash three Dreadlings on you — no more, no less. I thought surely that they would have thrown you on his doormat, but you survived. But I digress. Once these mortals rot below long enough, their fear can be harnessed. That is where you and I come in and do our jobs. You get the fucking picture, sweetheart?"

"I do," Celia responded. Her heart rate slowed as she realized Gainsmore was not going to kill her.

"There's a cosmic war, fought in the shadows. I'm sure you know that much. A war for souls. Lucifer told me it's quicker to make you return to work than for me to kill you and look for a replacement. Thus, you're one lucky cunt."

Celia stood silent awaiting Gainsmore's next words.

Gainsmore grinned at her. "I killed this fat fellow a decade ago on Bay Street. I stole his body, and, yes, his company."

"Without consequence?"

"I had to return to work, and so will you."

"Fuck," mumbled Celia.

Gainsmore replied, "Fuck, absolutely."

Celia looked at her death-watch. The face had changed. It showed a tiny map with red and blue dots scattered about. "Collect the red?"

Gainsmore grinned. "Help the dark army rise and keep the mortal shell you fought so hard to steal. You of course have the choice to refuse, if you choose..."

Celia looked around the warehouse at the snarling arachnid faces around her. "I will return to work."

"Vacation is over then. A wise choice. Now, give me that fucking scythe of yours."

Celia didn't want any of this. She longed to sit in condo soaker tub with the massage jets on and breathe in cinnamon candles while indulging in new pleasures. She scolded herself for overstepping her boundaries, and now she saw no other choice but to do as commanded. She walked to Gainsmore. Eerily, Dreadlings spread apart, forming an aisle for her to walk down. The hunched beasts snapped and hissed as she moved closer to Gainsmore. She flicked out her right hand, summoning her scythe then reached out and handed it to Gainsmore.

With her blade in hand, he walked to the center of the warehouse and directed a Dreadling to come closer to him. The shadowy little gargoyle sat obediently by his side, all the while staring down Celia with repulsive bright red arachnid eyes. Gainsmore swung the scythe into its heart without hesitation while the other Dreadlings watched, unphased. From the beast's disintegrating remnants, a black still beating heart was taken of the tip of the blade. Gainsmore punched it into the side of Celia's scythe blade. The moonlit texture flooded with a spreading darkness that eclipsed the blade. All that remained was a shimmer of moonlight around its edges, and the runes that had been added were now soaked aglow with red blood.

"Now you can summon Dreadlings. Now you can bring us sinners." Gainsmore snickered then walked toward the door. On his way out, he stamped the ground once quickly with his scythe, and the hundred Dreadlings exploded into ash and dust. He looked back at Celia again. "It's a bold move to steal a body that belongs to a saved soul, but I suppose you didn't know that. When you do something like that, the other side might take note. Be thankful Lucifer didn't just have you killed. I don't know his plan, but you must be sprinkled in there somewhere, or you'd surely be doomed."

"Wait," cried Celia.

Gainsmore sneered, looking over his shoulder.

"What do you mean doomed?"

"I'd rather not mean anything. I'll tell you this, though. I've never seen anyone do something so stupid as not to check if the body they stole belonged to the Heavens."

"What will I do if they notice?"

"I'll tell you what I'd do if they noticed. I'd summon a damn slew of Dreadlings and move this fat ass like you've never fucking seen."

Celia didn't know what to make of their encounter. She'd expected to be thrown in the lake of fire by now and stripped of her demonic status. Instead, she'd been awarded more power, but at a cost. Slavery and servitude had found her again. She'd stolen Billy's time to free herself. Now, that freedom would elude, her perhaps forever this time. Her death watch beeped with her first alert: *Jane and Finch - 2am: Joseph Bennet*. She was to collect a sinner at an ungodly hour of night.

Celia stood in Gainsmore's warehouse, lamenting alone. "There is no rest for the wicked," she mumbled.

12

Frank Rosenbaum had been a paralegal for most of his life. He valued people, and he valued helping them more than anything else he'd ever done. Never once had he taken advantage of a client's misfortune for money, unlike his parasitic peers. In fact, he had done more cases pro bono than anyone he knew. It hadn't hurt his bottom line either. For Frank it was never about the money; he got along just fine. It was about the difference he made in a client's life. Frank understood now, it was that nature about him that led him to his purpose in the afterlife. He was an afterlife advisor, helping people find their eternal purpose. On this day, he would have to be more than a simple advisor.

A glowing purple-fringed portal opened, and Frank stepped out, grateful as always to be home. He needed the keys to death, and he needed them yesterday. The familiar clouds and golden gates of this place warmed his heart.

"Hello, Batariel."

"Good to see you, Frank." The angelic guard welcomed him with open arms.

Golden gates parted, and Frank walked among sister and brother once more. The overwhelming sense of oneness almost brought him to tears every time he felt it, but there were pressing matters afoot. The marble streets stretched as far as one could see, and diamond pillars catching divine light held much of the astonishing architecture together. Warm, joyful greetings flowed into the streets as Frank walked by his white-robed peers. He was going to the veil, a garden wherein one could sit at holy waters' edge and pray. The pond would bring about answers for those who needed help. Today, Frank would pray for Billy Walker, the man who wrongfully sat outside the gates of fire and brimstone thanks to reasons beyond him. Frank passed the sweet smell of divine foliage and took rest upon a smooth yet ornate aquamarine bench. He pressed his hands together and prayed for answers.

It wasn't long before the answers literally flowed to the waters' surface. Cast in reflections through the water, he could see that Billy had stood his ground, but defeat had overtaken him in numbers, and those numbers were Dreadlings. The pond showed the clawed beasts had overpowered him and victoriously dragged him through Hell's gates. The image faded in the water, and the answers Frank truly wanted rose from the depths of his conscience. He would get Billy out of there, but he knew he would need weapons and the key to death just in case. Not the big guns, he thought, but something...

Frank left the garden after a while with his newly acquired equipment in hand. Although he'd never done anything like this before, he was determined to succeed. The familiarity of helping people find their purpose in the afterlife was something he cherished. Now he would do that, but this time it would be more of a chore than ever. Frank prepared to fight for Billy in new ways. He knew what Billy was meant for now. His destiny had changed when he'd called out in the faith of prayer that night at the bridge on New Year's Eve. His destiny had also changed when that demon girl had marked him with her scythe and later stolen his body.

"Off to the realm of stench and tyranny again?" questioned Batariel at Heaven's gates.

"I'm afraid so, my friend," replied Frank.

"Is it your first reclamation?"

"Yes."

"Here Frank. The document you came back for, proof of innocence." Replied Batariel handing Frank a worn scroll with Billy's name on it and proof that he did not belong to Hell. "Now go. Save that young man and fear not; have faith."

Frank smiled. "Fear not; have faith." He was nervous, but his faith told him he wouldn't have this task if he couldn't handle it. If he was meant to do this, it was because he could. He tucked his weapons away neatly and gently into the inner pocket of his suit jacket and walked with purpose through a glowing violet portal.

Frank shuddered. The rotting stench of sin and the screams of many were something you never grew numb to. His feet stepped out onto yellow, stained brimstone. Determined steps seemed meaningless as the gates of Hell drew farther away with each movement. It was happening; he'd heard about this from stories of past souls claimed. When they had come to collect, Hell played games. Frank ran toward the gates, they faded farther away with each stride. Frank thought back to the story of his teacher, Julia. She had warned of a time when she came to take back a soul stolen by Dreadlings. Frank remembered her describing the gates exactly as fleeing with each step. He smiled, remembering the tools he had, then he muttered, "Thank you, Julia."

Frank did a fast hundred-eighty-degree turn and summoned a portal, then jumped through as fast as his old soul let him. He came out exactly as formulated, right in front of the red-hot flaming gates of Hell. There was a gatekeeper surprised that someone was there. It was again the giant half slug, half man who wriggled up and sneered at Frank through fiery twisted steel bars.

Frank's five-foot-five frame and weathered hunched appearance did nothing for intimidation. He didn't need a striking physical appearance to get his message across, and he knew it. He smiled at the towering slug man.

"My name is Frank Rosenbaum. I am here for Billy Walker with this reclamation proclamation," he said holding up the worn scroll. "Bring him here now, or there will be consequences."

The towering slug man looked down at him. His glowing neon-green antennae lit the darkness around Frank, and so did the gates. Slime dripped from the slug man's mouth as he was about to speak, narrowly missing Frank as he stepped to the side. "No Billy Walker here for you."

"Why wouldn't you lie? You serve the father of lies. You know what? You never shared your name with me. Mind if I call you Schmendrick? Yeah, I like that, Schmendrick it is."

"Leave now!" raged the behemoth slug man, leaning toward the gates with mucous-covered skin aglow.

"Okay, Schmendy, I can see this is going nowhere." Quickly, Frank pulled out a large crystal key he'd retrieved from the pond he'd prayed at. He slammed it into Hell's gates. As they screamed open, Frank raised his voice. "I have a surprise for you..." He reached into his jacket pocket and pulled out an item that struck fear into the eyes of the giant slug demon.

"No!" protested the slug man. "I'll tell you. He's inside Theodore."

"Theodore?"

"The toad, he's inside the toad."

"Well, you better give that thing a massive laxative then, because if he's not standing in front of me in the next five minutes, I'll start throwing these things. We clear, Schmendy?"

The slug man cursed loudly in a forbidden dialect and slithered away, sloughing a trail of glistening discharge and wriggling maggots off his body.

Thousands of red-eyed Dreadlings peered from the darkness of rocky crevasses in wait, yet Frank stood his ground. He looked back at them and clutched one of his weapons at the ready. Shrieks and contorted sounds of anger seeped from the darkness. Frank muttered his mantra, "Fear not; have faith," repetitiously. Before he knew it, an utterly terrifying sight arose at Hell's horizon, with horrendous accompanying sounds. The tremors of a thirty-foot cyclops toad being paraded angrily toward Hell's gates. Frank stood still and continued to mumble the mantra in his mind.

Theodore parked himself meters away from Frank. The toad seemed settled by the slug man's command, but its cycloptic eye still moved and swiveled about ominously. The slug man spoke in an ancient cursed language to the beast. Frank quickly stepped back with caution. First the round, bloated, head of a many-chinned man popped out. Like a living cork, the man clogged up the process, peeking from the toad's repulsive rectum. Sweaty and wide-eyed, with throbbing and pulsing forehead veins, the stuck man was being pushed out by the toad as he peeped out the rectum in shock. Then, a wild explosion of twenty people covered in Theodore's festering sludge shot across the ground.

Frank took an old handkerchief from his jacket pocket. He stepped back a little and tried to filter out the unbearable smells by covering his nose. The old paralegal gagged and choked at the aroma, but still he held his spherical weapon in his right hand. The lot of Theodore's discharge all scrambled to their feet. Some were clawed and carried away by Dreadlings, but others who tried to run were less fortunate. The slug man had given Theodore the nod, and the toad had begun target practice with his tongue yet again to eat his live victims.

"Hey! Hey!" Cried out Frank. "I'm here for that one!"

Frank pointed to Billy as five Dreadlings sank their clawed fingertips into his back. The slug man turned a blind eye to the Dreadlings and left with Theodore. "I said that's who I came for!" Frank yelled ineffectually. He knew the Dreadlings didn't care; they were like animals acting on instinct. They didn't care who or what Frank was there for, but he'd hoped the slug man would have done something. Frank's fears were coming true; he would need to fight back.

The old paralegal put away his handkerchief and reached into his deep pockets for another his weapons of choice. He pulled two out, holding one in each hand for good measure. With all his might, he cocked his arm and began to throw them at the clamoring beasts. The wails and sights that followed were astonishing, even to Frank. The holy water balloons he'd filled from that sacred pond before he'd left were no laughing matter as they burst on the beasts. Like acid, the blessed water pierced their black scaled hides as they lay paralyzed and disintegrating.

Frank grabbed Billy by the arm and yelled, "Run, young man!"

Frantically, they ran through flaming gates. Dreadlings not hit by holy water chased and bounded after them. Billy looked back frozen in horror, but Frank's hand grasped his forearm and pulled Billy into the light of an expanding portal.

• • • ● ● • ● • • •

"Oy vey," Frank sighed, walking over and collapsing onto a shimmering gold park bench, looking over at Billy.

Billy simply nodded.

"You can't speak, can you, son..."

Billy shook his head.

"Of course, they took your voice."

Billy nodded again.

"Well, they were worried you might have picked up something important from that book I gave you. There is some powerful knowledge in it. They can't very well have you open your mouth and preach about it, so they kept you quiet. You saw what goodness lies in the hearts of people all over the world, I take it."

Billy nodded and sat down beside Frank on the golden bench. He knew they weren't alive by Earth's definition anymore, but still he felt his natural senses. Contrary to Celia's prior lamentations over her lack of senses, Billy felt the warmth of a sun in the sky, the breeze of the day, and the soft fabric of his new clothes. He examined his attire while sitting beside Frank. It was the same glowing white silk suit Frank wore. It shimmered beautifully as it caught sunrays. Billy wanted to ask where they were and opened his mouth to speak out of habit.

"I know, son. I'm sorry they took that from you. I can tell you, though, you'll get it back soon. There're a few things I'd like to say first, though. One, is that this is not Heaven, not by any definition, but it is still holy ground. You are technically still on Earth, but you are in a veiled part of Earth shifted from their reality." Frank let out a little chuckle and continued. "It's been called the Bermuda Triangle by the mortals. Rightfully so; the veiled area around it is a triangle. You can come here anytime but you can't enter Heaven. Not until you fix what you caused when you took that mark from the reaper. We know your time was cut short, and for that we're sorry. They'd like to offer you something, another chance, a job."

Billy sat up and listened intently to Frank.

"My name is Frank Rosenbaum. When I was a man on Earth, I helped people. When I died, they knew exactly what I needed from the afterlife. You know what it was, Billy?"

Billy opened his mouth and gestured cynically to the silent opening.

"Don't get smart; it was a rhetorical question. I needed to help people; that was and is my purpose. I believe you have a similar purpose. You can be the difference. You can stop them from doing this to anyone else ever again."

Billy nodded. In his heart, he knew Frank was right. He could feel it. If it were up to Billy, no one would go through the nightmare he'd just endured.

"Come with me for a second."

Billy followed Frank. He beheld the translucent wonder of a rainbow bursting jovially through a waterfall, followed by shimmering sunlit deposits of amethyst, ruby, and other gems encrusted around a calm crystal-clear pond.

Frank stood over the small pond that ran from the waterfall.

"This is it. Here is where you will make your choice. Stay here if you like, but Celia takes your body and with it more power. Step into the pond and you'll fall back to Earth with a new body to fight these demons in disguise. Now, kneel down, cup your hands, and drink from this pond."

Billy hesitated.

"It's not water in the normal sense. It's holy water, kid, not wet to the touch but healing in its effects."

As Frank had commanded, Billy took in the sweetest water he'd ever tasted. Invigorated, he stood up. "I feel...*hah*! My voice!"

"Alright, alright. Calm down, young fella." Frank smiled. "There's more we have to go over before you make your decision."

"You called Celia a demon?" Billy questioned.

"She tricked you, kid. She took the most desirable form she could think of and melted your heart with lies. Deep inside you is a good nature that she played on. We've seen demons pull off things like this before, but lately it's gotten out of hand. It's not easy for them to steal a mortal's body, but Celia did."

"What is she then?"

"She is a reaper, that much is true, but she is certainly also a demon. Those from below that serve as reapers, they're all demons. When they come to collect the bad, they send the bad, Billy. No one gets away from Hell, not even their own demons. Well... Except you." Frank chuckled. "But you're not a demon, and you didn't belong there. You were a good man who was beaten down in his last days."

Billy scratched his head. "I can't believe I couldn't see past her façade."

"Well, it was good enough not to cause suspicion in the mind of a depressed man who was under the influence."

"I suppose so," Billy said.

"Celia saw your vulnerability and played on it, young man. At one point she even put a hex on you to forget your morals and lower your guard. Listen, take your time to decide about this. I know accepting a job that you don't even know that much about is a big ask. I will try my best to answer any questions you have."

"No, Frank, I know my decision. If I could stop something like this happening to anyone else, I would. Can I ask you something?"

"Ask away, kid."

"Why the second chance? I'm grateful, but I mean, I saw so much good in that book you gave me. I killed my landlord!"

"Do you really think you had control of that weapon for even a second, Billy? Did it not feel like your hands were pulled along with your body anytime you swung it?"

"Yes."

"Celia killed your landlord, son. She had to make the bond with her blade so when she stole your body, she could still use the scythe as a mortal. Once she made that bond, I'm sorry to say, Billy, you were on your way out, and control of your mind and body faded rather quickly."

"What a mistake it all was," Billy huffed.

"It doesn't have to be. There's something I have to show you before you decide to do, this..."

"What is it?" Billy interrupted.

"Your new body. I don't want you to be alarmed when you see it."

Frank stepped to the pond's edge, waving a hand over the water. Like a movie screen, it showed the form of a young girl all of twelve years. She was barely five feet tall. Her hair was worn in a wavy brunette pony-tail.

"Oh, c'mon! Are you kidding me with this?"

"We need you to go under serious cover to end these possessions. This is no joke. This is all we've got right now. Besides, it's the ideal form for you. You'll take anyone by surprise, kid." Frank continued trying to sell the new body as Billy crossed his arms and shook his head.

"There are others in your city. Demons who have exploited mortals unchecked for too long. I'll show you. Take this, man."

Frank pointed to the pond, where the image of an all too familiar face glistened softly in the water. Billy cringed. He should have known the man's fat shell was housing such corruption. Devlin Gainsmore and his bloated, arrogant figure faded in the pond water as Frank continued.

"You see, Celia wasn't the first to do this kind of thing. Hell doesn't give a damn about it either. They just put these reapers back to work in mortal shells with even more power as their reward! Lucifer must see chaos on Earth and applaud. Gainsmore and Celia, they are taking sinners to Hell before their time is actually up."

"Can't you send in angels to stop them or something?"

"That kind of thing is not in the cards, kid. It's against the rules. They're wearing mortal shells. The angelic warriors of Heaven fight in a realm we can't see. Sure, sometimes they test a human's morals and hide amidst them, but they'll never harm a mortal body, even a possessed one. You, Billy Walker, will be their reckoning. You will be our Reaper Hunter. It's time we did something about these shady shenanigans!" Frank cried out.

Billy laughed. He could tell the old man was worked up. "Shenanigans?"

Frank's white and silver hair-laced brow furrowed. "Tomfoolery and what have you. Don't get smart; you know what I'm saying here, kid. You can stop them from taking out sinners before their time. You can stop them from raising an army of Dreadlings from the fear of the suffering souls below."

"What are you saying here, Frank? Are Dreadlings..."

"What, people? No, Billy, they aren't people. Those beasts are born of fear. In the depths of Hell, the tortured souls of the mortals manifest those beasts through fear. The more they have to torture, the more fear drips from their souls to manifest those vile creatures."

Billy looked deep into the pond. His new form reappeared. A little brunette pony-tailed twelve-year-old girl stared back at him as if the lights were on but no one was home. "You ever hear the term, you hit like a little girl, Frank? I am literally going to hit like a little girl. What the fuck am I suppose to do with this body?"

"Hey, you watch your mouth, young man, and be grateful for this second chance! You'd be surprised what you'll be able to do. This little girl's body was that of a formally trained ballerina! She was a prodigy until the fatal car accident that ended it all. Besides, you'll have a powerful scythe that can cut through demons like a roast chicken at Shabbat dinner!"

Billy shook his head. "Why a little girl?"

"Because no one looks twice at the face of innocence. They walk by you, and BAM! You hit 'em with your blade and send 'em packing back to the lake of fire."

"You make it sound so easy. Why not try your hand at it..."

"Because it's not my destiny Billy... It's yours."

"Where did this body come from anyway?"

"We resurrected it. As far as anyone knows it's still in the ground," replied Frank.

Billy paused in thought for a moment.

"Tell me, if I do this, will I ever see this again?" Billy gestured to his natural male physique.

"I don't know, and I'm sorry it's come down to this painful choice. I will say this, though." Frank paused and put a hand on Billy's shoulder. "If they didn't believe in you to do this, you would still be where I found you the first time."

The pair stood in silence at the pond's edge. Billy was first to break the silence after a few minutes. "Why do they do this?"

"Who do what?" Frank stumbled out, a little confused.

"Why do these reapers steal bodies? I thought Celia had it pretty good, to tell you the truth; she had me fooled."

"Bah, bubble-headed flirtatious deceptions and lies. The mortal pleasures and senses are too tempting, sometimes even for ethereal beings. Taste, touch, even the sweet smell of flowers. All things denied in the depths of despair, even if you just work there. And God knows the demons aren't about to experience them up here. So, they took what they could get."

"So that's it for me then. I'll never know the smell of coffee in the morning again?"

"Hah, there will be senses again, don't worry. The first thing you ask about is coffee, though? Your not listening, Billy. You take this chance, and it's true, you will be similar to the demons in the sense that you'll not eat or need food. The second you are back in the garden, though, you'll be able to experience all your natural mortal senses again. Think about it, kid. You're at an advantage. Celia is in your mortal shell. Lusts for mortal temptations will fill her mind. She'll be vulnerable. You should try to catch her off-guard. Demons are wise, but they are just as easily tied down by mortal temptations as a true mortal."

Billy looked again to the still waters of the pond. He rubbed his chin, as he often did when he concentrated. "Let's do this then. There's probably going to be some poor sap out there like me. Someone charmed by a demon into utter foolishness. I've made so many mistakes. I should have just died, Frank."

"I'm not going to preach to you, kid. This is your chance to fix this, but only if you want it."

"And if I don't want it?"

"We have another lined up, someone like you. To tell you the truth, we asked you first because you got shafted the worst."

"How will I find Celia in such a huge city?"

Frank smiled. "Look for me. I'll be inside their technology."

"What?"

"You think all those screens people put up and carry around are only good for wasting time? We can use them to communicate across dimensions far beyond what the mortal eye can see. Look for me in them, and I'll guide you."

Billy nodded. "I guess this is it then?"

"Hold on a second. You can't just leave without your weapon."

Billy knelt down by the pond again and waited to hear Frank out.

"You'll have both kinds of sight, mortal and ethereal. You'll have better hearing than before and be able to pick up the slightest of noises. If you use your scythe right, you'll be able to transcend matter like the demons. That will take some getting used to. Having a knack for portals doesn't always come easy."

"Portals?"

Frank smiled again. "You can use your scythe to cut open portals if you need to flee to this garden, or anywhere for that matter." Frank snapped his fingers, and from the sky a scythe much different than Celia's drifted down.

The blade was not shrouded in moonlit textures; instead, its edge was touched by a fire so bright, it was blinding, like the sun. Frank gently handed the scythe to Billy.

"I can go anywhere with this thing?"

"Well, it will be here, mostly, unless you think of a different place beforehand. The garden gives you life; you are tied to this realm for now, kid. When you're here, just jump back into the pond and think about where you want to land. You'll come out right where you should."

Billy stepped closer to the glistening pond. He could see the warmth of a Toronto summer and the smiles of those enjoying it. "Was I gone long? It felt like a lifetime, you know, down there."

"Six months, Billy," replied Frank. "There's one last thing I have to say, kid."

"What?"

"It's about Tina."

Billy's eyes grew wide. "Tina?"

"Celia was able to take advantage of her. She stole the time that Tina had left. The family was deceived into happiness. They truly thought you two got back together. Celia stole everything from her." Billy gritted his teeth, and Frank paused, seeing his demeanor change. "I'm sorry."

Billy's fist clenched as he mumbled, "Fuck." That was the best he could do to hold it together, out of respect for Frank. He remembered that he in fact was still the beneficiary for Celia's estate in her will, and now he knew that Celia had been watching him for a while, casing his life for the taking.

"I'd be angry too, kid," Frank said, trying to reassure Billy. "It's a human emotion, and that's all we are is human. Find Celia, use that anger to send her back to where she truly belongs."

Billy reached out and took hold of his new weapon. His hand clutched the new scythe so tightly. The shaft was clear like glass, but strong like steel and as light as a proverbial feather. It twisted like vines around the glowing fire-fringed blade rather ornately.

The blade was thicker and shorter than Celia's. As he wielded the weapon, he could tell it was perfect for a smaller frame. Billy could see he'd be able to grasp a smaller section of the vine-like handle that jutted out with his new smaller hands.

"Drive it into the chest of a mortal shell and you'll rip out the demon within. Once they are on the hook, so to speak, you can send them below with a portal. If you hold the blade in too long, its light will destroy the demon — it's your call, kid."

"Just a touch..."

"Just sink that blade in, and the scythe will do the rest. It'll exterminate Dreadlings and cast out demons. It was made to end them, so end them or send them."

Billy readied himself. He took another look into the pond before he leapt. He hadn't been this angry in a long time, but that anger made him feel alive once again.

"Remember, look for me in their technology."

Billy nodded.

Frank's voice echoed in his consciousness as Billy fell through the water, slowly, effortlessly, below. There was no sensation or feeling, not until the world seemed so big.

13

Billy heard the snap of a portal close behind him. He wasn't sure what area of Toronto he'd stepped into. He only knew that his stature had changed dramatically as he took it all in. The deserted alley he now walked led him to some beat-up steel doors and overflowing garbage bins. He saw a white van at the alley's end with its doors open wide. He walked up to the driver's side mirror and stood on an old wooden skid. He was now indeed a twelve-year-old girl. Billy looked as he'd seen himself in the garden's pond reflection. His brown hair was kept neatly in a shoulder length pony-tail. He wore sparkly jeans and a purple long-sleeved thin hoodie.

Dammit, he thought and stepped away from the van mirror.

"You lost, kid?" asked a worker carrying two boxes.

"What part of the city is this?"

"It's Little Italy, sweetheart. Are you okay?" The man rolled up his white dress-shirt uniform sleeves in the summer heat. Then he took a gentle posture and knelt down to soothe what he thought was a lost child. "You can come in the restaurant. It's safer inside, okay? We'll call your mom."

"I appreciate your concern, but I know exactly were I am now, thank you," Billy answered, walking down the remainder of the ally.

"Hey, kid. You sure you're okay?" hollered the man.

Billy turned. "I'm better than I was yesterday."

"Strange little girl," the worker mumbled.

Billy walked the summer streets of Toronto and rolled up his hoodie sleeves. There were a few second glances at a wandering young girl, but no action taken. Now, Billy wanted to check in with Frank as quickly as he could. He took in the city in a strange new way. His young eyes observed storefronts and restaurants differently. He knew what he was looking for and pushed on past groups of people. There were quite a few blocks before Billy came across what he'd been seeking. The familiarity of a fast-food chain with a digital drive-through menu screen brought about Frank's wrinkled and familiar smile. Billy ran over, seeing the old man's image in the order screen. There were no cars at the moment as Billy stepped into one of the two order lanes.

"Hey there, kid. We've got word on Celia. She was spotted in the transit system subway tunnels, waiting on the northbound side."

"How did we find her?"

Frank smiled. "We've got eyes, like they do. Just be ready to take her by surprise, and remember, you can't hurt a mortal with that blade, so there is no harm in swinging away when you see something or someone that doesn't belong. Got it?"

Billy smiled and nodded at Frank, then he said goodbye. Before he stepped away from the order lane, Billy was startled by the anxious honk and plea of an obnoxious man in a silver truck.

"C'mon, kid, go in the restaurant if you wanna order something!"

Billy turned in frustration. "Didn't you just get here? There's two lanes, asshole."

"Hey! Your parents teach you to speak like that! Where are they anyway?" shouted the man as Billy disappeared on foot.

Only a couple blocks over, Billy set foot in the subway system. The crowds below were easily negotiated with a new and agile little frame. Billy was surprised at how easily he felt himself move through a crowd now. The turnstile security gates were no obstacle as he slid through right after a woman just ahead of him. Billy stopped as he approached the subway tunnels. He looked to his left and then his right. To his right, a yellow LED transit route billboard told him he would be headed northbound if he boarded the next car.

Over that pixelated billboard, Frank's face made another appearance in a sort of stippled digital way. "We know she headed that way. She was seen getting off at the Eaton Centre. Go, Billy. Stop her, before she kills."

The doors slid open, and Billy boarded the first car among the commuter rush. He sat cross-legged in a single seat by the car's doors. Across from him, an older gentleman with a gray, trimmed afro read his newspaper. Most everyone paid no mind to Billy, except for an elderly woman with curled white hair who rested both of her hands on a silver cane. She took in each passenger around the car until settling upon Billy.

"Sweetie, do you know your way home? Where are your parents?"

Billy could see this lost child business becoming a common theme. He decided to ignore the question and looked out the subway car window instead. The old lady seemed to exude more judgment for Billy's nonexistent parents than concern for Billy after that.

"Sweetheart, if you're scared and lost, I can help you. What is your name?"

Frustrated, Billy responded dismissively, "It's not important."

The interrogation continued. Billy could sense her real interest was punishing this little girl's absentee parents. Billy didn't blame the old lady; he might have been keen to do the same under different circumstances.

She wanted to be the hero who brought a lost little girl to a police station and had the parents punished in the public eye. Billy told himself he had no time for this as she began to continue.

"Your name is important, and so are you, young lady. So please, may I know your name?"

"Well, they call me Billy."

"That's not your real name, is it sweetheart? Is that a nickname? Billy is not a girl's name."

"It is now, lady," he said, standing abruptly as the subway car slowed. It was exactly the stop Billy needed. Swiftly, he grasped the subway support pole and swung out the sliding doors, disappearing into the hustle of the crowd. Slipping through the swarming people was becoming something of a breeze.

It was not long before he was in an enclosed glass walkway connecting the subway system to the shopping mall. The hot sun magnified through the glass, and Billy hustled through, scanning around for himself, or what one might call his former self. He wondered just what, if anything, Celia had changed about his appearance since the incident. Would he recognize himself now?

Juice bars and storefronts flooded with tourists and shoppers would make it difficult to find a single person. Billy was frustrated. He'd have rather found Celia in a dark alley and taken her by surprise than looked for her in a crowd like this. Frank was right; Billy couldn't just wait at Tina's condo. He knew Celia would be there eventually, but who knew what damage she might do beforehand and who she might kill? Billy was entrusted to stop her from killing people before their time. The more people she managed to shortchange for time, the more might miss their chance at salvation, just as Frank had said.

The new swarms of shoppers who pushed in from the streets were a variable that he could do without, but he got by. Although he dodged through easily, Billy's height was another thing that made the hunt for his old body a struggle. Every face was looked up at. A double chin that could do with a shave, the exposed buxom cleavage of a fit young woman. Billy smiled and told himself he could have picked her up in his prime. Then, there was the thick-rimmed glasses of judgment from an old man watching Billy dart about in search of Celia. All were taken in from the obscurity of his small stature. Billy had an idea. He raced over toward a mirrored elevator and slipped through the doors before they closed.

"My, aren't we in a hurry, little one."

Billy didn't respond to the lady standing next to him. He didn't even take in her appearance as he stared down from the rising elevator through the glass on its other side. When the doors opened, Billy shot out through the crowds once more. The third floor gave the best vantage point in the mall, and Billy knew it. It was where he'd proposed to Tina. In the height of the Christmas season, he had waited for the perfect moment. Tina loved the holidays, and she loved that enormous tree. When the mall had erected the gaudy fifty-foot thing, he'd lured Tina to the third floor and proposed by its peak. He smiled, reminiscing about that moment.

It was summer, and the tree was absent. The memory had brought clarity and peace to his mind that was welcome, though. He realized then that he was not angry at Tina for her mistakes. He was angry at himself for how distant he'd been after his diagnosis. He should have known that his sulking and his coldness were not the answer for someone that needed security in a time of uncertainty. Tina had always been like that, needy, and in normal times, Billy had desired to be needed by her. He looked over the balcony at the third floor and whispered, "I'm sorry, Tina."

After a few quiet moments of reflection, Billy decided his daydreaming had gone on too long. He caught the time from a nearby decorative storefront clock face: 7:00 p.m. He'd been perched there like an owl without results for quite a bit. If he was to catch his prey, he was going to need to do something different. This lookout had not worked for him. He stepped over to a nearby mall information display. From that he began his mental checklist of where or what exactly Celia would be doing in a place like this. *If I was a self-indulgent demon who loved mortal pleasures, where would I be?* Billy asked himself. A list of possibilities came to mind.

The café on the upper balcony looking down on the people below, the makeup store, the spa store with scented everything. Billy thought about it; he'd often bought Tina scented bath oils and bombs from that very shop. He ruled out Celia going to the makeup store, even though her obsession with lipstick in the short time he'd known her had been next-level weird. As he looked at the lit map, it was decided.

Billy brushed past a family and stepped fast down an escalator. It was only a few bends and turns until he saw the familiarity of aproned employees passing out scented samples and shelves lined with candles and oils. The scents inside were everything Billy remembered. His eyes glistened for a moment as he remembered the good times with Tina. Not just the moments of passion, but the pure moments; the times when he looked at her and saw their love cast like a reflection in her eyes. He wiped his eyes on his purple hoodie sleeve as a young employee came up.

"Little girl? Are you lost?"

"No!" snapped Billy and ran out of the store.

He heard the employees commiserating with one another over the exchange as he disappeared. It sounded like one had said, "Poor girl," as he fled. Billy had felt surprisingly vulnerable at that store. His past was still his past, and Tina was a big part of it that was still alive in his heart.

Billy retraced his steps after striking out in the scented spa store. Back up to the top floor, he looked about for any sign of either Frank or Celia, but both were absent. He needed a lead, not just a sighting from an hour ago. If worst came to worst, he would sit outside their old condo and hope Celia hadn't killed too many people in the meantime. He'd only been here for such a short time, and already panic and urgency had set in.

What an outrage that a demon could run amok among mortals. Billy walked past the café he'd wondered about earlier. The scenic balcony had a large number of people. Indoor trees and plants around the café offered a small degree of seclusion, but not enough to hide everyone. Billy noticed a man in a new looking expensive midnight-blue suit. His red hair was shaven at the sides and neatly styled into a faux hawk on top. Damned if he wasn't glad that he'd been a redhead now, thought Billy.

Billy had recognized himself. He looked better, healthier than he had in his own skin. Not only did Celia have expensive taste, but she'd certainly taken care of her new possession.

Billy gritted his teeth. The tiny clenched fist of a twelve-year-old girl shook. His white-knuckled hand was all he could do to contain the immediate anger that arose. He could see the aura around people, the dimness or light of their soul around their bodies. His absence from inside his old body left it without a glow. Billy wanted to march over and plunge his scythe into Celia this instant. He thought for a moment. Was now the perfect moment for surprise, or was he jumping the gun, fueled by the impatience of anger? As she sat and sipped a latte, he would slip into the café and literally stab her in the back. Billy prepared himself, remembering that Frank had told him to use that anger against Celia. Now was his retribution.

14

Celia sipped a warm latte infused with more sugar than necessary. She'd taken so many sinners before their time now, and Hell had given her immense power over the Dreadlings. Still, she was not satisfied. She wanted the power, but she wanted sweet freedom too. Pleasure before work was the only thing she'd ever really wanted. At any moment she knew she would have to put pleasure on hold to collect yet another sinner. What a shit circumstance she was in, she thought, sipping her latte. Since her encounter with Devlin Gainsmore months ago, Celia had not seen or heard from the man. It was just as well. She didn't want to. She thought back and cursed the moment he infused her scythe with the black heart of that Dreadling. That moment was a reunion with her chains of servitude. Celia's mood quickly soured, and no longer could she enjoy her latte. The relaxation she sought in this café had disappeared. Her attention drifted from self-pity to her death-watch as it told her of yet another sinner to harvest.

"Dammit," she mumbled.

It seemed to her that sinners were dropping like flies these days. She understood she was in a huge city with a large population, but lately it seemed like they never stopped dying. This time her watch read that a man addicted to gambling would pay the ultimate price with his life because of his debtors. Celia didn't know or care how the man would die; she just knew she had to be on Danforth sometime before midnight tomorrow to make sure he stayed dead. Her death-watch had indicated that if she didn't make it to shorten the man's time on Earth, he could somehow live and possibly find salvation. Celia couldn't have that. If mistakes were made, she didn't want to find out what punishments could follow for her. After all, she had already been lucky out of Lucifer's sheer convenience. She left a bill and change on her table for the waiter and stepped out of the café.

Billy watched Celia move in his body. She didn't move like he used to. There was a feminine way about her and an arrogance that pulsated from her demeanor. From behind the information kiosk across the way, Billy continued watching. He had fully intended to sneak into the café and catch Celia off guard, like he and Frank had originally discussed. Now, though, she'd hastily left. Billy watched with purple hoodie pulled over, as if to hide. Celia caught an escalator down one level, and Billy eyed her carefully so he wouldn't lose her in the crowds.

Frank's familiar voice rang out as he appeared in the few screens above the information kiosk. Billy's back was still turned away, but he heard as he watched Celia.

"Looks like she's headed for those exit doors, kid."

Billy took a quick glance at the kiosk map to the north exit. Then he took one last look at Celia's direction. She was absolutely headed where Frank had said.

"Excuse me." Billy cut through the crowd again with the wisdom of an adult and the agility of a child. The escalator moved too slow, and his patience waned. He slid down the last few feet of the rail, startling an elderly man.

"Damn hoodlum!"

Tiny feet slapped the tiled mall floor, and Billy saw turnstile doors spin in the distance. He swayed and dodged past lollygaggers with their phones in hand, paying no attention to their trajectories. He could see her there, standing at the curbside, flagging down a cab. *Dammit,* he thought. *No taxi will stop for a little girl.* He was going to lose Celia.

Closing in, Billy hustled. He saw her catch the attention of a yellow cab. The familiar flick of his wrist brought out his glimmering scythe. The thought of knowing no mortals could see his weapon put him a little at ease. Celia's back was still turned as the cab pulled up beside her, and Billy held the scythe subtly at his side. This was it. Billy was almost within striking distance. He pulled the blade back and closed in on Celia, but something felt different. Celia's aura had somehow changed, and a darkness only Billy could see flowed from within her. He could even smell it. It was that same sulfuric burning of Hell. The force that followed it blew him back as he tried to take that swing. Billy seemed to be fighting something invisible as he stood up and pushed against nothing to take that swing again. Then he recalled the smell. It was the burning smell he recalled when the Dreadlings were around. The darkness that had blown him back materialized, and Billy was quickly on his back as familiar shadowy claws pierced him again.

Billy fought the pain of twisted evil claws. Parallel rows of, red, slanted, glowing eyes stared through him chillingly. He couldn't seem to move as the beast pressed him flat on his back against the sidewalk. He winced in pain and saw the cab taking off with Celia inside. Left helplessly pinned down on the sidewalk by a Dreadling, Billy tried to fight it off.

"Fuck!" yelled Billy. He rolled around, doing all his little frame could not to get clawed again. So many people had begun to gather around him. Mortal hands went through the Dreadling and touched Billy's tiny arms to try to help him up. One person shouted, "She's having a seizure. Help her!" Another yelled, "No, I heard you shouldn't move them."

It probably does look like a seizure, thought Billy. He should have been on guard, he thought. He should have expected anything, even a Dreadling guarding her. His new scythe was his only barrier between claws and teeth as the beast's gnashing continued. Billy still held and twirled the crystal vine shaft in one hand, but now he'd managed to wedge it between himself and the beast.

Although the surrounding mortal crowd tried to help Billy, they couldn't. Billy was being attacked spiritually. The Dreadling's mouth snapped down murderously at him with yellowed jagged fangs. With each lunge for Billy's face, the beast's tar-like mouth dripped together and tore back open. The public concern over a little girl who'd fallen to the sidewalk and wasn't getting up was yet another distraction Billy didn't need. Still, he fought with the heavenly shimmering scythe at the ready. He didn't know why, but now he thought back to his rec league days of hockey with the boys. The good times, before his diagnosis.

He realized the way he was holding the scythe felt familiar. A wonderful recollection came. He knew how to stickhandle, despite his little frame, and this weapon was powerful and feather-light. One hard crosscheck and the beast flew in a burst of ash and smoke through a concerned and kneeling middle-aged man by Billy's side.

A remarkable handspring brought Billy to his feet without much effort at all. A benefit of the young body, he thought. Stunned, the crowd gave Billy space as he stood up.

"Little girl, are you okay!" someone yelled, but Billy was already running and gone. Unrelentingly, he ran after the Dreadling. It wasn't until two floors up in a parking garage that he stopped and lost sight of the bounding beast. Amidst the shadows of the lot, its dark, translucent body disappeared. Disappointed, Billy thought his cover was surely blown. The Dreadling would undoubtedly have the means to show Celia that Billy was on the hunt for her. Even worse, Billy wondered if the beast could see right through to the real him inside.

Billy thought about things for a moment, standing there in the darkness of the parkade. He faded into the shadows and walked quietly between a slew of sports cars and SUVs. Slowly, he backtracked and listened with a newly heightened sense of hearing.

He could hear...something. Something not normal, not of this world. The sound was so faint, yet it didn't belong. Billy continued to take it in. Its noises seemed more audible as he listened, standing still for the moment. A fire-like flickering and hissing, and it sounded like it moved about above him. Billy closed his eyes and backed between the tight space of a truck and a white electric car. He stood there as if unaware, all while listening to the noise of what he was sure was the beast. With his breath held and ears perked, the noise grew louder and nearer from above and behind. The hissing and flickering came closer, and Billy smiled; his trap was set. The sudden, eerie, quiet calm gave Billy the cue. He flicked out his wrist and summoned his sunlit blade. All in one fluid motion, the scythe was summoned and swung without warning. The death screams of the shadowy beast above made Billy cringe. Burning black ash and orange flaming cinder rained down from its explosive end. The scythe had done its work. The powerful blade had spun so effortlessly in Billy's hands. He looked around the quiet lot, not a soul in sight. Billy cut open a portal and thought of a quiet destination. He dusted himself off, stepping out into an alleyway near to the mall entrance. Still, Billy felt somewhat deflated that he hadn't sent Celia packing at his first chance. Frank peered down from a huge electronic billboard in the sprawling Dundas Square tourist area across the street. Billy ran over and stood in the square, looking up at Frank with his purple hoodie pulled over his head.

"Was a close one, kid. You can't win all the time."

"I wasn't sure if she'd seen me."

"She didn't, kid, we saw. Seems like it's how we thought; they've given her authority over the Dreadlings. She has their protection."

"Have you ever seen that before?

"Well, I've seen a lot in my time."

"It's bad. Isn't it, Frank?"

"We don't lie, Billy. It's not in our nature anymore. The truth is, yes, I believe it is. There's normally this cosmic order about everything. We collected our people, they collected theirs. The shmucks are making riskier, more daring moves these days."

"What do we do about it?"

"We play chess. Remember something for me, though. You're not just a pawn out there; you're the Queen. You're built to move all over the board that is this place. Remember, when you open those portals with your blade, you can go anywhere and even send them packing anywhere. These demons are in mortal shells, and with those limits they can't travel through portals like you. There is only one way out of a mortal body, and we all know what that is. Why not check on our other favorite demon, Mr. Gainsmore? Good luck, kid, and Shalom."

Frank fizzled off the Dundas Square billboard display, and Billy stood alone among the masses again.

He felt like a machine, a little soldier who was not bound by the rules of mortality in this body. He didn't need to do anything except hunt, and that was what he would do now. With Celia's escape, he had another target in mind for the moment. Bay Street was a short distance on foot. Streetcars picked up commuters as Billy walked by them. He rounded corner after corner and still used the familiar landmarks he always had as guidance in Toronto. As he came upon the Bay Street strip where he'd once worked, he had an idea.

For the better part of the night, Billy would find a perch to sit atop. He looked around and found something perfect, a quiet fire escape across the street. Billy slid once again into the darkness of an alley, and when the time was right, he cut open a portal. He dropped so gently onto the fire escape he'd eyed that he didn't make a sound. Now, he sat comfortably yet high up enough that no one would bother him. Perched in the night, Billy would watch. He knew the hours of Devlin Gainsmore were unorthodox. He came and went whenever he pleased. From the days Billy worked for one of the big banks, he'd heard that Gainsmore came and went at strange hours. A man like that lived by no one's rules, but Billy felt no fear of him.

Billy watched quietly across the road toward Gainsmore Holdings Tower. For now, he would watch the Toronto summer night life go by from above. Billy slid his hood over, curled up in the corner of the fire escape and took it all in without so much as a blink. He was reminded of things that he'd missed. He'd missed it all, really. The people, the cars, the lights, but most of all the architecture. Toronto was a beautiful city, one that lived in Billy's heart even on the worst of his days. Although the night had not brought about answers, the incredible sunrise he witnessed lifted his spirits. Toronto never slept, and neither had Billy. The glass buildings of Bay Street proudly shimmered as the first glimmers of light washed over them. Billy hadn't moved an inch, and still he perched in wait, anxious to see if the tubby businessman would make an appearance. This was his only lead at the moment for Gainsmore, but it was something. The man did after all have a floor in the building. Billy pondered his options.

It was go after Gainsmore or do the same perching like an owl across from his old condo for any sign of Celia. Basking in the sunlight, Billy relaxed and leaned on the rail of the fire escape. He thought about what it would have been like if he'd ripped Celia out of his former body. He would have done it just like she'd done to him. He imagined smiling at her as she recognized him underneath it all. Below, Billy watched as a couple of strolling twenty-somethings held each other's hands. They were debating where they wanted to eat breakfast this morning. Billy eavesdropped as one teased the other about always wanting the same thing.

Other crowds dressed for work pushed along, buried periodically in their phones, glancing up quickly to avoid bumping into one another.

Billy was starting to like not having a dependency on eating, drinking, or resting. Although he did miss a good iced coffee. He climbed down the fire escape ladder and let it extend. He'd eyed the front entrance to the building long enough that an expensive blue and white car had pulled up out front. Billy didn't know the make; he didn't care. He knew by the license plate who it was. It read: *Gains*. Billy moved swiftly across the street and stood to the side of the building by one of the entrances where several ornate and squared concrete pillars hid him well. He waited closely in the wings. Just a few steps to the front entrance and Billy would casually strike the demon down without warning.

First a minute passed, then two. It wasn't until he'd heard the luxury car start again that Billy became confused. Peering out from behind the structural support pillar, he watched as the car pulled away. The tinted windows made it difficult to see inside, but Billy swore Gainsmore stared him down, as if he knew.

What the hell?

He came out from hiding and watched the vehicle disappear in the distance, turning left down another street. Billy needed to get in touch with Frank and find out just what exactly the plan was, because his was not working. The way this whole thing originally sounded had been much easier when Frank had sold it to him, but now Billy was uncertain.

The familiar hustle of Union Station brought Billy exactly what he was looking for. People gathered, looking to catch the next subway car or to grab a quick meal from an underground vendor. Billy was only interested in finding Frank. A digital billboard brought about Frank's warm and wrinkled smile.

"Frank..."

"Before you say a thing, I know you tried out there. You don't have to apologize. Come to the garden. We've got a lot to discuss."

Not expecting that, Billy was disappointed. With the Dreadling's unexpected attack and the prospect of Gainsmore somehow knowing Billy was after him, he certainly did need Frank's guidance. He walked over to a public bathroom and found a vacant stall at the end. Two young women joked at the sink about something Billy didn't hear. Billy paid them no mind. He just needed to get to the garden. There was no alley, no dark spot from public view; this stall was it, really. Billy closed the door, put the toilet seat down, and stood on it for a moment. Then he took a short swipe with his summoned blade at the space in front of the toilet. Billy could see the garden on the other side of the portal. He leapt for it with scythe in hand. As he disappeared, the motion sensor flushed the toilet, and the stall door swung open. The two women heard the bang of the door. One peered in at the empty stall then stared wide-eyed at her friend.

15

Billy came out of the rift reunited with the sweet-scented breeze and familiar warmth of the garden. He didn't know he'd missed the garden this much until he was back. Colors and scents he never could have imagined on Earth surrounded him. He loved it here. For a moment he thought he should perhaps have taken up Frank's offer and stayed for a while. Then again, the garden was rather small, perhaps a little larger than a football field. An eternity here might prove rather boring.

He spied Frank now. The old man was sitting on a shimmering diamond bench by the pond's edge, and the little waterfall was spilling in peacefully. At the pond's other side, the gold bench they'd first talked at also shimmered in the light of day. Frank's back was to Billy as he approached.

"Hey kid, have a seat. Listen, I think Devlin might be too dangerous to confront just yet."

Billy stepped around the bench and sat next to Frank. The old man's face was filled with concern.

"Your recon has proven useful. I don't want to risk your afterlife. You can stay in the garden if you don't want to go through with this."

"What are you saying, Frank?"

"I'm saying, I didn't know there was going to be an army of Dreadlings involved in all this. When you went to confront Gainsmore just now, we saw...something."

"What?"

We can see through your eyes when you're down there on Earth. For just a moment we looked closely at Gainsmore as he drove off. Buried deep in the man's eyes we could see — a legion."

"A what?"

"There are more demons in that body than just one. It appears somehow Celia has done the same. They can summon Hell's Dreadlings from within."

"I'm not afraid, though, Frank."

"Heh, I knew you'd say that. Let me tell you something, then: I'm afraid for you."

"Why?"

"Because if you get dragged through a portal by a Dreadling, I don't know if we can get you back this time. Hell is making risky moves. The way Gainsmore looked when you were hiding behind that pillar, he sensed something. That's why he drove off. If you're going to go on with this, you need to talk to someone who's fought more than a simple Dreadling before."

"Who?"

"A friend."

Frank clapped his hands, and a portal was opened before Billy's eyes.

With subtle ripples, the other side showed clouds and gold gates. Was this Heaven? Billy was excited. The snap of the portal shutting behind them did not distract from the beauty Billy took in. There was a blinding light, then a feeling of love and warmth that pulsed through his entire being. The overwhelming feeling of oneness brought tears to his eyes, and he froze as his heart filled with a peace he'd never known before. Frank took Billy by the hand and guided him.

"This way, kid."

They stepped to the shimmering golden gates, where a towering figure stood. His glowing yellow armor of light was almost too much for Billy to behold. He shielded his eyes.

"You know he cannot come through here, Frank."

"I know, Batariel, relax. It is you we are here to see."

"How can I help you?" Billy stood mesmerized not only by the commanding resonance of the guard's voice but also his appearance. His jaw was strong, like it had been chiseled from stone, yet his dark skin was as perfectly smooth as glass. *He is surely an angel*, thought Billy. Then, as Billy's thought finished, Batariel looked down at his little twelve-year-old frame and smiled. He'd heard Billy's thoughts and responded, "Yes, I am."

Frank continued, "Billy, as you know, is to hunt down certain stray reapers who have gone rogue on Earth."

"Yes, a noble quest indeed."

"We've encountered a problem."

"What is it?"

"We've been detected before we could even strike. These reapers, they have the Dreadling hordes at their command."

"My, that is a problem."

The angel stood pondering. "You understand we don't fight in the mortal realm, Frank. That is why Billy was chosen as the hunter."

Frank nodded. "I know, but you have fought the demon hordes. You have vanquished worse than a Dreadling. Can Billy do this alone?"

"Hell does not play fair, but Billy has been given a body half celestial and half mortal. He cannot be slain by normal means." Batariel smiled at Billy again, then continued, "I understand you already vanquished one Dreadling. Well done, child."

"But are his gifts alone enough, Batariel? Is he enough to take on the Dreadling hordes lurking inside those hosts?"

"You have been given gifts, Billy. The scythe can cut down many demons. The weapon is enough to cut down the hordes, but he who wields it must not waver in faith. And by this, I mean faith in ability and self. You have to know that you are made capable. If the battle becomes too great for you, escape to the garden, like Frank has said. There you can regroup and strike again. It is the garden that feeds you, and it is the garden that sustains you. I have seen in your mind, Billy Walker. I know your past. To be confident with your new weapon, do not wield it the way you would assume. Wield it with familiarity and comfort. Like you did when that Dreadling had you pinned down on that sidewalk."

"You mean, like a hockey stick?"

Batariel smiled. "Familiarity and comfort, Billy Walker."

"Thank you, thank you, my old friend," Frank said.

With mutual respect, they wished each other well, then Billy followed Frank through a portal back to the garden.

"Well, kid, take a look in the pond. Wait for the right time. It's up to you now. You heard Batariel. Let your faith guide you. He believes in you, and so do I."

Billy smiled at Frank. "See you soon, old-timer."

"I'll be here, watching and waiting."

Billy knelt by the picturesque pond once more. The crystal waters formed a vision of those he sought. First it was Gainsmore, still in his extravagant luxury car driving through unknown parts of the city. Then he spied Celia. She was following someone by the shadows of the night. It was a middle-aged man who looked rather desperate. Billy caught a glance of their location. The man stumbled through Princes' Boulevard. He neared the familiar expanse of the Canadian National Exhibition stone arch gateway. Billy watched as the man stumbled through the night in fear.

He passed the gothic stone entrance into the vacant fairgrounds. Billy could see the familiar ornate angel perched atop the entrance. He didn't know what was happening exactly, but he knew he had to help this frantic running man or death was certain. Billy watched him run. He assumed Celia was following to steal his remaining days, much like she had his. The pond waters changed, showing Celia close in pursuit, still somewhere in the shadows. Billy looked into the pond and thought a little longer. Perhaps he could buy this man more time. He let his mind drift to those exhibition gates. He would come out exactly where he desired. He let one foot dangle over the still pond water and leaned forward. As the tingling sensation of the otherworldly water washed over him, he heard Frank's voice one last time before he fell completely through.

"Go get 'em, kid."

16

Celia had tracked this man across the lakeshore area from a bar near Danforth Avenue. She'd watched him from the shadows since he'd been carelessly chatting up someone at the bar. Now, she waited impatiently in the shadows for his death. She just wanted to harvest his soul and enjoy the mortal luxuries she'd longed for in the first place. She watched as the man headed for the Canadian National Exhibition's stone archway. He fumbled a few times as he looked over his shoulder. She wondered why he'd headed in this direction. Was there some sort of safe haven awaiting him? A friend's place, or perhaps a place he knew he could hide.

Although she would have rather been at the Steel Stallion again, or better yet the condo with that ripped stripper, Celia's curiosity grew. She wondered just how this man would die. If nothing happened in the next few minutes, she'd kill him herself. He was not just being followed by her, and she knew it. One thing Celia didn't mind about doing all this again was watching nature take its course. To her the entertainment of knowing someone's death was imminent was always enjoyable. The monotony of the old stab and soul pull was so drab. Sure, she could have just hit him with the scythe and torn out his soul if she'd wanted to, but where was the fun in that? She liked a little excitement, and right on cue, it sounded like she was not going to be disappointed. Celia heard squealing tires. Cars were coming up to the vacant fairground gates, and fast. She wasn't the only one looking for this man. She'd known it from his behavior earlier in the night. The chase had started a few blocks back when the fellow had fled on two different streetcars from two men. Celia had been on him with each move, but he hadn't seen her. It was these squealing tires and the evil behind the wheel that he was running from. He didn't have a clue about her. As desperation grew, Celia watched the man run with winded lungs. He gasped for air, leaning behind the last stone pillar in a line of many at the fairground gates. Multiple cars had squealed to a halt at that moment. Celia grinned.

They'd found him, and he knew it. He should have quit while he was ahead. The troubles of his gambling addiction had led him to this fateful point. Since he'd cheated the wrong people out of their money, he knew he would be cheated of his life. His heart beat thunderously, painfully. He prayed they didn't see him hiding behind that final stone pillar.

The slam of car doors and the pounding of feet shook him. He peered across the vacant exhibition lot. There was a dark blue van with tinted windows and a black SUV, both at the stone archway. Another car, an expensive one, blue and white, pulled in slower from behind. Wide-eyed, with his gaze stuck on the people who wanted him dead, he foolishly gave his position away and tripped slightly. His shaking legs had failed him.

Guns were quickly drawn, and the gambler turned his back. He gave it everything he had to run again, hoping the pillar obscured his view. He ran so desperately that he paid no mind as strange noises of tearing in the sky above, mixed with gunfire, echoed into the night. Something or someone small had dropped from above, but still the man ran.

He heard the sound of car engines screaming away from the lot, and it wasn't until he was much farther away that he looked back. He wondered how he had not been shot.

So much gunfire had rung out, but no harm had come to him. He took it all in from a distance and thought he saw something terrible. It was a little girl. They'd somehow shot a little girl. Tears at his cowardice streamed down his cheeks. His mistakes had killed a child. Even through the tears, his fight-or-flight instinct controlled him, and flight was all he had. He disappeared into the night.

Just as Billy had foreseen, he'd dropped from overhead and stopped a murder. Gunfire had rung out, and his little frame had managed to absorb all of it. He'd seen guns drawn before he'd taken that plunge, and the trajectory of his drop had been true. The gunmen, seeing they'd slain a little girl, fled in fear to their vehicles. All except one vehicle squealed out of the parking lot. Billy knew immediately that it was the Rolls-Royce of Devlin Gainsmore.

"Unbelievable," said Billy, standing up and dusting himself off. The bullets inside his body caused no pain. He wasn't aware quite how this new body worked, but it was clear bullets were no obstacle. He heard the sound of metal dropping to the asphalt and saw the last of the bullets ejected by his body. His purple hoodie even closed up the holes that had been ripped through it.

"What *are* you?" asked Devlin Gainsmore, staring hatefully at the child across the lot.

"I'm one badass ballerina with the soul of an angry man," quipped Billy.

"I can smell your righteous stench from here. It was you outside my building. We could sense you, smell you, lurking by those fucking pillars."

"Are you sure? I just took a bath, well, sort of. I don't think I stink?" Billy quipped again. He walked closer to Gainsmore, slowly closing the gap.

He'd had no idea Gainsmore was the man this poor sap owed money to, but he wasn't surprised. There was certainly more going on in Devlin's portfolio than just a real-estate empire. Billy now stood a few meters away and stopped, staring down the evil within the man. Gainsmore took in all five feet of Billy with an unimpressed sneer. Just where the hell was Celia? The whole reason he'd dropped here was because of her. *I guess now I'll have to kill two birds with one stone,* he thought, *or two demons with one scythe.* That was if he could find her.

Devlin was the first to make a move. The demon in disguise flicked his wrist and with his dark scythe in hand began to stamp the ground. Dreadlings ripped out like flickering shadows from within him. So many tore away from within the man's flesh.

"Behold!" Gainsmore's voice reverberated demonically. "We are legion!"

"Nice to meet you, legion, I'm Billy. I was once your tenant, but now I'm your reckoning." Faster than the closest Dreadling could strike him, Billy had summoned his blade of redemption and sliced the first beast into a haze of raining cinder.

The fat businessman's eyes had eclipsed with the darkness inside him. He looked more confused about Billy's statement than alarmed at the Dreadling's destruction.

"What?"

Billy replied, "Yeah, you should fix the fucking plumbing in your three-story walkups, asshole."

Billy spun his scythe back and forth in a figure eight and then held it low, just like a hockey stick. He watched as Dreadlings closed in around him. The first of the horde dove at him, attacking with claws flailing. Billy swept the blade up and cleaved off its arachnid-like head. Black and orange burning ash burst into the night as the creature died. Billy smiled; he was going to hold his own. He felt a new vigor as he wielded his weapon. He mumbled quietly, "Thank you, Batariel, and thank you, Frank."

16

Chaos had erupted around the vacant exhibition grounds. Masses of Dreadlings rallied against Billy. Some jumped off statues, others off the sides of vacant exhibition buildings. All tried to lay their ethereal claws into him. Things were smooth with the scythe for Billy now, and smooth was fast as he sliced away with precision. The more Gainsmore summoned Dreadlings, the more tricks Billy pulled from his purple hoodie sleeves. Overhead, one, then two Dreadlings swooped down to tackle Billy's little frame from the side of a building, but he was too agile. He could sense this little body was once very good at ballet, just as Frank had said. The execution of a stunning pirouette came naturally as Billy held out his blade. The spinning scythe skewered both beasts through their chests with demonic yelps in the summer night air.

Every Dreadling that ran for him seemed slow now. Billy's reflexes were unmatched. Beast after beast met the inescapable end of pointed agony. Billy glanced over at Gainsmore. The man was dripping with sweat but seemed far from beaten.

"I'll summon every last fucking one of these bastards if I've got to," he yelled.

There was no fatigue for Billy, no burnout. He ran, he dodged, and he sliced his way ever closer to Gainsmore. Pirouettes and slashes guided Billy through the horde as they exploded with the slightest touch of the blade. Billy felt himself dancing as he destroyed demon after demon, and, most importantly, he was closing in on Devlin Gainsmore.

The man stared Billy down as two more of his Dreadlings were sent bursting to ash in his face. Gainsmore and his horde seemed relentless, but Billy managed to get close enough for a swing. Scythes clashed with otherworldly sounds of impact, and Dreadlings poured endlessly out from the exhibition gates. Billy held strong and vaulted back using his scythe for balance. He saw the Dreadlings' numbers grow too great. They dangled off the stone exhibition gateway, they jutted from behind pillars, and they did everything they could to strike at Billy. One of the vile little gargoyles even used the stone angel at the gateway's peak to vault down toward Billy. They'd surrounded him with their numbers and started to constrict into a tight circle.

He thought of Frank, he thought of Batariel, and he thought of the escape plan. It was at the forefront of his mind; it always had been. Billy sliced a portal through dimensions in that vacant fairground. Then he slipped through to the garden just as a claw from the horde had managed to slice his wrist.

Frank sat happily on the decorative golden bench and watched the gentle waterfall cascade into the crystal pond. Billy had popped in quite a fair distance from the pond. He looked at his injured wrist. Nothing; the garden had healed him. Billy ran through flowing, shimmering lavender fields across the garden toward Frank and the pond. Not a word was exchanged. Frank just gave Billy a nod and watched the kid plunge into the water. Then, Billy repeated the process several times.

He was getting the hang of things. Frank smiled. He watched in the water as the kid got the drop on the beasts time and time again. When the Dreadlings' numbers really started to dwindle, Billy heard a chuckle from the old-timer on one of his runs through the garden. Frank saw that the horde didn't know what had hit them, and he knew that indeed he had chosen the right hunter for the job. Billy cut the beasts down from above, he cut them down from behind, and he cut them down as he pleased.

When the number of Dreadlings was countable on two hands, Frank couldn't contain his cheers. He watched with a wide grin from beside the pond. The old paralegal leaned forward to look at the action reflected in the water. Billy had jumped once again through the water and slipped away from a pack of Dreadlings. He landed above the three clamoring beasts and plunged his blade down upon them. As Frank watched him walk toward Gainsmore through a cloud of

Dreadling death debris, he pumped his fist and shouted in excitement, "That's the ticket, kid!"

Billy had by his count executed over half of Devlin's pets. This little frame Frank had picked was meant for this dance of destruction. Billy had overwhelmed the forces of darkness, slipping through to the garden, slicing through them with his righteous sunlit blade. Billy Walker was their reckoning.

"Enough!" yelled Gainsmore, panting like a tired dog in the summer heat. The runes on the side of his scythe's dark blade lit a glowing blood-red shade. Gainsmore stamped the shaft of his scythe against the ground, and the few Dreadlings left burst to dust and ash at his command.

"You fight well, child, though not well enough to cast this demon into oblivion."

The stocky businessman unbuttoned his expensive beige suit jacket. He held his dark blade at the ready.

"Come, travel through your portal and see where it takes you now," challenged Gainsmore.

Billy was wary. He did want to leap from a portal and thrust his blade into the demon inside. Then he'd perhaps even leave it there and see what happened, but he didn't. There was a brief stand-off. Devlin moved cautiously to the right while Billy circled to the left. The portly man moved so incredibly quick, it seemed unnatural. Unexpectedly, he threw his blade at Billy. The spinning scythe's shaft shrank as it whirled through the air with deadly accuracy.

Billy sank to his little knees and held out his blade. His young reflexes saved him again. He'd sent Gainsmore's blade ricocheting away after it nearly decapitated him.

It was no matter to Devlin; his blade reappeared in his grasp with the flick of his wrist.

"When my blade infects your righteous soul, I am going to follow you down just to watch your second death."

"Yeah?" responded Billy. "What makes you so sure I haven't already been down there?"

"No one escapes the second death."

"You sure about that? I had to get passed through a giant cyclops toad's rectum, but I escaped."

Again Gainsmore looked surprised, and Billy used that to his advantage, striking hard and fast. Their blades met in a clash of sparking defiance. Billy leapt back, spinning while trying to skewer Gainsmore like he had his Dreadlings, but the demon was prepared. He hit Billy's blade so hard, it flew out of his grasp and skidded against the asphalt. Devlin's dark blade shimmered with blood-red runes aglow, like it hungered for death and destruction. Despite Billy toppling onto his back to dodge the strike, he summoned his scythe again and clashed with Gainsmore.

"You will fail, child."

Billy didn't respond. Instead, he swung twice at Gainsmore's head, but the fat man parried. Then Gainsmore stepped back, raising his hand. With that motion, a swirling black mass of serpent-like coils arose from the ground. Billy knew what he wanted to do; he was trying to send Billy down Hell's bloody rabbit hole, just like Celia had. The black portal swirled behind Billy, and Gainsmore took another swing, trying to push Billy through it.

"No fucking thanks," Billy responded.

Gainsmore's fat body still dripped with sweat. It seemed the exertion was finally too great for his sedentary carcass to bear.

Billy smiled. He knew now the man's body would give out at any time.

"Smells like a pig roast out here," Billy quipped as Devlin struggled to push him in the portal, clashing their scythes again.

"Fool," growled Gainsmore, shaking.

Billy saw the opening he needed. The heat of his sunlit blade grinding against Gainsmore's shone inches away from the demon's sweat-beaded brow. Billy ducked down, dropping his blade and his posture. His righteous blade swept up from under the bloated businessman and came to a glowing rest between Devlin's legs. Billy stepped back, watching the portly man collapse into a quivering heap on his side.

The portal Gainsmore had summoned sank into the asphalt as if his control over it was ruined. Molten cracks seared and ripped at the smoking flesh of the corrupted demon's dying shell.

The once swollen body of a man of excess was burning away. Billy watched as Gainsmore shivered and shook, putrefying into something far beyond human. Flashes of the demon within the man horrified Billy. He stood back and let his blade do the work, but to his surprise, he didn't want to see it.

In a matter of seconds, all that was left was a pile of ash and the dark blade of a demon now gone. It was clear to Billy that Gainsmore had been much more powerful than Celia. He had exuded such power, yet still he'd feared the little girl with the motivating rage of a betrayed man. The image of those stained bones and horns that jutted and tore out from Gainsmore's deteriorating fatty carcass flashed through Billy's conscience. The last bits of the demon's bones turned to cinder, and Billy picked his sunlit blade off the ground. A foot away was also Devlin's own dark blade. Billy knelt and lifted it with his left hand.

Frank's voice rang out in the night. Billy looked overhead to a digital billboard advertisement along the nearby expressway. "Well done, kid. Bring that dark blade with you when you come to the garden. Maybe we'll find a way to destroy it."

17

Celia lurked in the shadows. This night had taken quite a turn. A whirlwind of excitement and fear bubbled up inside her. She watched these unexpected events unfold in front of her eyes. A child had dropped from the sky and was now overwhelming a demon. Devlin Gainsmore, whom she thought was certainly more dangerous than her, was obliterated. She watched from the side of a nearby building through the shadows into the vacant parking lot. There was something peculiar about this child. She moved so well with that burning blade. At the child's hands, Celia had seen the Dreadlings burst with a fragility she didn't think they had. The Dreadlings of Hell were not to be taken lightly, and a horde of them should have overwhelmed anyone, but not this child.

The girl had fought with the confidence and fury of someone that wanted revenge. Celia had seen very few fight like this. Celia was more than afraid — she was terrified. As Devlin Gainsmore summoned a portal of dark matter in a desperate attempt to cast the child through it, Celia could see through his human form. She supposed it was her duty as another demon to help Gainsmore. Perhaps summon her horde of Dreadlings and take a few swings at the righteous child. Celia was not ashamed, though, that she was more interested in survival. Gainsmore had fucked himself over being here, she thought. That gambler wasn't even on his radar. It was clear Gainsmore had become too consumed with money and revenge since he had been willing to chase people down for it. Celia didn't give a damn. She was curious to see if the demon could hold his own.

The child clashed blades with him. She was certain it would end soon, and she was right. A savage swoop between the fat man's legs sent him curling into a fetal mess.

Just where would Gainsmore end up now that the child had won? Would he be cast back to Hell?

Celia thought back to Hell. She never wanted to be in the heat, decay, and stench of that place ever again. She watched the little girl stand over the smoking man's burning carcass. Then she witnessed her answer as not only did the faux humanity of Gainsmore burn away, but also the demon within. He wasn't going to Hell. He wasn't going anywhere. He was just — gone. That frightened Celia. All that remained on the ground after that was the dark blade of Devlin Gainsmore.

If the child did that to Gainsmore, then she was certainly doomed. She didn't stand a chance. She needed to run or at least disappear. Celia watched the child pick up Gainsmore's ancient scythe. Then the child cut a portal into the air with her sunlit blade. A purple glow flickered around the edges. Celia could see through the other side from her hiding place. The shimmering of gemstones, a waterfall, the lush greenery and flowers of an inviting garden. Just where was the child escaping to?

"Fuck," Celia mumbled in the darkness. She knew she was being hunted now. She needed answers, she needed safety, and after seeing that child destroy all those Dreadlings, she needed more power. The possibility of complete extinction was not something Celia was interested in.

In fact, it brought her to the harsh reality that she would indeed rather work in Hell than not exist at all. All she had wanted was to have a little fun, and now she walked the vacant fairground lot alone in self-pity. Still, she was blind to her own mistakes and blamed Gainsmore and anyone else she could think of for her new circumstances. It was unfortunate, but it appeared that Celia would have to ask for help. That meant a hard choice was to be made. Hellfire, brimstone, and all that went with it. When the snap of the child's portal was heard and Celia was sure the child was gone, she raised her own blade overhead. Then she summoned her own portal and sliced off Billy's head with her own scythe, letting the pieces fall lifelessly down in that lot. A swirling mass of dark energy encompassed her celestial form, and she rode it down, down to misery and decay again.

Darkness subsided, and Celia stepped into a smoke that dissipated, revealing yellowy brimstone. Sparse pits of molten rock bubbled, and wallowing mortal souls tried to pull themselves out to freedom. Celia kicked one in the face, and he flew back into the molten rock with a satisfying fiery splash. As Celia walked past tortured souls, she eyed the familiar birthing pits of the Dreadlings. Giant mucilaginous maggots fed on the fearful screams of people and that fear accumulated into black tar-like pits. Celia could see the Dreadlings growing by the hundreds inside the massive maggots. Celia remembered the beasts clawed their way out of the those wriggling puss-filled monsters. When the maggots swelled, the Dreadlings would burst them open to find their freedom.

Celia was in search of an area far beyond this one. She summoned another portal and felt it swirl around her, then she walked out to a much deeper and darker area of the abyss. More tortured souls wailed as she walked by, ignoring their pleas. A little ways down, Celia did see what she was looking for. Demons more powerful than your average Dreadling poked and prodded mortals back into a burning lake of fire. They were the ones. They were known as the burning children. Celia watched them with blue flames flickering about as they tortured the mortals. She hated the creatures. One eyed her and screamed.

"Yeah, you guys suck. Hope you know that," she told them.

They snarled, and many turned to scream at her. They couldn't speak, and she liked it that way. Useless halfling creatures. Their bodies were always ablaze, like their father's. Thick grayed hides like cattle and faces like bulls to match terrified their victims. Bright blue flames danced about their flesh. Their four arms wielded a bloody spear in each, poking sinners back into the bubbling molten pits across the landscape.

Celia knew she had to speak with the ruler of this plane, or the one that ruled them all, and you didn't find the ruler of them all — he found you. Celia was of the first level of Hell; she would seek out Amalon of the fallen. She walked slowly along an uneven stone pathway. At the path's edges, a few men begged to be taken down from spikes that impaled them and the ground around the path. Centipedes ate at each of them.

"Take me down, please," one man called.

Celia smiled, walked over, and covered his mouth. "There now, ask for help," she said. His voice was gone.

The burning children continued to scream piercing, animal-like noises as Celia carried on down the path. She wasn't afraid of them. She was, however, afraid of their father. One stared her down as it skewered a mortal and tossed it back into molten rock. She moved forward unphased. She was close to Amalon's throne. She could see it in the distance. Ash and bloodstains led to the top. The raising granite-like steps formed a pyramid, and he sat looking down to his children below. Celia placed her foot on the first step, and before she took another, Amalon's accusing voice shot down from heights above.

"Who would tarnish my throne with their feet?"

Celia knelt at the first step, still unable to see the demonic ruler at the height he was. "Please, I beg you," she responded.

His voice shot down again and resounded like it was right in front of her. *"I know what you've done! Suffering should be your reward, foolish demon!"*

"Please, I—"

"They have plans for you. You have seen it."

"Seen it?"

Amalon continued, "You have seen the garden!"

"Yes," Celia responded. She remembered the portal the child escaped through.

"Listen to me, demoness. You will be given a new body. One without mortal limitations. You will kill that child, and Hell will harvest sinners again without interference."

"Yes, Amalon."

Although this was not the escape from servitude Celia wanted, she would at least exist. Existence at all was better than oblivion.

Amalon continued, "Come forth, demon."

Celia took one step onto the first stair and instantly stood in front of the demonic ruler. She knelt and looked fearfully at the black stone floor. The flicker of blue flames about his body gave off such heat. With the wave of the demon's clawed hand, Celia was given a new body.

"Now, give me your blade, demon," Amalon commanded.

Celia summoned it, holding it above her head with both hands.

"You will kill the child, you will destroy the garden, and you will do what we ask." Amalon slashed his right wrist with the dark scythe blade. Blue blood glowed in the darkness, shooting wildly as he pressed the wound against the scythe blade.

"When you stand on Earth once more, the prince of the air will find you and seal your fate."

Celia nodded reluctantly.

"Take thy weapon and do thy work!" Amalon commanded.

"Yes, Amalon!" Celia cried out and stepped cautiously away from the beast's throne.

Celia walked the endless stretch of Hell's first plane to the front gates. She saw not one, but two old friends. Theodore charged toward her, bounding noisily until he was only feet away. He'd recognized her old form now that it was back and expected food. Celia laughed. The foolish toad always expected a meal from her. She had looked after him for centuries after all.

"Not today, Theodore. I have new work to do."

His new keeper, Vilkaris the Foul (whom she'd appointed as her successor) slowly slid over. The slug-man questioned her as he drew even closer, "A promotion?"

"Yes. You're due for one by now, aren't you?"

"No, I'll feed the fucking toad, thanks," he said sincerely.

"At this point, I think I would rather do that."

"You gave it up. It's my task now!"

"Easy, Vilkaris," she said with a smile. "Take care of him. Remember, he likes his meat..."

"Seasoned." Vilkaris grinned.

"Yes."

Celia held out her newly cursed sickle and summoned a swirling mass of dark energy to take her back to Earth. She had the start of a plan and the means to execute it. She knew nothing down here was granted without the permission of a fallen angel, and Amalon was certainly one of them.

Others of the fallen commanded their own planes of Hell, except Lucifer. He prowled the Earth like a lion, waiting to devour the unaware with temptations. He was the prince of the air. Celia had to meet him. Through him she would seal her fate; she had no choice in the matter.

A portal of dark energy brought Celia into the vacant dressing room of a popular clothier. She checked herself out in the dressing room mirror. Damn, she was hot again, or so she thought. She certainly looked more like she used too. The new form was welcome. She was thankful anonymity was hers again. Her features seemed a little different. Her black hair was cut short a little past her chin and flowed down lower in the front. She was fit-looking but had curves that she knew she would use to her advantage given the opportunity. She wore black leggings and a light blue tank top.

Celia swung open the dressing room door and walked out. She was greeted by a sales associate. "Oh, I didn't see you go in there; my apologies. Did everything fit you okay?"

Celia smiled. "I will pass on them today, but thank you."

She headed for the storefront and glanced back at the confused associate as she saw there was nothing in the stall. Celia smiled.

Her happiness was temporary as she thought about what was ahead. She would meet Lucifer, or rather he would meet her. Celia walked over near the very mall café she had sat in days before. She took a seat at a bench out front and realized as she tried to smell the baked goods inside that the pleasures of the mortal senses were not something she could enjoy in this new body. It seemed she was not mortal at all again. She cursed under her breath, missing taste, touch, and scent. Only a few minutes passed before she felt a tap on her shoulder, and she looked up. To her left was a stunningly handsome, tall man.

He wore a tailored black suit with white dress shirt and scarlet shimmering tie. Accenting the tie was a gold clip with a barely noticeable inverted pentagram. It gleamed at its edge, catching the sun through the mall's glass ceilings.

"Celia! What a pleasure," he said warmly with a perfect smile. "Come, sit with me for a drink in the café."

It was him, the father of lies. His handsome visage and demeanor were a wonderful front for his true nature. Celia followed closely and took a seat in the back corner of the café after him. His sky-blue eyes dropped Celia's guard easily as he looked her. She was instantly attracted to him, despite the circumstances. Her mind had drifted away from who he was as she took him in. The way his shirt rested on his solid chest, the way his chiseled jaw looked as he smiled. She felt her cheeks flush. *Dammit,* she thought, *pull yourself together, Celia.*

"Don't be embarrassed Celia, it's perfectly natural, I have that effect on everyone," Lucifer said, responding to her thoughts. "I am, after all, the most beautiful creation you will ever see, even like this." He gestured at his mortal form. Drinks quickly followed. The server also fawned over her new customer. Celia noticed multiple unnecessary check-ins as they tried to have a conversation. At one point, after the third interruption in five minutes, Celia couldn't help herself. "*Yeah, hi,*" she said with a fake smile. "We are fine. Nothing has or will change in the next five minutes so... *Thank you.*"

The sever walked away, irritated and mumbling. Celia swore each time she had come back, her button-down blouse had been pulled a little lower.

"Now, now, Celia. Jealousy is a sin, isn't it," said Lucifer with an arrogant smirk. "Who is to say nothing will change in the next five minutes for you; you never know."

Celia looked puzzled at Lucifer's comment, and she could see it was his intent.

"Let's continue. It appears this all started when you met Rubella on the CN Tower and decided you wanted a vacation in a mortal's body. In your profession, you simply have to collect sinners and send them to where they belong. Instead, you stole a mortal's body. You then pursued a wild, lust-fueled lifestyle, falling into the mortals' tempting pleasure traps. Then you killed three Dreadlings and plotted to kill another reaper out of sheer paranoia." Lucifer clapped his hands. "Well played, Celia."

Celia lowered her gaze submissively. She folded her arms in protest, like a child scolded by a parent.

Lucifer continued, "You didn't even bother to see if the body you sought had a saved soul in it. He was indeed a saved soul, Celia. You saw a suicidal man at the brink and thought, that's my guy!"

"I'm sorry," she said meekly.

"Hah, of course you are. Do you want to know a secret?"
"What is it?"
"Well, it's about the righteous little girl everyone is so afraid of these days."

Celia was all ears.

"I thought that would interest you. That little girl is not a little girl at all. That is the very victim who you screwed over to start this disgraceful scandal in the first place."

Celia saw Lucifer's demeanor change. His mortal shell was the same as it ever was, but behind it, Celia saw flames. She had her ethereal vision again, and it was clear Lucifer was livid.

"Do you have any idea how long we had gone on undisturbed collecting sinners? Then you submitted to petty self-indulgence." Lucifer's quiet and accusing tone was deliberate. He never caused a scene, but he certainly drove fear into Celia.

"Wha...what can be done?" Celia fumbled.

Lucifer smirked. "I commanded Amalon to aid you. You will take your scythe to the garden where Billy Walker dwells. You will sever his connection to the garden and with that banish the child from the garden. When Billy is weak, you will strike. *Understand?*"

"Yes."

"Good." Lucifer's demeanor calmed again as he smiled. "Once you infiltrate the garden, slam that cursed blade into the ground and watch. That is your task. Simple enough, isn't it?"

"How will I do this?"

"You saw it yourself; Billy Walker took the dark blade. We will know the location of the garden and through it we will enter. That blade will allow us to open a portal to the garden. You will wait by the north storm tunnel of the Humber River until you see that portal open. Then you dive inside."

"I have to go into the river?"

"Yes."

"I–I don't want to go in that filthy water."

"You're going in that river, Celia, and remember this: succeed or fail, it's relative. Either way, you will be as you wish."

"As I wish?"

"Yes, you will be as the mortals."

Celia thought for a moment. Would Lucifer really reward her with a mortal vacation again if she carried out this task?

Lucifer smirked, hearing her thoughts. "You *shall* be as the mortals."

18

Billy was home. The garden felt like his sanctuary now, a place he truly belonged. His connection to it felt stronger each time he was there. It was comforting knowing Frank was always waiting for him on one of the two ornate benches. The old man sat comfortably with one leg crossed over the other and hands in his lap. Billy took in the sweet, fragrant air, saturated with scents of the wild lavender fields.

"Hey there, kid. Looks like you brought back Gainsmore's scythe like I asked. We'll have to destroy it. I don't exactly know how yet; it's not really my area of expertise. But bring it here son."

Billy walked over and stood beside Frank. He held the weapon outstretched with both hands, and Frank received it, resting it on his lap. "Well, that's one *hell* of a weapon," Frank said, smiling. Billy chuckled. "I think we'll store it somewhere around here, until I consult with Batariel."

"Where?"

"I'm open to suggestions," replied Frank.

"Have you tried dipping it in the pond? I mean, when you took those balloons down below and whipped them at Dreadlings, look what the water did to them."

"Could be risky." Frank walked to the pond's edge looked at the dark scythe, then cupped a bit of water in his hand and sprinkled it on the blade. "Ah, just as I suspected. Nothing."

"Why do you suppose the water did nothing?"

Frank passed the blade back to Billy. "It's not a living thing is my guess."

"Well, I'll take it to the other side of the garden and bury it for now then. Perhaps in the lavender fields?"

"That'll do. That's a big area, though, so you better mark it."

Billy nodded. He looked at the dark blade. It was pitch-black in his hands. Not like when Gainsmore had wielded the thing. Now, it was deep among the lavender until they knew what to do with it.

"Listen, kid, relax for a bit. I'll go talk with Batariel about that blade. I might be a while, but when I get back, we'll know how to destroy it."

"Why not take it with you? Let them deal with it above."

"No, darkness can't enter the heavenly realm, not even in the form of a reaper's blade. I wouldn't be able to step through the portal with it."

Billy nodded.

Frank smiled. "See you soon."

Billy ran with the blade to the fragrant lavender fields of the garden. A warm breeze swept over the flowers as he entered the fields. He wasted no time in burying the blade, digging a shallow area with his own scythe and covering it up as though nothing was there.

He placed a tiny amethyst gemstone he'd picked up from around the pond to mark the spot. Then he meandered back and sat near the pond's edge. He let his feet dangle in the clear water for a while as time passed slowly. Billy looked into the crystal pond and couldn't help but feel thankful. He was thankful for Frank and the second chance to right the wrongs he'd been dealt. Sitting quietly, Billy realized that Frank was truly the only friend he had now. As sad as the realization seemed, he smiled. One true friend was enough anyway he told himself.

Celia had caught a taxi from Toronto's Harbourfront neighborhood. The driver was confused when she'd asked to be dropped off by an underpass, but she didn't care. She paid the fare and stepped out into the night. There she waited in a downpour, miserably, until opportunity knocked in the night. Celia, already soaked, stepped near the flowing river's edge. It didn't matter that the river flowed hard and steady. All that mattered was that it took her into that storm drain ahead.

Celia held her breath and took a dive. The landscape blurred into obscurity as she was swallowed. The only sound was a snap when the portal they'd told her would be there closed. Celia hated this part. The in-between. The cold, the darkness, and the sound, almost like a scream as she was torn between realms. This time it seemed to go on longer than all the other times she'd traveled like this. When she saw light, she walked cautiously from the mouth of the portal. She was in a fragrant field of purple flowers, and my how everything smelled wonderful. Celia couldn't help but stand there in a stupor. She breathed in the sweetness of the air and thought jealously, *So, this is how they live.*

All she had to do was slam her blade into this sacred ground and her job was done. She would be free of these tasks. Free to live as she liked in a new mortal shell as her reward.

With her sickle in hand, Celia stood calm in the fields of lavender. She was nervous. Her hands shook as she readied herself. She counted down hesitantly with each breath, and on the third, she plunged the cursed blade into the ground.

Blue flames licked the blade and spread about the lavender, devouring their beauty. Then a cloud of misty blue blood sprayed about the air around the scythe. The mist gathered and thickened until bones took shape. Then muscle swirled and wrapped around a wicked frame, until finally, Amalon stood before her in gray, muscled flesh. Celia stepped back, taking in the beast's larger than life form. He was massive. He walked on hooves, yet he stood erect like a man. Blue flames flickered about his cattle-like hide. From behind him, he pulled out a massive axe that looked to be made of bone, and with it in hand, he spoke to Celia.

"Tell me, demon, where is the child?"

Celia stood dumbfounded at the sight of Amalon made flesh and larger than life. "I–I don't know this place. He could be far across it," she responded.

Amalon grunted, and smoke billowed from his mule-like nostrils. Slowly, he stamped through the bright purple lavender fields, killing them in his wake. With each of the beast's steps, Celia watched the atmosphere change. A plague of death was spreading among all living things and darkness throughout the sky.

"Amalon," said Celia. "How do I leave this place?"

She'd never seen the beast's expression change, but it did in this moment. He laughed a vile laugh. "Stay or go, it is irrelevant, like you now. Your part is done."

So much for an exit plan, thought Celia. She stayed back and watched the garden ripped apart by evil. She stood in the burned lavender field watching Amalon rain destruction on the land. It was very satisfying for her.

It wasn't long before she saw Billy in his new demon-slaying form. He sat with feet dangling innocently at the edge of a beautiful pond that ran off from a quiet waterfall. Amalon approached slowly. How dare he, she thought, how dare he hunt her and be awarded any sort of redemption. When she found him, he was at the brink of disaster. A depressed, separated alcoholic, literally teetering on a damn railing. Who would have known he had prayed for redemption moments before she arrived? Celia trailed behind Amalon and waited with a smile to see Billy destroyed. If a fallen angel couldn't bring him back to the second death, nothing could. Soon Billy would be where Celia thought he belonged. Perhaps she would make a special trip down just to feed him to Theodore for old times' sake. Then she would enjoy the mortal spoils Lucifer promised. Celia looked back at the scorched field. She saw her scythe still impaled in the land. She skipped over and picked up her blade from the scorched field, dreaming of what was to come.

Billy stared into the pond. He hadn't been this relaxed in as long as he could remember. The only thing that interrupted his leisure was a sudden waft of heat. One that wasn't your typical warm tropical garden breeze. Billy sensed something strange. He looked over one of his little shoulders and saw blue flames rising up in the distant horizon. Immediately, his stomach sank. Something was moving through the air toward him, and it was big...

Amalon's ancient blood-stained axe of bone whipped toward Billy, almost out of nowhere. Billy had mere seconds to move. There was only one way to go for Billy Walker. Forward he dove, disappearing into the crystal waters of the pond. The familiar sensation of the in-between left Billy weightless for a moment. On the other side, he walked among human beings again. He'd been spat out in the same Little Italy alleyway he'd started his journey in. Nobody was around. It was a sticky summer night, and late. Everything was closed. Billy didn't hesitate. He sliced another portal open to the garden. He needed to get back there for that dark blade. Billy thought about things for a moment. Perhaps the demon who'd tried to slice him into oblivion wasn't after the blade. Either way, Billy had to stop the madness before it was too late.

With another portal cut, Billy set foot in darkness. He emerged to see the lavender fields and willow trees that once swayed in gentle sweet breezes now scorched. He pushed forward with his righteous scythe leading the way.

The sorrow of evil's arrival had even overflowed into the sky. The sun bled scarlet in defeat, and as it set, night took hold. Billy held his blade overhead, and it transcended the eclipsing darkness, lighting his way.

He knew he might not be strong enough for the battle that lay ahead, but he had to try. He ran about the scorched lavender fields in hopes of seeing the tiny gem with which he'd marked Gainsmore's buried axe. He scoured the land, taking swipes at the ground. He wished he'd marked the spot better for himself as he swung and stamped about for it. It wasn't until he saw blue flames flickering on the horizon again that he saw a tiny glimmer ahead on the singed ground. That little amethyst marker had worked. Billy saw the burning beast in the distance. Now it was a matter of who was quicker, the half man, half mule king of the Dreadlings, or the man in the body of a child.

Dammit, thought Billy. He ran with all he had. He was not winded, but how he wished his tiny legs carried him faster. The buried weapon was not far off, but the beast of reckoning was closing in. Billy ran with everything he could summon to reach the shimmering gemstone first. Immediately, he began swinging his scythe wildly to dig. Swipe and swing after swing of his righteous blade brought the dark blade to the charred garden's surface. Billy touched the twisted wooden shaft of the instrument of evil. He stood up victoriously, holding darkness in one hand and light in the other. The sickening scream of the one known as Amalon sent terror even through Billy's tried heart. He didn't know if the dark blade was what the beast wanted, but he knew he had to get out of this place with it somehow. Though he hesitated for only a second to think, he knew there was no time to waste. Ash kicked up from the ground, and Billy ran straight for Amalon.

The beast dwarfed him endlessly. The only advantages Billy seemed to have were his speed and stature; he prayed it was enough. A feint to the right sent Amalon's stained bone axe dropping down scarily close. Billy caught a close glimpse of the weapon. Skulls of those struck down by the demon king were impaled on spikes down the back of the blade. One such spike had five heads stacked like a kebab, some rotting and others now just bone. Billy rolled past Amalon and never looked back. He was headed for the pond, but what had become of the water, so perfect, so clear? As he reached the only exit from the garden that he knew of, he could see he needed a new way out, and fast. The crystal pond was turned into a mass of bubbling tar. The alchemy of the beast had destroyed Billy's only solace, his only sanctuary, and now he grew angry.

So enraged had Billy become that he believed he could do it. He believed he could slay the mighty demon. Stranded now by the tar pit, he stood firm, shaking, with each scythe in hand. Amalon kicked up ash and burned sacred ground with each kick of his hooves. His strides grew as he saw Billy take a stand. With the two blades in his grasp, Billy held them out like extensions of his arms. He didn't know if the demon had a weakness, and he didn't care. He wanted the beast destroyed.

Billy looked the mule king dead in the face and yelled, "If you can shift shapes like the other demons I've met, you'd think you'd pick a better face. Not even a mother could love a face like that unless she belonged on the farm too."

Without a thought, without hesitation, Amalon charged harder at Billy. It happened so quickly that Billy wasn't sure he'd dodged the beast's axe. There was pain, and Billy could see the color red on his hoodie, *so much red*.

For the first time since he'd had this body, Billy was bleeding. He looked down to his side. There was a small bone fragment sticking out at the side of his waist. The pain that spread from the wound was like nothing Billy had experienced on Earth. He lifted the purple hoodie he wore at the waist and could see it was a terrible wound. The axe had shot fragments of bone at him when the beast swung it. Billy felt as though he was passing out. Weakness was consuming him as an unfamiliar poison spread through him.

"The second death awaits, Billy Walker," growled Amalon. "This time, there will be no interjection from the Heavens. We will hide you in the deepest depths of suffering."

Billy was defeated. He knew it. With his last ounce of strength, he remembered Celia. He remembered how she raised her dark scythe overhead when she was in control of his body. Billy did the same. Lifting that new dark blade above, he closed his eyes. He desperately thought of a familiar destination.

This alley had become all too familiar as Billy fell from a swirling black mass above. His uncoordinated effort to escape had sent him through one of the portals he'd seen Celia use. He didn't know why the evil weapon worked in his hands, and at that moment, he didn't care. Billy bounced off the hood of the familiar Italian restaurant's parked delivery van and then rolled off onto the alley's cobblestone ground. He was thankful. The demon in the garden had failed to bring him to the second death.

Billy had escaped using their own tools against them. The purple hoodie he wore looked as though nothing had happened to him. Billy felt around his waist for the now absent wound. He was stunned it was gone, but the pain, the unbearable pain, remained. His little frame stumbled about that alley of Toronto's Little Italy. It was at the alley's end, near the restaurant entrance, that Billy's eyes closed and he collapsed from the unbearable lingering agony.

19

Celia wondered what was in store for her now that she had done her part. The garden had been consumed by evil and decay, and she had happily watched from the shadows. Billy had escaped, she'd seen it, but he was, terribly, mortally, wounded now. He would likely die somewhere in the Toronto streets.

She watched now as Amalon disintegrated into ash among the charred ground. He would return to his throne below now that he'd destroyed the garden. The sanctuary of the hunter was truly in a shambles. Celia knew a strike from Amalon's blade meant certain death, even if it was a shallow strike. One poison bone spur from the axe and a soul was driven mad with pain. Over and over, she had seen Amalon drive troublesome mortal souls mad with pain. Celia thought about Billy and his escape again. She wondered just how he was able to wield that dark blade of Devlin Gainsmore.

It was no matter; he was dying now somewhere, and he couldn't escape to the garden. Celia grinned. She had her condo and her money waiting for her now. She was going to live the high life again, free from the boundaries and duties she'd wished to escape. A mortal vacation awaited her.

Celia had wondered just how she would escape this wreck of a garden at first. Now she smiled, knowing her scythe remained. She would use it again to escape the scorched garden. Picking up her scythe, she summoned a swirling portal of dark energy. She stepped into its cold grasp and hoped that this was the last time she would need to do this, at least for a while. She knew it was the last she'd see of Billy. No one survived Amalon, but did the second death await him? Would he be dragged below, or would he somehow be given another chance to hunt her down by the Heavens if he died again? Her paranoia grew thinking about it all. She took a deep breath and shook her head, saying to herself, "No one survives Amalon."

Stepping out of her portal exactly where she wished, Celia was inside her condo once again. She needed to settle herself; her nerves were still rattled. Not only that, she felt dirty. She drew an aromatherapy bath and took off the ash-stained clothes from Amalon's garden desecration. She felt alive again, just as she had when she'd stolen Billy's body that first time. Lucifer had indeed come through with this new body. Celia studied herself in the bedroom's full-length mirror as bubbles swelled up in the round on suite spa tub. She was a little taller than she had been before, perhaps 5'6" now. Her curves seemed similar as she cupped her new breasts. Celia grabbed a scarlet bra from Tina's dresser drawer. It would be nice to shop for lavish clothing, pretty makeup, and lacy things again. Celia held up the rose-patterned scarlet bra, and just as she'd thought, Tina's things fit just fine. She smiled at her new reflection and tossed Tina's pretty bra aside. She thought of all the devilish things she was going to do in this mortal body this time around.

Celia turned off the water and melted into a blissful moment of eucalyptus euphoria and tub massage jets. Her concerns, her worries, all melted away in that steam-filled bathroom. Fifteen minutes passed. Celia was drifting away in the tub, her head resting on a waterproof pillow at the tub's edge, and when she shut her eyes, she heard a whisper...

"It would be a shame to drown with so little time in your new flesh."

The strange whisper awoke her in a panic. It was Lucifer. He sat across from her, grinning on the toilet, wearing a shimmering silk crimson suit. Celia covered up, folding her arms. Lucifer grinned again.

"Don't cover up on my account; besides, I gave you that body. My, my, I did a fine job picking out that body for you. I don't think you'll have a problem at all finding a man or woman to fuck. Not with a build like that. *That is, after all, what you are after.* Isn't it, Celia? The mortal experience, if I'm not mistaken."

Celia dared not speak her mind. He could send her to Hell with a blink and strip her of her of everything. In the moment, she was rightfully afraid.

"I am grateful. For this body."

"I know you are, Celia, but I wonder, will you still be as grateful when I ask something of you?"

"What is it?"

"I think you will find this offer more than generous considering your continual defiant actions. I am going to need you to use that blade of yours and command the Dreadlings one last time. They will be different now, more powerful thanks to the blood of Amalon that still stains your blade. They will help clean up your mess."

"My mess?" questioned Celia.

Lucifer's friendly demeanor was quickly eclipsed by an accusing gaze. Celia could feel an intense aura of anger emanating from within him as her heart beat faster. When he felt her fear, Lucifer smiled warmly again and said, *"Billy Walker did not die."*

Billy's eyes opened up to ash and darkness. A blackened fog filled the land he awoke in. He brought himself to his feet surprisingly easily. His stature had changed. He was tall, he was himself again. The small frame he'd borrowed to fight evil was gone. He looked at his hands and arms. Billy thought it strange to be this big again; he'd gotten used to the other body over time. He hadn't wanted to get used to it, but being that size for that long had become the new normal.

Billy waded and choked through rising ash and fog. His steps were cautious and uncertain. It was not until he came to a small clearing that he knew where he was again. The once richly colored gemstones were now jagged and black. They all surrounded the once crystal pond waters that now resembled a pit of tar-like muck. He was at the ruined garden again.

Billy looked to his right, and there was Frank, sitting at the once golden bench. It shimmered no more. His back was to Billy as he sat facing the tar pit, slumped forward.

"Frank?" Billy called out.

The lack of a greeting concerned Billy; his stomach sank. He stepped closer and spoke a little softer, hesitantly. "Frank?"

Given the state they were in, Billy did not expect one of Frank's typical cheerful responses, but he'd certainly expected something. Frank wore the white jacket he'd often had on, but now it was stained with ash and shimmered no more. Billy was within arm's reach of Frank and rested a hand on the old man's shoulder.

"I'm sorry Frank, I—"

The old man turned to face Billy. His eyes were frosted over with the gray, lifeless gaze of death. Frank's neck had been slit, and from the wide wound, bubbling tar like that which filled the pit dripped out and down his neck.

"No!" screamed Billy over and over through tears, but as he cried out, something happened. White light surrounded him as the garden began to fade away. Billy could feel a tingle around his abdomen that caused him to look down. He was flat on his back somewhere in the darkness of an alley. He could see clearly as the light formed objects and faded away from his surroundings.

"Do not move," said a voice of authority and power.

He was back in the body of the child, and the pain that once consumed him had subsided. Billy surmised it was thanks to the man leaning over him. Billy was shocked, confused even. He didn't know what had happened. Had he really been in the garden?

"I..." Billy let out.

"Peace, be still," said the mysterious man. His clothes were tattered, and he had an untrimmed bushy beard. He wore a dirty green baseball cap and looked like a bum, but Billy knew better. The man's hands shimmered with warm light, and as they ran up Billy's side to his heart, he saw darkness purged from within his body. He knew Heaven had found him.

"You can sit up now."

"I was in the garden again. I saw Frank."

"Hallucinations. Frank can't get to the garden now, and neither can you."

"Why?"

"They've destroyed the pond, and they've destroyed your connection to the garden."

Billy sat on the steps of a closed business's back door. He pondered for a moment and studied the man. "How did you know?"

The angel answered, "Just because Frank's not in the garden doesn't mean he can't keep an eye on his friends." The gentle angel smiled, and Billy saw past the derelict exterior people judged him by. The glowing golden aura within the angel had cast out the demonic poison inside Billy. They sat silently together for a moment as Billy gathered his thoughts. It was the angel that broke the silence first.

"We saw you before you were cast below by that demon. We tried to warn you once before all of this, but she had control of your mind."

Billy had a flashback. The man that now sat beside him in the alley was indeed the angel from whom Billy had thought about taking time. It was the bum Celia had torn him away from near Dundas Square. Then he remembered standing in front of a church as Celia had mesmerized him with some type of hex. She has indeed completely controlled him and walked him straight to his demise on that midnight winter bridge.

"When I left the garden, the wound had disappeared, but the pain was so real."

"The wound was spiritual. It may have been gone physically, but the demon king Amalon had infected you with a darkness that would have consumed you. Your waning faith was your downfall."

"But I didn't think my faith was waning."

"Did you think you were going to die a second death?" The angel smiled, looking at Billy.

"Yes."

"Then your faith was weakening."

Billy nodded. He knew the angel was right. One look at Amalon and he'd doubted everything Frank said he could do. Billy stood up and brushed off his little shoulders. The stained purple hoodie he'd worn was like new again.

"I thought angels were only allowed to test humankind. I'm not ungrateful you saved me, but I remember Frank saying angels never meddled in mortal affairs."

"It's true, but you're not exactly mortal, are you? And Hell is not playing by the rules. So, what is the harm in exploiting a gray area?"

Billy smirked. "A good point."

"I must tell you when the demon king Amalon destroyed the garden, he also destroyed many of your righteous abilities."

"What do you mean?"

"You will be vulnerable in these days, Billy Walker, that's what I mean."

"Vulnerable?"

"You are no stronger than a mortal now. The only difference is that you wield a righteous weapon."

Billy frowned. "No more stopping bullets and disappearing to the garden then."

"No."

"But I still have this." Billy flicked his left hand open and summoned Gainsmore's dark scythe. The onyx shimmered, and the runes on the blade's sides glowed red, like when Gainsmore had wielded it.

"You can wield that blade?"

"Yes."

The angel looked a little confused. "How?"

"If I think about it, I can summon dark energy portals," Billy said with matching bewilderment.

He also didn't know why or how it was possible, but he knew it was. There was silence between them as the angel rubbed his beard in contemplation.

"I suppose you're a child of two worlds. Frank fished you out from the depths of despair, yet you were not allowed to pass through Heaven's gates." The angel stood up. "Wield both the blades then, child; you will need them. From what I understand, the forces of Hell know you're alive."

"How could they know so fast?"

"It's like Frank told you. They have their eyes, and we have ours."

"The Dreadlings?"

"Yes, they prowl about in the darkness of the night, waiting, watching. I will be among the shadows like them, Billy. When the time is right, I will stand with you." The angel stood up and walked down the alley. "And Billy... That reaper who stole your body. She hasn't been seen since the garden was destroyed." With that warning, the angel disappeared down the alley, and again, Billy was alone.

20

Celia didn't know where to begin. She knew the request, she knew the requirement, she knew she had no choice. Where was she to find Billy Walker? The man who was now a feared hunter of demons, slaying them with the body of a seemingly helpless child.

Dammit, Celia thought. For now, all she could do was sit at the breakfast bar in Tina's condo. She looked around at it. Perhaps she would sell the condo once Billy was dead. She'd leave for a more exotic destination. Celia knew Billy would seek her out here, and she intended to use that to her advantage. He certainly would not recognize her now. She knew Lucifer had given her a new body not for her sake but as a safety net in case Billy was indeed still alive. The element of surprise was not something to be taken lightly.

Celia swiveled the barstool and looked over at the decorative clock on the wall. Tina had strange taste. The analog clock was a working piece of art and appeared to be melting down the wall. It was midnight. Celia was more hungry than tired. Besides, sleep was not on the table. The mortal experience was hers again, and she was discovering that the blissful moments were often overcome by bullshit. She stood up abruptly and grabbed her clutch purse. Then she headed out into the Toronto summer night.

First, she needed to set up a defense and use the Dreadlings like Lucifer had instructed. The Church Street condo's entrance was a clean and shimmering glass lobby. Stepping out from it and flicking her wrist, she summoned her scythe. Celia stamped the wooden shaft against the sidewalk and summoned two Dreadlings, and then two more and so on. Like alpha predators, they scaled walls and sat on guard near the entrance, watching, waiting for Billy.

One peered down from the top of the building's overhang and screamed at Celia.

"Just find Billy Walker and do as I ask. Then you can fuck off."

Blankly, its arachnid face stared at her with fangs twitching. It screamed again and climbed higher.

They were different, stronger, like Lucifer had said. The shadowy beasts had blue veins pulsing and glowing. "The blood of Amalon," Celia whispered. Two gathered and sat again atop the protruding lip of the building entrance. Celia commanded them, "Find the child, find Billy Walker, and kill him."

Celia stood in a streetlight's luminescence as her pack of Dreadlings leapt into darkness through the streets. Oblivious citizens chattered and held hands, unaware of the wretched darkness lurking beyond the veil of life. Celia watched them bound like wild dogs on the hunt. She only wished she could be present when they found Billy and tore his vulnerable body apart. She smiled and walked into the night. Now, she would find someplace tasty to eat, then she'd return to the condo and call it a night.

• • • • • • • • • • •

Billy was tired, so tired, and cold. A breeze caught his little frame in the subway tunnels. He didn't know where he was going to sleep and didn't know what he would do for food. The connection to the once healing and sustaining garden was gone, and he missed it deeply. He hadn't taken it for granted, but he never thought it would or could have been lost to him.

How he wished now that Frank would appear on a digital billboard or ATM screen and tell him, "It's going to be okay, kid."

Billy felt very much alive now but defeated. He snuck into a lonely empty subway car. Rhythmic sounds of the cars pushing through dark tunnels and passing by blurred lights didn't bother him. It reminded him of the times he use to clear his head on the way to work. He flipped his purple hoodie up, tucked his feet up, then nodded off a little. Although he wasn't concerned with the fellow passengers, he was careful not to drift completely away. Billy still thought of the possibility of Celia and her Dreadlings. He knew from the angel's warning that they would find him; it was just a matter of when and where...

Time drifted by slowly, and Billy's intermittent nodding off had gone on for the better part of the night. He got off the looping subway car with what little sleep he'd gained and exited up a stairwell to Union Station.

The sun had risen and blindingly announced itself through Union Station's arching windows. The old and decorative clock read six in the morning. Billy felt like a sitting duck as he took in his surroundings. He was to wait for an angel disguised as a homeless man, was that truly the plan? He was starving, thanks to the loss of the garden's life-sustaining connection. He wanted food and had no money. Billy eyed another troubled young soul, perhaps all of twenty years, begging for change. They caught eyes, and the young woman waved gently at Billy to come closer.

"I have more than enough change for the both of us," said the young woman with generous open hands. "Please," she said, motioning for him to take some coins.

Billy was not ashamed. He took what she'd offered. "Thank you," he replied. "How did you end up here, like this?" He didn't want to be rude, but she was so young, perhaps all of twenty.

A faint smile touched the corners of her lips. "It is not important how I ended up here. It is important how Billy Walker ends up here." Somehow, he was surprised again. Heaven truly did have their own eyes, just as Frank had said.

"So, you're an angel."

"Yes."

"No offense, but are you all homeless?"

She raised an eyebrow. "Not all of us, but what a way to test humanity." Then she looked up. "Besides, who is truly homeless when they have a place above waiting for them?"

Billy smiled and told her he'd be right back. He was grateful he'd found another angel or that she had found him. He approached a vender who sold muffins and other breakfast goods. It wasn't long before he walked back over to the angel and thanked her again. Though the sweet taste of a blueberry muffin danced in his mouth, Billy asked, "Have you seen... her?"

"No, not even a Dreadling, but we know where she is."

Ravenously, Billy made the last of his muffin disappear and sipped from a plastic bottle of orange juice to wash it down.

"Was that your first time eating since you lost your connection to the garden?"

"Yes."

The angel smiled. "It's no wonder you were so hungry. Without the life-sustaining manna, I too would starve."

"But you beg for change? What is the use of that if you don't actually need to eat?"

"When I see the person with a cold heart and a mind set on the material world, do I beg for change? Or do I beg for their change..."

Billy sat beside her. "I see your point."

"Come with me, Billy."

"Where are we going?'

"To find Celia."

Anxiously, Billy followed. It was only in accompanying the angel that he grew to realize the cold-heartedness of humanity. As the tarnished angel walked past neglectful mortal eyes, Billy took in the hardened glances. Quick looks of unease, some of disgust, but most of them, the worst of them, were the ones who pretended the angel did not exist at all. Their sneers suggested that recognizing the very existence of a downtrodden youngster was beyond them. That broke Billy's heart. He knew then that he had at times been no better than the majority. There were times he'd stopped to help, but there were times he'd walked down Young Street and ignored someone desperate and huddled over a vent for warmth. The times he looked the other way were equal. He wiped a tear away with his sleeve.

The angel glanced over her shoulder. "*Good.* Your eyes tell of your mind's redemption."

It wasn't long before Billy could see his old condo in the distance. All that he and Tina had worked hard for stolen by a demon. The angel guided Billy through an outdoor parking lot and into a parkade garage. They walked up the stairs all the way to the top lot. There they had a clear view of Tina and Billy's old condo.

"You see that?" asked the angel. Billy nodded; he did see it. Dreadlings in scores scaled the sides of the building. Celia had barricaded herself inside with a horde of Dreadlings on guard and at the ready.

"We'll never get near her."

The angel sat down in the vacant parking spot, legs crossed and hands clasped together in her lap. Billy was confused for a moment, then he realized she was praying. He remained silent, waiting for what seemed like the longest prayer in the history of prayers. He knew they needed a miracle, and he hoped the angel had one, because he didn't know how to make one. The angel slowly stood up, a little drowsy, like the prayer had taken something out of her, perhaps draining her in some way.

"Are you okay?"

"I'll be fine."

"What did you pray for?"

The angel smiled. "I prayed that on this day we would not fight alone."

Billy nodded. He prayed for the same.

21

Celia nervously sipped an iced coffee, made by the very machine Billy had bought Tina a year ago. She'd been watching her Dreadlings hourly. Nothing, not even a glimpse of the man turned little girl turned demon killer. It wasn't until a startling shriek from a Dreadling perched on her balcony that she was shaken enough to spill her coffee. Surely, it had seen the child.

Celia peered cautiously from her balcony. The Dreadling's shriek had put the eyes of vengeance upon her. It was Billy and someone else, a ragged woman in tattered clothing, stained khakis and a hoodie. Both of them looked over at her balcony. Celia faded into her condo, heart pounding. They couldn't possibly have seen her face this high up, and that was her advantage. It hit her hard now: the fight was about to begin. Her Dreadling army versus Billy and his righteous allies.

Dreadlings' shrieks and screams continued as the dark beasts mustered to attack in broad daylight. Celia watched from a window across to the parking lot where the pair had been spotted.

The translucent golden armor of an angel adorned the homeless girl, and with her first blow she struck a sword of shimmering light through a Dreadling's skull. Blue mists of Amalon's blood burst from within the mutated beast, and it disappeared into a cloud of blue, burning ash. Celia listened opening her bedroom window a touch. She thought she heard the angel instruct Billy, but it was faint. She thought she heard the angel say her name.

Celia watched, and Billy burst away quickly from the Dreadlings toward her condo. Such youth and young agility kept Billy out of harm's way. Celia saw handsprings and flips as he dodged vicious Dreadlings. Billy had made it out of sight so quickly that Celia couldn't keep track of his little agile frame.

She couldn't see what had happened, but she heard the death cries of Dreadlings shoot out in the daylight. The sickening sound of the misting of Amalon's blood was clearly heard. Billy was killing them with his righteous blade and somehow, he had the backup of an angel. Celia shook with fear. She had broken the rules of reaping. She had dared to venture into the world of possession, and now she knew where it had gotten her. Her days of reaping didn't seem that mundane now and a mortal vacation had certainly not been worth all this. As Celia flopped down on Tina's beige suede sectional, she thought of the insanity of all this and nervously, foolishly, she laughed. The soul she had cast to Hell now chased after her, killing demons with the agile frame of a dancing twelve-year-old ballerina.

"Fuck," she whimpered as her nervous laughter turned to tears of stress.

Celia told herself to pull it together. She began to think of how she might make her last stand. Between her weary, stress-filled breaths and thoughts, she heard a knock at the door. This was it, she thought. Somehow, Billy Walker had gotten in and was standing outside her door.

Celia flicked her wrist, summoning her dark blade, and walked on light feet to the peephole. She peered out into the hallway.

There stood a man in the brown attire of a delivery driver. He looked familiar. Celia had seen him bring packages to the building on other occasions. He saw her eyeing the peephole, and a twisted grin crept onto his face. "I've got a last stand here for, Celia... No signature required."

"S–set it down at door," Celia said shakily.

Surprised, she watched as he did exactly that. When he boarded the elevator, she quickly grabbed the package, taking it inside and placing it on the quartz breakfast bar counter. Celia picked up the closest kitchen knife and sliced the box open at the seam. Inside she saw a note, handwritten in gothic lettering on weathered and singed paper. Below it, red tissue paper covered something. Celia picked up the note, it read:

Hi there Celia,

I see you got my package! Why not use this gift I have been so gracious enough to have delivered to you by one of my loyal demons...

Remember this as well. No one knows what you look like... You could walk out the front door casually and they would be none the wiser... It's almost like someone gave you a new body for this exact reason?

So why not take your last stand on your terms? I'll be watching you, Celia, so make it spectacular. Use it somewhere big and open. And Celia, don't ever say I didn't do anything nice for you...

Win or lose, you shall be as the mortals.

L.

Celia looked at the red chestnut box again. It was small, about the size of her fist. She released the copper clasp at its front. Inside, she moved some more red tissue paper to the side. There was a little sphere, so beautiful, so eye-catching. Celia stared into the sphere for a second that seemed so much longer. As the swirling colors and shifting stars mesmerized her, she knew exactly what it was. Lucifer had given her a dark temporal anomaly. She took it out and slipped the little marble-like thing into her pocket. Things were serious now. She had to get away, like Lucifer had said. She would use her newfound anonymity and escape. She couldn't hide from Lucifer, and she couldn't hide from the angels in her midst. If she ran and betrayed Lucifer, she would most certainly be cast down. If she didn't rid the world of Billy Walker this time, she knew there would be literal Hell to pay. Outside her condo, she heard the chug of one of the three elevators moving. Was this it? Was a fierce little executioner in a purple hoodie on the way to cut her down?

Celia let the condo door slam behind her and ran. Shimmering mirrored elevator doors opened as she disappeared. Behind her the fire escape door closed gently and quietly, and she moved down the stairs. Casually, she stepped out into the gentle sunlight of the day.

In her scramble, Celia had grabbed a pair of Tina's old torn-up jeans and the closest T-shirt she could find. Now, with her hair pulled back into a ponytail and wearing the silver designer sunglasses she fancied from Tina's collection, she stepped to the lobby. She didn't dare glance to the lot across the street where she knew the Dreadlings fought. She would act like the blind mortals; the supernatural didn't exist to her for the time being. Celia did subtly look for Billy in the purple hoodie, though. As far as she'd seen, there was no sign of him. With each step, her pace increased, and when it was safe to, she fled even faster.

Heart pounding, she crossed over Front Street and walked past the iconic and familiar red brick Flatiron Building with its slim structure and ornate copper top. Celia couldn't stand this; she hated the fact that she was the mouse and no longer the cat on the prowl.

She was not alone. More Dreadlings were her answer. She wanted a distraction to get away far away for now. Celia had only summoned about a dozen to occupy Billy and his ally. Celia slipped out of sight then subtly flicked her wrist and stamped the ground, summoning even more of the beasts. They would distract that angel, and if they didn't slay Billy, she would use Lucifer's new toy on him soon. Celia had an idea, a big idea.

22

Celia crossed a nearby green space and from there went down an alley. The landmark buildings she'd become familiar with guided her. The CN Tower, the sprawling skyscrapers of all those Canadian banking institutions... She was on the right track. Soon she would be exactly where she would make her final stand.

Celia felt for the gift Lucifer had given her, rolling it around in her pocket, and smiled. Once she unleashed his temporal anomaly, there would surely be chaos. She laughed with a dark and twisted satisfaction. The eyebrows of a few passers-by rose at her outburst, but she didn't care. Her laughter bred arrogance, and her arrogance bred naivety. In her mind nothing would stop her now, not even Billy's new allies. Once Lucifer's temporal anomaly took hold, she would have a new control.

Celia approached her destination. It was odd seeing the city like this, but it was morning, and at this hour things were peaceful. Workers arrived, and small crowds rose from the subway stairwells, but Dundas Square was for the most part quiet. Celia had work to do. She looked at the tourist spot taking in every corner, alley, and store. Her attack would be well orchestrated. First, a Dreadling sacrifice. She flicked her wrist, summoning her dark blade. Then she held it out and recalled all those Dreadlings that remained from the fight by Tina's old condo. She then stamped subtly the sidewalk out front of Dundas Square, summoning only one Dreadling this time. Her internal intentions were shared with that single Dreadling. It was to be the bait. Its purpose was to run Billy to Celia's Dundas Square trap. She watched as the shadowy beast leapt and bounded up buildings back toward her Church Street condo. It would make itself seen, and it would lead Billy right to his end.

Celia waited patiently now. Her mind drifted to mortal delights once again. Perhaps a latte would hold her over while she waited to see Billy's second death. Celia spied a nearby café with an outdoor balcony looking directly on to Dundas Square. She didn't know how long it would be before the bait brought her enemies into the web she'd weaved, and she didn't care either. Celia was going to end this once and for all. She had sacrificed too much not to be rewarded. After all the time she'd served, she believed she deserved a simple vacation. The chains of an eternity of demonic servitude were not fair in her eyes. Not while these mortals experienced unbelievable senses that they took for granted. Standing in the café line-up with the sweet smells of baked goods and sugary lattes enticing her, Celia was experiencing the emotion she'd missed of late: happiness. Sure, she'd had a few laughs and smiles watching souls suffer in her days below, but that only went so far. These sensations she'd taken in during these last few months, she could not go on without them now. She was consumed by taste, touch, and smell and couldn't imagine how these mortals managed to take them for granted.

Celia thought back to when she used to watch them from afar, back when she was reaping their unknowing souls. She'd always wanted to know what they experienced. The freedom to lust. The freedom to give in to the wildest pleasures of a mortal's senses. She sneered thinking back to the other demons she'd worked with.

None of them really new the extent of what they were missing. Even those demons that could possess a mortal shell had not truly experienced the depths of the mortal experience. No, now as she stood in this new body, she was determined to experience it all. All she needed was to rid herself of Billy Walker, but first — a latte.

Celia took a seat on the second-floor balcony overlooking Dundas Square and watched the crowds pass by. She would perhaps not even have to use the temporal anomaly Lucifer gifted her, if the Dreadlings ripped into Billy in Dundas Square.

She imagined the Dreadlings ripping his soul from within that little body of his and dragging him back to the depths of despair. Maybe he would end up in Theodore's rotting stomach again. A grin crept up her cheek as she breathed in the maple scent of her latte. She took a sip and sat back. It wasn't until she was on her last sip that she saw her plan falling into place.

Taxis and crowds of people gathered around the mall entrance across from the square. Most importantly to Celia was the sight of an odd little girl in a purple hoodie: Billy. He ran, dodging through the crowds toward Dundas Square. Celia grinned. This was it, it was time. That angelic ally from earlier was absent, and that was good, but she didn't want any surprises.

She held off for the moment, watching her single Dreadling leap into the center of Dundas Square. Fountains of water shot up in rows from little spouts in the tourist area grounds. No one could see the looming beast but Billy. Celia watched him look around as if in search for her, but she leaned back in her cozy café seat and watched from above. It had turned out it wasn't her that little Billy had been looking for at all. His angelic ally had somehow run up behind the summoned Dreadling and stabbed a sword of light through its shadowy hide. The water-spouting fountains around them carried the dead beast's blue ash to the heights of its reaches.

Come hell or high water, Celia didn't care how Billy was defeated, but he had to be. She stood up from her table, flicked her wrist, and stepped off to the side in the shadows. Quietly, rhythmically, she stamped her scythe's handle against the café's chestnut wood floor.

Dreadlings poured into Dundas Square, appearing in flashes of dark energy from everywhere, crawling down from the sides of buildings, jumping from billboards above, and rising from the depths of subway tunnels. They numbered in the hundreds now. Celia watched as Billy Walker and his angelic ally were hopelessly surrounded.

Just for a moment, she had stepped out from the shadows into the morning light, but that moment was long enough. Tina's silver designer sunglasses reflected the sun as she looked down on Dundas Square. Across from the café, a deadly little dancer looked up at the glare. Celia froze, and Billy eyed her. It was as if he knew now, somehow, who she was.

23

Through the hustle and distractions of the people, Billy saw something. The faintest glint, so brief, but it was still there. He'd caught it in a glance when he looked up and to his left where the morning sunlight had reflected off her silver sunglasses.

Those are my damn sunglasses, Billy told himself. Tina loved those glasses; she took them in the separation. There, standing on the café balcony, was a young woman Billy did not recognize. She brushed aside her shimmering black hair and stepped back cautiously after exchanging a strange look with Billy. She had made a fatal mistake. Not only was she wearing silver designer sunglasses that were uncommon, but she was wearing the baby-blue t-shirt he'd bought Tina on their trip to the east coast.

"I see her, I see Celia," Billy cried out to his angelic ally.

"Go, end this then."

"But the horde."

Dreadlings crept close in a black, strangling mass around the square. Tightening, constricting, like a serpent, they moved in a circle around them. People walked right through the beasts, obliviously unaware of Billy's ethereal enemies in their midst.

When all hope seemed lost and Billy held each scythe in his hands, he saw something. Those in tattered old clothes, those cast aside by society, had gathered. At least seven so-called homeless stood around Billy, protecting him. They were always there, waiting, watching in the shadows, hidden in plain sight.

Billy stared down Celia on the balcony, and she backed away. Behind him, Billy heard one of his allies. The older man with the long, gray beard who'd healed him in the alley. He had found him, just as he'd promised. Shimmering golden armor of light now adorned him as he spoke. "On this day Billy Walker, you shall not fight alone!" He struck down a Dreadling that tried to claw into Billy from behind.

Billy slipped away, slicing through Dreadlings in his wake with his righteous scythe held like a hockey stick. He heard pedestrians speaking in the square. "Someone phone the police, there are schizophrenics dancing in the Dundas Square fountains!" He realized just how quick he needed to be about this all. The people were clueless. They only saw derelict people swinging their arms about wildly at nothing in the Toronto streets. If only they knew that Hell had already kicked in their door and was now in their house.

Dreadlings pounced down from all angles. Billy could feel his tiny frame starting to take in more breaths. He prayed that he wouldn't wear out. The garden's manna was not his anymore. He truly was just a man in a child's body with a holy weapon, and he didn't think it was enough, but he knew he had to try. Billy dodged the clawed hand of a Dreadling and did a handspring toward the front entrance of the café where Celia had been seen.

Caution went out the window for him now that Dundas Square was the scene of chaos. A crowd of spectators had gathered, and now a news crew had pulled up and was shooting. Billy heard sirens, but he couldn't let that distract him.

Where the hell was Celia? His gaze darted about the surrounding area. The glimpse of a baby-blue shirt racing to the underground spurred on the chase again. Billy flicked his wrist and wielded his righteous blade. He sliced unmercifully through Dreadlings on his way to the subway. Two of the beasts dodged his holy weapon, and one even sank a clawed finger into Billy's shoulder. Something was wrong; that same searing pain was there again, like that of the wound the demon king Amalon had caused him in the garden.

His vision blurred, and Billy still swung violently at every beast that crossed his path. With all his little might, he'd made it to the subway stairwell. He couldn't let this be his end. She was in his sights, she was in his grasp, and she was not going to get away with destroying his life or anyone else's. Billy took in a deep breath and fumbled down the stairwell, almost falling down the stairs.

"You good, kid?" a young man asked, but Billy ignored him clutching a railing to hold himself up.

He saw Celia swerving through a crowd. She was boarding one of the subway cars as the doors spread open. "Dammit," he cursed under his breath, clutching his bleeding shoulder. The Dreadlings could hurt him not only spiritually but physically now. Billy lunged for the subway car doors, but he was too late as they closed in front of him. He thought all was lost again until a glimmer of hope came to mind.

He would use the dark blade taken from Gainsmore again. Now he would see what he could truly do with it. Billy flicked his left hand, as he'd seen Celia do many times, and the dark scythe appeared. Its shaft was the perfect size, like it had adjusted just for him. Billy lifted the dark blade overhead. He was going to summon that all-too-familiar swirling mass of darkness he'd ridden to Hell in. This time he was in control, and this time he had a different destination in mind.

Billy looked ahead to the car Celia had slipped inside. It was pulling away, and fast. No matter how strange it would seem, he had no choice. To pedestrians waiting for the next train and passengers on board, Billy was going to disappear and reappear in front of their eyes. He knew what they could and couldn't see and began. Gusts of ferocious winds swept up from below him, and the familiar cold, swirling black mass surrounded his tiny frame. Someone looked up as the wind swept across their face, but as fast as a blink, Billy was gone.

Two train cars back from Celia, Billy was among a small group of commuters. A few stunned looks arose about the cabin as a little girl seemed to appear from nowhere. Billy knew they couldn't see the dark energy carry him here, but they had certainly seen something unusual. He clutched a support pole to steady himself. The confusion seemed to be chalked up to something else as the few who witnessed Billy's arrival went about their business again. One shook it off and buried himself in his phone screen. Billy clutched his injured shoulder and moved cautiously up the aisle. He could see just ahead into the second car.

It didn't contain many passengers, and it didn't contain Celia either. They hadn't reached their next stop yet, and he couldn't risk losing her. If she changed clothes or gave him the slip now, he thought he might not recognize her again. He had one thing going for him, though: she wanted him dead again. He thought about that for a moment as he stepped into the next car. Wherever she went in the world, he would try to send her back to Hell, and she knew that.

Billy slipped past a bickering couple who never gave him a glance, and now he saw her. She sat at the front of the next car with her legs crossed comfortably in her seat, seemingly without a care in the world. Billy was stunned as he saw a smile creep up the corner of her lips in a convex mirror at the front of the car. Did she know he was there, watching, waiting...

24

Frank was panicked. He hadn't spoken to Billy in days, and he was unable to cast a portal to their common ground. He had a place in Heaven. A nice house amidst the clouds with marble pillars out front and golden railings inside. Frank was anything but happy staying in his heavenly home right now, though. He was worried about his friend.

Batariel had alerted the divine council of the tragedy in the garden, and now Frank had the opportunity to ask for help. Frank knew the nerves he felt were his flaw alone, but speaking to divine beings was something that always made him feel inadequate. Batariel, keeper of the heavenly gates, was divine, but the rapport he'd developed over the years with the angel overshadowed Frank's feelings of inadequacies. Frank got ready, running a black comb through his silver hair. He didn't need to but nervously adjusted his shimmering white tie that matched his suit. He closed the door to his home and walked down golden sidewalks in his heavenly neighborhood. It wasn't long before he came to his neighborhood's transportation portal. It was a shimmering diamond-carved archway that much like the pond in his hunter's garden took you to where you desired. Frank stepped in. He emerged on the other side of the portal and stepped up to some sprawling aquamarine stairs. At the height of the squared steps, at the top, was a temple on the mount. He was among them now. Frank bowed and then knelt, awaiting their greeting.

Five spheres of energy, each aglow with a different color, pulsed and spoke in unison to Frank. "Frank Rosenbaum. You seek answers; you seek help. Those below who have desecrated our work severed your hunter's connection to the garden."

"Yes, the garden, it's gone. I can't get there."

"We can see your fear. We can feel your heart."

"I am afraid," Frank replied.

"Be not afraid, Frank Rosenbaum. To bring about change, a simple seed planted will be enough."

Frank raised his head only slightly and saw that from above, a shimmering white seed emanating light fell down to his hands.

"Take it and heal the garden."

Frank smiled, looking at the shimmering seed in his palm. Still, he did not know how he would get to the garden. The connection to it was severed, and his connection to Billy was also severed. Frank could no longer use the pond to cast his image into the electronic devices of Earth.

"How–how will I get to the garden?" Frank stuttered.

"You will," replied the divine council in unison.

Frank watched as they faded from view. The old paralegal stood up. There was hope in his heart now. Hope that when he found his way back to the garden, Billy would be safe and Frank would see him again.

• • • ● • ● • • •

"You've gotten your answer, I see." Batariel smiled looking down at Frank with the glowing seed in his right hand as he stepped through Heaven's opening gates.

"I know I can restore the garden, Batariel, but they never told me how to get back. I can't even feel the connection I once had to the garden, and even worse to Billy. I can't open a portal to the garden...I..."

"Calm now, Frank. Be calm."

Frank took in a deep breath and tried to calm himself, then continued. "Batariel, if I don't hurry, I'm not certain Billy will be able to fight without the garden's healing connection. From what I've heard, Hell has given their reaper an army of Dreadlings tainted with the blood of an unspeakable demon king."

Batariel smiled. "That might be so. Hell may not be playing by the rules, but remember this, when the rules are broken, we will keep the peace."

Frank looked up at Batariel as warmth and comfort filled his heart. *The angels... The angels among the people*, he thought. *They will watch over him until I can fix this.*

"Thank you, Batariel."

"Safe travels my, friend," said Batariel as Frank disappeared into the clouds ahead.

Frank walked down mountainous pathways veiled in the clouds and reached the first plane below Heaven faster than he thought. A place not unlike a two-way mirror, where those above could use things called looking tables to see their loved ones still below. Frank smiled at a family gathered around a looking table. Like a television, it showed a feed of what or who they sought below. Frank heard a white-haired man who despite his hair color was not so old speak with concern about a young relative. It appeared they looked upon one of their grandchildren and requested divine intervention in his troubled life. Frank didn't want to pry and pressed on to another area. He was looking for an empty watching table. There he would find Billy and see just exactly how bad or good the situation had become.

Frank walked over to an old round stone table with crystal-clear glass in the middle. He sat back, and clouds parted, revealing a cushy armchair so padded, Frank almost melted into it. He shifted forward and looked into the glass. Without a word, images of what worried Frank's soul began to swirl about hazily. Then as the image came into focus, it was young Billy Walker in an alley, straining for breath and passing into unconscious oblivion.

Frank fought back the tears. "Oh, kid, I'm so sorry." He continued watching Billy. A mysterious disheveled man had appeared nearby. Gently, he lifted up Billy and took him away.

Frank smiled. He could see the light emanating from within this man. The kid was alright. Batariel had been right. The angels among the people had found Billy, and that comforted Frank. Now he needed his next concern addressed. How was he getting to the scorched aftermath that was the garden? His white dress pants pocket was aglow. It was indeed the pocket he'd placed the seed in, and it now beamed and pulsed brightly. He took the seed in his hand and watched as clouds shifted apart, leading him to an ancient brick archway wrapped in beautiful glowing golden vines. He kept his pace down a worn brick pathway that twisted until he reached a hedge maze. Everything around him was perfectly trim and immaculate.

"An old man with the seed of a Hunter's Garden. I haven't seen that in longer than I can remember. In fact, last I remember a garden being overthrown was the battle of the fallen."

Confused, Frank held out his hand with the glowing seed in his palm.

"Hah, that's not for me. You will need to hang on to that."

Frank took in the gardener's features as he smiled back at him. He wore a neatly trimmed short white beard, but he was not so old-looking, physically. He had the strong build of someone who toiled with heavy tools and lifted many things around the garden. He wore a sleeveless, forest-green tunic that drifted past his waist to his upper thighs and loose black flowing pants.

"What is your name?" Frank questioned.

"I am Otsuka. I tend to the garden, as all who want to serve should."

Frank nodded. "Will you help me get to my Hunter's Garden?"

"I will. Judging by the fact that you have that seed, I'd say the garden is not in good shape."

"We can't see in there since the attack. They've left it in a state of darkness and decay. It could be swarming with Dreadlings for all we know."

"Come with me..." replied the gardener.

Frank was wary of what lay ahead. Reluctantly, he followed.

They approached a trimmed and symmetrical hedge maze. Once at the opening, Frank stopped at three sparkling diamond archways. Shimmering white gates of light opened so gently at each archway. The walk through was so surreal and so peaceful. Harmonious songs of birds and teasing scents of blossoming flowers distracted from the circles they seemed to keep walking in. It wasn't until ten minutes passed that Frank spoke up.

"Look, Otsuka. I appreciate your exemplary grounds keeping skills, and this maze is beautiful, but I can't be touring this thing all day. I've gotta help this kid, understand? The kid is in real danger."

Otsuka stopped. It appeared Frank had spoken too soon. They'd come to a clearing in the center of the maze. Frank saw an open field filled with purple lavender and butterflies. He breathed in the calming scent that reminded him of his time with Billy in their garden. Then Frank saw four simple cobblestone pathways, all leading to a well in the middle of a small green grassy area.

"This is your gateway."

Frank looked at Otsuka and frowned. "Down the well?"

Otsuka nodded.

"I might be already dead, but I can still feel a good fall when it happens, you know? How does an old man traverse a tiny stone well?"

Otsuka smirked and pointed. There, as Frank stepped closer and closer down the cobblestone pathway, a wound rope attached to a reel came into view. It appeared the well had a wooden bucket somewhere down inside, and Otsuka thought Frank was game to ride it. Frank looked over his shoulder.

"It is the only way back to your Hunter's Garden."

Frank shook his head. "I used to be able to teleport there at will, you know that."

Otsuka gave Frank a nod then replied, "Someday, again."

The muscled gardener wound the rope repetitiously about the reel. When a wooden bucket no bigger than a whisky barrel appeared, Frank knew he was meant to step in. The old man boosted himself up to the well's edge using a large stone that was settled beside it. Carefully, he stepped in the wooden bucket and curled up with knees tucked. Otsuka worked the bucket gently down the well and smiled one last time at Frank.

"What if there's a Dreadling horde!" Frank cried out.

Otsuka's smile drew to a grin. "Plant the seed."

The light of the well disappeared as Frank drifted deeper down. In time, he knew not what direction he travelled; up and down seemed relative as darkness took over. The only thing he knew for sure was that the seed in his pocket pulsed and shone brighter as his journey pressed on. He reached in his pocket and clutched the seed tightly. He didn't dare take it out for fear of losing it in the well. It wasn't until he felt a smothering feeling of something hot, warm, and sticky that he hoisted the seed out from his pocket and pushed his fist to the sky. With his fist closed around the seed in his palm, he knew where he was now. The old man flailed and kicked about through a mucky, stinking black substance. He cast himself out of the tainted pond. He was at the garden, or what was left of it. As his hand opened and the seed cast a gentle light around him Frank, took in the charred remains of the place.

The overwhelming smell of something made him gag. The vile new scent was unlike anything he'd ever taken in. The burn of it singed his nostrils but lingered long enough to twist into an organic smell of death.

Frank held his breath and wished he didn't have to breathe in this realm. But like everything that materialized in the garden, he too was now temporarily organic. Frank removed his stained jacket then wiped his face with a handkerchief from inside his lapel. He slipped off the rock he'd pulled himself to at the pond's edge and heard...*them.*

"Skreeee!"

Their war cry echoed, striking fear into the old man's heart. There wasn't even a moment to say his favorite reassuring mantra. Dark claws pierced his right arm, and Frank fumbled as one pierced his left arm also. The seed slipped out of his palm, but the pulsing of white light from it burst dozens of surrounding Dreadlings into black ash. Strobes of holy light flashed as the seed seemed to fall in slow motion to the ashen ground. Frank watched the seed pulse and the beasts try to get at him before they exploded in holy light. As the seed took hold in the tainted ground, Frank looked to the sky and said, "Thank God."

"Even though I walk through the darkest valley, I will fear no evil, for thou art with me..." recited Frank. Exhausted, he leaned back against a large stone near the pond and saw the seed continue to take hold, sinking into the blackened ground. The holy seed's light had started to spread swiftly. All around him, Frank watched darkness overtaken. Dreadlings burst into black ash by the dozens, and flowers sprouted in the hundreds. The old man could feel the youth of the garden returning all around him. Even in his bones he felt the life force returning around him. He sprang up, feeling the healing energy overtake him. The old man ran off toward the resurrected lavender fields, dancing with a youthful vigor in celebration.

"Haha! Goodbye! Good riddance and good day, sir!" he boasted pointing in the fanged face of a snarling Dreadling as it exploded in the spreading light. Frank's celebratory pranc-

ing seemed to be timed perfectly as the Dreadling intruders exploded in holy light.

As he danced about, Frank saw gray stone shells crumbling away. Amethyst, ruby, emerald, and more all burst from inside lifeless gray exteriors. The once beautiful and ornate benches he sat at also returned from a tarnished blackened state to shimmering gold and diamond. What warmed Frank's heart the most, though, was seeing where it all began. The waters of the pond where Billy had made the choice to take a stand at had returned to clear perfection. Frank smiled. He could contact his hunter now, and if he wasn't too late, his hunter would be well again.

25

Celia knew Billy was on her trail. He was playing into her trap perfectly. Just one more stop and she would lead him to the second death, or so she hoped. She heard the announcement, "Spadina," echo overhead from the car speaker. This was it. It was time to lure Billy Walker to his eternal destruction.

Celia stood up and caught the car doors as they slid open. She rushed through the exits and toward the stairwell leading aboveground, but she was cautious that Billy was never left behind. The demon hunter's little frame was wounded, not terribly, but Celia could see in the glass exterior of a building nearby the clutching of a shoulder.

Billy moved increasingly slower with every passing moment. Celia smiled; he was poisoned by the unholy infected blood of her Dreadlings. She could see it ahead now, her final stand. Celia knew it was obvious to Billy where she was headed, and she didn't care, as long as he followed. She picked up speed. There were a couple of workers at the ticket booths to the baseball field known to many as the SkyDome, but Celia passed them. She spied a single guard who stood at what seemed to be the only open door to the sprawling stadium.

"You can't come in here. Not until three."

Celia smiled and flicked her wrist. Then, in an instant, the worker felt the sting of his mortal end with Celia's dark scythe in his chest. His eyes wide as he fell to the ground, clutching his chest, Celia winked at him and then blew him a kiss as the light left his eyes. He never saw death coming, and she always loved a mortal's shocked expression when it did. Celia opened the glass door and set foot inside the vacant stadium. She only saw one man out on the baseball field as she walked out onto it. He seemed to be inspecting the setup. It was no matter, thought Celia. He would not be the first mortal caught in the crossfire.

Celia slunk quietly into the dugout and waited. She pulled the temporal anomaly out from her jeans pocket. The swirling dark matter inside spun about with an otherworldly glow.

Three minutes passed before she heard the inspector on the field speak.

"Hey, you can't be in here kid. Hey, kid, you alright?"

Billy Walker had reached his mortal limits and collapsed on the field. Celia saw the inspector hold his little frame and speak to him.

"Kid! Hey kid!" The inspector pulled out a cell phone and was about to dial, but Celia knew the time was now. She stepped up from the dugout, taking each step slowly, cautiously. There on the pristinely groomed pitcher's mound she watched Billy struggle to his knees.

Celia took one last look at the temporal anomaly, and then she threw it with all her strength at the pitcher's mound. The man comforting young Billy Walker looked up in time to see the marble smash and a purple haze swirling around them and the stadium. This was it. Lucifer's gift would end this vessel of vengeance known as Billy Walker. He wouldn't stand a chance now. He was weak, he was wounded, and the garden was in ruins. Celia was pleased.

The morning light faded as the anomaly took hold in the city skies. Day turned into night as the sun was eclipsed and its remaining outer ring barely burned in the sky. Celia had slowed time. As long as this crimson eclipse held, Billy would surely die.

The inspector on the mound shook with fear and looked to the skies, taking it all in like nothing he'd ever seen before. Behind the inspector, a mirrored rift with smoking and glowing purple frayed edges opened. Celia's temporal anomaly had created an opening to the very gates of Hell inside the stadium.

"Wake up, wake up kid! We've gotta get the hell out of here!" *No service* read the inspector's cell phone as he looked at it a second time.

The inspector's voice echoed through Billy's mind, and he rose to his feet with what he had left in the tank. He could see her now. Celia stood there, grinning from the shadows of the dugout. She stepped menacingly up from the dugout stairs onto the field and flicked her right wrist. Billy shambled forth and flicked his right wrist, summoning his righteous sunlit scythe. Behind him, the screams of the inspector turned his head. From the summoned rift, something was coming. The ground shook, the astroturf tore, and Theodore the thirty-foot cyclops toad had the inspector's legs dangling from his amphibious mouth.

"Fuck, no," cursed Billy. He rolled forward as the vile creature's webbed feet smashed down on the pitcher's mound, almost squashing him. Billy dripped with feverish sweat and still shivered from the Dreadlings poisonous attack earlier. The infection still tore through his vulnerable little frame.

He caught a glance of Celia in his peripheral vision. She had thrown her dark blade at him. The shaft shrank as it took to the air, spinning, hurtling forth destructively. Angrily, Billy managed to swat it away with his blade. Celia flicked her wrist, and it reappeared in her hand. She taunted Billy by acting surprised that the blade was back in her hands.

Behind him, Billy heard the screams of the field inspector. Theodore had swallowed the man whole. The amphibian abomination seemed satiated for a moment. Still, its single menacing eyeball darted about watching, stalking Billy. Billy rolled away as the toad hop toward him, and he fought through sweat and delirium to avoid Celia's attacks. Celia ran for him, throwing her blade not once but multiple times. Each time Billy gave it everything to dodge. It wasn't until the blade caught him in the left leg that he knew he was in trouble. It hadn't severed anything, but it had certainly spun its tip into his calf. Billy fell at first base, and Celia walked ever closer, smiling all the way. Theodore hovered over Billy at first base in wait, like Celia was in control. The beast's red veiny eyeball watched over Billy. He blinked and out of excitement he opened his mouth. The beasts tongue shook and vibrated with the anxious thoughts of devouring Billy.

Celia spoke first to Theodore, "Ah ah, wait Theodore…" Then to Billy, as she closed the gap between them. "Let that feeling sink in, Billy. That cold feeling of death."

She was right, it was so cold. The blade in his leg…he imagined that was what it felt like if to be stabbed with an icicle.

"It's alright, Billy, let the cold spread. Soon you'll feel it in your heart and then not at all."

Billy fought so hard to take the blade out, but Celia was in control. It wasn't until she was a few feet away that she finally flicked her wrist and held her scythe again. Billy couldn't walk. He could barely move, but he still had both blades. He held his dark scythe up quickly, and from that summoned a black mass that took him away. He wasn't far away at all, but he at least was safe. Billy was way up in the stands now, somewhere in the high hundreds.

Billy leaned into a guard rail and miraculously overhead on the Jumbotron monitor screen. He saw…*him* and heard him. "The garden lives! The garden lives!" Frank cried out, echoing across the stadium.

Then, just like that, something felt different. Something felt fixed inside him. The searing pain in his right shoulder from the Dreadlings' claw, the fever, the cut in his leg, it was still there, but it was fading. His connection to the healing manna of the garden was coming back.

Billy grinned down from above at Celia, still standing by first base. She was stunned. He could tell the return of his supernatural protection from the garden was something she never thought she'd see. Above them, the eclipse was at its peak. Celia looked up at the shifting eclipse in concern. Billy suspected it was tied to Hell's takeover of the stadium. Whatever Celia had brought about when she threw that sphere from the dugout, Billy now knew it was all temporary. He knew he'd have to fight. Perhaps he could drag it out just enough for Hell's supernatural takeover to end. Then, he smiled at the thought that maybe he would be rid of Theodore forever.

Angry at the garden's resurrection, Celia stamped on the ground in a rage, summoning every last Dreadling she could. They poured from the nosebleeds. They rose from the dugouts. They came from the outfield walls with their shadowy claws. They ripped up the walls and stands. The Dreadlings had materialized physically in this eclipse. So many rows of arachnid eyes aglow now peered ferociously at Billy.

Dammit, thought Billy. No angels, no allies. He'd played right into Celia's trap like a fool.

He heard Frank speak again over the Jumbotron. "Come home, come to the garden, kid!"

Cutting a rift in the air with his divine blade, Billy jumped from the upper deck into the air and disappeared. The calm sanctuary that was his garden greeted him with the scents and warmth he'd missed. It was as pretty as he remembered it. He ran toward Frank. The old man embraced him like a father with open arms.

"Thank God, kid, thank God you're here. There will be time for greetings later, though. Finish this, get the drop on that toad, and send Celia where she belongs this time, okay?" he said with a smile.

Billy ran over to the crystal waters of the pond and looked below. He envisioned precisely where he would drop and then leapt into the water.

As the sky tore open above the hideous toad, Billy fell on the beast's muzzle, and like a cowboy riding an unbroken horse, he rode Theodore. The toad screeched and thrashed about, kicking up dust and ripping up astroturf around the field. Billy had sunk his scythe into one of its nostrils.

Deeper and deeper, Billy pushed in the blade until it disappeared into the toad's cavity. He held on, wildly bouncing about in the outfield, until a mighty mucilaginous sneeze cast him away, slimed and sliding across the outfield. Billy rolled to the right as a webbed foot smashed down on the turf and then to the left as the toad stamped again. *I can do this*, he told himself.

Dreadlings raced to him, and one by one he danced away, cutting them down with pirouettes of destruction. He looked through the masses of them for Celia, but she'd fled.

"Dammit!" Theodore's tongue darted at him, and he rolled forward. Billy was angry, and fueled by anger, he did everything this twelve-year-old ballerina's body would allow. He slashed and spun his dance of destruction, dodging Theodore and impaling Dreadlings that dared to strike. The slam of Theodore's webbed digits almost got him, but Billy danced away, spinning as the vile creature missed again.

He'd made his way deep into the infield now, and a back handspring across home plate brought him face-to-face with a creeping Dreadling. The demon clutched the clear shaft of Billy's righteous blade with its claws and dripped a dark substance from its mouth. Billy didn't try to push against the creature; instead, he summoned the other dark blade in his left hand, holding it low like a hockey stick. He impaled the Dreadling with a rising surprise slash and then spun like a little tornado with both blades outstretched as others closed in. Ash rained down from the darkened sky, and Billy danced with darkness and light.

With every Dreadling he slayed, Billy thought about how to end Theodore, who pounded wildly toward him. A massive sticky tongue shot past Billy like a bullet, barely missing his hoodie sleeve. He thought about opening a dark matter portal with the dark blade and sending the beast down below. Then he thought better of it. That would cast the innocent field inspector into the depths of Hell. He couldn't let that happen. No, Billy had another idea. He didn't like it, but it was his best chance.

Theodore's bloodshot cyclops eye caught Billy, so menacingly, so hypnotically. Billy had remembered the beast's paralyzing gaze. Theodore's eye took hold, and Billy stood frozen in place, knowing full well what would follow next: the warm stickiness of the tongue against his clothes, the sudden pulling as it retracted and brought him off the ground. Billy would let the beast take him. It was the only way.

He flew through the air toward the mouth of the toad. The last thing he saw was Dreadlings swarming in the stadium, still all over the field, still coming down from the nosebleeds. Even though he couldn't see her, he swore he heard Celia's laugh echoing through the vacant SkyDome.

This time Billy was prepared as he fell. He slid down the toad's warm esophagus toward the belly of the beast.

By this time, he'd summoned both of his blades again. His righteous blade lit up the toad's innards. He saw the weak point. Theodore's swollen rotting ulcer looked as promising as he'd remembered. When he pierced it, the deafening screams of the toad rang through the baseball stadium and beyond.

Billy smiled and sank the blades in deeper, then slid down and eviscerated the beast. Theodore burst with a stench of rot and death that flooded the baseball field and stained the astroturf. Billy rolled out and away, soaked in the awful toad's fluids.

It was almost immediately after that when Billy saw the white-haired Englishman he'd been stuck inside with before. He'd slid out, along with some others. The Englishman began to run for freedom across the stadium nude. Somehow, he was broadcast on the Jumbotron, and his Louisville was seen swaying in the wind. The Englishman looked back, stunned at the toad's destruction, and as he ran, he hollered to Billy, "Thanks, old chap!"

Billy wasn't sure if the Englishman could see his true form or his young earthly vessel; he didn't care. The man took off materialized in his birthday-suit through a stadium exit. Beside Billy, covered in bile and mucous, like he was, lay the field inspector.

"You good?" Billy asked, looking over.

The inspector sprang up, stunned. He froze, only for a moment, and looked at the bubbling remains of the cyclops toad. Then, thanks to Celia's temporal anomaly and the astral eclipse, he was able to see the Dreadling hordes that had also materialized. The inspector let out a high-pitched scream and ran off through the same gate as the escaping Englishman.

Billy looked up at the eclipse. The tides were turning. The shifting of the sun to its former state brought about panic in the stadium for the Dreadlings. Theodore's bubbling remains sank into the stadium ground. Fluids and intestines littered the field, but the creature's bones and flesh oddly sank away.

The Dreadling horde's piercing war cry burst a shot of adrenaline through Billy's heart. He flicked his wrists and stood his little ground, waiting as they dove from the stands above to the field. The waning eclipse seemed to be sending the Dreadlings back to Hell quite fast. In their last efforts, they charged again. A back handspring past second base kept Billy free from the horde's reach. Then, pirouettes and a ballet jump called the grand jeté sent Billy jumping over one Dreadling and gave him some space. He was in command of this little body, and its muscle memory seemed so fluid as he fought.

Billy slashed at the horde as they climbed over one another to get at him in left field. His blades effortlessly pierced with each pirouette. It wasn't long before he'd slayed a dozen, then two dozen. Home plate saw fifty or so of the beasts charge past toward Billy, and as he got ready to strike again, he heard Frank's voice echo through the stadium.

"Forget about the Dreadlings, kid! Come to the garden!"

Billy listened. He tore an opening to the garden with his righteous blade, disappearing and leaving the horde behind.

Standing by the pond, Billy saw the warm smile of his friend once again. "Welcome home, kid."

Frank patted Billy on the shoulder, and they sat at the familiar golden bench near the pond.

"That was quite the show down there."

"Yeah, I should have scalped some tickets beforehand. I could have made a killing."

Frank laughed. "You see that?" He pointed to the pond.

Billy watched as the pond water showed the Toronto skyline and the red eclipse ending. The day was theirs again.

"That was a temporal anomaly. Celia weakened the veil between worlds to summon that toad and that Dreadling army."

"That was some crazy shit, Frank."

The old man chuckled. "I know."

Billy kept watching the pond while Dreadlings started to burst and smoke like overdone popcorn in the returning sun.

"Does Celia still wield power over the Dreadlings?"

"We don't know, to tell you the truth. I know that the hundreds she summoned are bursting to ash in the returning sun, as you can see. As for whether or not she can call on them again, I'm not certain."

"I should take her out now while she's on the run."

"You have the garden's healing protection again, but it doesn't mean a Dreadling can't drag you to Hell through a portal if they get hold of you. So, be careful and escape here if you need to."

Billy smiled. "You see those dance moves, old-timer? They can't handle this."

"Hah." Frank gloated and smiled a little. "I told you that body was good! Jokes aside, though, we've still got to be cautious. Down there, they would take you so deep below, I don't even know that I could find you. It'd be worse than Theodore's digestive tract this time."

"I didn't think anything could be worse. So, what's the plan now, Frank?"

"Wait here. Here you can keep an eye out for Celia more easily. We've tried to follow her on foot before, and it wasn't so great. You can watch for her from the pond and scan the city faster, you know? When the time is right, we can strike that final blow. We know what she looks again now anyway."

"How will I know when it's time to strike?"

Frank put his hand on Billy's shoulder once more. "You will."

26

Afraid now, more than she'd ever been, Celia stumbled breathlessly into a piss-smelling stairwell between boarded-up buildings. She was angry, and hungry, and on the run. Her last stand was a disaster. Theodore had been eviscerated in the fucking SkyDome before her eyes. Like the coward she was, she'd fled at the first sign of the tides turning.

Now, she wandered the streets of Toronto. She knew going back to her condo was no option. Billy Walker was her mistake. How was she to know that one man marked for death by disease would also be marked for righteous revenge by her selfish actions? She had created a monster.

The sorrow of her current state sank in deep in the summer heat. It was her new reality. There would be no more blissful mortal delights while Billy Walker lurked about, hunting her. Instead, Celia was consumed by emotions she'd never had to embrace: worry, anxiety, fear. She was living the mortal experience and all that it entailed. She flicked her wrist, tightly clutching her dark scythe as it appeared. Then, she tried stamping the ground to summon a single Dreadling. Celia stamped on the concrete stairwell ground over and over in a panic. Nothing.

A young man looked at Celia, confused, as he saw her empty hands slamming nothing with fury and panic in the stairwell. "Do you need help?"

"Fuck off!"

The young man just shook his head and walked on.

She'd lost control. Her new mortal heart sank, along with her body. Celia slid onto a deflated cardboard box and sat in the stench of that stairwell. She let her gaze drift into a trance of anxiety and worry.

She knew she had two options: run for days or kill Billy Walker herself — if she was lucky. After the acceptance of her consuming self-pity, Celia stood up and walked the city streets. Her anger spread infectiously. It spread like tainted vines of darkness. Murderous thoughts fluttered through her mind again. The thought that all she'd gained, all she'd sacrificed, could be jeopardized by a man cast into the slender frame of a twelve-year-old ballerina. The way he'd moved about, dancing as he slayed her Dreadlings — it infuriated her and it terrified her. She told herself that she was a demon, born in fire, older than Billy Walker could ever contemplate. She told herself that if anyone could send him back to the afterlife, it was her. She tried to build up her confidence, and then a familiar voice shattered it.

"He's coming for you, Celia."

She knew it was Lucifer. His voice echoed everywhere and nowhere without a trace. His distracting voice had taken Celia's focus away. She tripped over a homeless person laid out on an air vent for warmth.

"FUCK!" she yelled, unable to suppress the rising anger. A couple walking by holding hands jumped at her sudden outburst. They shook their heads in disgust, and Celia sneered back at them. She'd decided then and there what she was doing: she had to run. She had no choice. She would take off to a distant place and hide from Billy, forever — hopefully.

Eateries were busy with patrons, streets were filled with traffic, and Celia was trying to subtly disappear. She would head to Union Station and board a train out of Toronto. She didn't know where, but she had to escape. She slipped by the greenery of a nearby park. An older man sitting at a bench threw cracked corn for pigeons like they were his only friends in the world. Celia walked through the flock angrily, and the birds took to the sky. The curses of their caretaker never touched her ears because Union Station was in her sights, and fleeing like those very birds was all that was on her mind.

Celia stepped up to the line with the rest of the lot and looked at her options. She instantly knew where she would go. She'd move about until she hit Montreal. She would go to Central Station. She thought about it for a moment. She'd do just fine there, she told herself. She did after all speak every language known to the mortals and even ones unknown.

"Montreal, please."

Billy knelt by the pond's edge and watched through reflections. Glimpses of Celia's whereabouts through electronic screens and even the occasional eyes of an angelic soldier would appear. She couldn't hide.

Frank stepped beside Billy and put a hand on his shoulder once again. "It's time, isn't it, Frank?"

"She can certainly run, but she can't hide."

Billy looked up at his old friend, awaiting his next words.

"She will fight you; she will have to."

"I know."

"She's a demon, kid, through and through. She'll stop at nothing to get what she wants. and you know what that is."

"Me, to die."

"Watch for her to summon portals. Remember how she cast your soul below in the beginning."

"I remember."

"Then, go. Before she boards that train..."

Billy stood up and waited a moment with Frank until he saw a glimpse of Celia's whereabouts through the crystal pond water again.

"See you soon, old friend," Billy told Frank and slipped through the pond into the lively Toronto streets.

Frank sat down, leaning back against a huge amethyst by the water's edge as his hunter disappeared. There he waited and watched to see what Billy Walker had in store for the demon that stole everything from him.

27

Billy heard the familiar snap of his portal closing behind him. He hadn't had much choice but to appear in plain sight. He knew no portal was seen by a mortal, but still, to have a little girl just appear from nowhere was not ideal. He looked around crowded Union Station; he'd appeared in a corner of the building. Men and women dressed in business attire paid no attention to him, and that was good. He'd seen Celia through the mirrored waters of the garden's pond. She'd walked through the crowds and made her way to the boarding area outside. She was looking to disappear, and Billy was not going to let that happen.

He casually flowed through the crowded station toward the train boarding area and eventually near a platform where many waited. Billy hung back in the masses, peeking through crowds from behind a trash and recycling bin combo. He hadn't seen Celia, but she couldn't be far, he knew it. He was looking for his silver sunglasses, but perhaps she'd grown wise to it. When he'd last seen her through the pond, she still wore them and that baby-blue shirt he'd bought Tina.

He scanned patiently until the baby-blue shirt and jeans of a young woman drew suspicion. Her dark hair and build looked like what Billy had seen of Celia's new body. It was her; he could feel it. The thought arose of flicking his wrist, summoning one of his two blades, then sinking it into her back. Then he thought better. Just how was he going to do this properly?

Perhaps he would wait until she boarded and then drop inside the train from the pond portal in the garden. Perhaps he would get in the train before her and slice her as she boarded. Now that Celia's summoned eclipse had ended, no one would see him wield his ethereal blades, so a public execution was a possibility. He continued to watch Celia as she stood there waiting.

Only ten minutes were left until she would catch her train to Montreal. *The longest ten minutes in the history of my existence*, thought Billy. He watched her, waiting, scanning the area in paranoia without knowing Billy was mere meters behind her. Then, something or someone seemed to tip her off. Celia turned directly around and looked Billy dead in the eyes as he was crouched behind those waste bins.

The panic in their eyes was shared. Billy saw her sharp breath, and she saw Billy's surprise that he'd been seen. It was time for fight or flight, and again Celia chose flight. A madness took hold of her as she climbed down and dropped to the railway tracks. She sprinted down those tracks and turned a few heads. One worker yelled, "HEY!" They were so focused on Celia's sudden choice that no one saw the little girl in the purple hoodie disappear inside a portal to chase after her. Billy's portal cut true, and he slipped away.

He ran across the garden and caught a quick smile from Frank, then he dropped through the pond, just missing Celia and coming through behind her. Billy's strides were not as long as Celia's and she was out-running him, but he had a solution. She was rounding a turn in the tracks under an overpass and glanced back.

Billy cut a tear with his scythe again and dropped through the pond once more, this time right in front of Celia. Her dark scythe clashed with his righteous blade, and like thunder they echoed through the railyard underpass.

"Nowhere to run, Celia."

"I'll kill you again!" she screamed, slashing unmercifully at Billy.

A pirouette to the right made Celia miss, and a split jump over her second swing made her miss a second time. He smashed his sunlit blade against hers twice as they battled and dodged. Celia leapt back and then lunged forward with a surprise slash, and yet again Billy spun backward, making her miss.

"You're as dead as the day I met you!" she screamed, throwing her scythe like a boomerang at Billy. This time it caught the edge of his thigh, and Billy fell to a knee, wincing in pain. Celia recalled her blade with a flick of the wrist and grasped it with a satisfied smile.

"What..." she said with an accompanying cackle and continued. "They told you ballet would save your life? I've wielded this weapon longer than your existence, Billy Walker."

She was right, thought Billy. If he was going to overcome her, he needed to do better.

Celia wound up and repeatedly threw her scythe, trying to split Billy apart. He swatted it away and rolled against the stone railyard in pain. The wound from Celia's blade still stung terribly. Billy thought about it; he needed to get back to the garden and heal. Things of this world didn't seem to hurt him, but Celia's blade was. He wasn't healing fast enough, like he'd thought he would, and Frank had been right. Celia was still an ancient demon and a threat. She began to close in and faked a throw again, trying to mislead Billy or catch him off guard.

In the midst of their battle, a distraction... A maintenance car came around the corner, and a worker in an orange vest stepped out.

"You've got about two minutes before a train comes flying down these tracks!" he pleaded with them, stretching out his hand for them both.

Billy and Celia were at a standstill for the moment with the truck in between them. It was Celia that made the first move, throwing her dark scythe so fast at Billy that he had no choice but to drop. The stone-hard ground hurt against his little knees. Behind him, Billy saw the shock of a man hold his hand to his chest. The worker didn't know what hit him and sank to the ground with the ethereal blade of a reaper still clean through to his back.

"No!" Billy cried as he saw the man go down. There was no time for sympathies, though, because Celia was over him with her dark blade back in hand, leaning in for the kill.

"I just wanted freedom!" She pulled back and swung wildly, clashing with Billy's scythe over and over as he tried to hold strong on his back.

"You were going to die anyway. What was the difference!" Celia screamed as Billy rolled back and forth on the tracks.

The clacking of a train in the distance, pulsing, pushing against the steel tracks, struck fear in Billy's heart.

He'd come full circle now. He was back in the same situation he'd met Celia to begin with. Only this time, he had no desire to die. With a strike that should have cut him in two, the twisted vine shaft of Billy's scythe saved him. He held it out like it was about to give one of his good old hockey rec league lads a stiff crosscheck. Celia pressed down from above him with all her weight, and Billy didn't know how long this little frame could hold out. Her body was so much larger, stronger, he could feel it. Now was the time, he thought. She had seemed to have forgotten what he had...

Billy summoned the dark blade of Devlin Gainsmore in his left hand and slammed the evil scythe from up and under into Celia's black heart.

Consumed by Billy's death, she never saw it coming. Billy kicked her back, and she stumbled away, falling to her knees on the tracks. He stood up. Blood dripped from Celia's mouth as she coughed and winced. Her scythe disappeared from her grasp, and Billy knew he'd won. Celia took one last look at him from her new body and with her last ounce of strength spat her mortal blood at Billy. He felt the winds of death flow through the end of the tunnel and stepped off the railway tracks, leaning against the adjacent wall just in time.

The red mist of Celia's mortality were her only remains as the train whistled by with a redundant warning whistle. Billy had indeed succeeded. He didn't know what would become of Celia, but there was solace as the wind of the train brushed his face. There was solace in knowing that another mortal would never be tempted by that demon's deceptions.

—

Billy sliced a tear in the fabric of reality and stepped into the warmth and glow of his garden. Everything seemed somehow different and yet the same. He saw Frank and drew nearer. The old man reached out and hugged him, but this time Billy leaned in from above and wrapped his much larger arms around Frank.

"I knew you'd set things straight, kid. The second they told me your story, I knew you were the one to sort them out."

"What will become of me now, Frank?"

"Take a look in the pond."

Billy walked over, somewhat reluctant but curious. He felt different; he could tell his stature had changed. In the water's reflection he saw that he was the way he used to be. Billy Walker saw himself for the first time again as the man he once was.

Frank came and stood beside him at the pond's edge, then clapped his hands together with a grin. "Mazel tov!"

"C'mon, Frank," Billy said with a joking smile.

"Look again, kid."

Billy looked down into the water and saw...her.

Tears welled as she walked through clouds and through the beauty of a rainbow-kissed landscape. Tina was more stunning than he remembered, and it was certain that he still loved her.

"She's waiting for you, kid. Listen, I need to tell you something."

Billy looked up from the calm reflection in the water.

"It wasn't her fault entirely, the infidelity. She still loves you, Billy. You know that?"

"You mean?"

"There is more to her story and more to yours, if you'll hear it."

Frank waved his hand over the water again, and it went clear.

"We learned about a certain deliveryman when he dropped a package off to Celia — that temporal anomaly from the stadium. The day you came home early from work, it was that same deliveryman with Tina."

The pond water shifted again, and to Billy's surprise the deliveryman he'd caught with Tina came into sight.

Billy quickly pieced things together but let Frank continue.

"That deliveryman, he's not a man at all. We didn't know how bad it was, but it's like I told you before, you got hit worse than anyone. That's why we gave you the chance to clear it all up."

"I've made peace with all that. Besides, I don't know if I have it in me to go after another demon after all that."

"I just wanted to let you know, kid, it wasn't Tina's fault entirely. That demon of lust — it seduced her."

"The past doesn't matter now. We can start anew, can't we, Frank?"

Frank smiled and put a hand on Billy's shoulder. "You're right. You can start anew. You don't have to go after this guy. We just wanted to clear the air."

Billy looked to the pond again. Tina stood peacefully in a field of the most colorful and heavenly array of flowers he'd ever seen. She was happy, truly happy. He knew she would be fine, and he knew he would do this one last job for Frank.

Frank spoke again. "You did everything we asked you to, kid. I won't ask for more. All we wanted was you to sort out the mess you stepped into when you agreed to let Celia mark you with her scythe, and you did that."

Billy looked at Frank. "Tina is happier than I've ever seen. I suppose one last favor for an old friend wouldn't be out of the question..."

Frank smacked his hands together and grinned. "One last time then!"

Billy looked into the water as it shifted, and so did his stature. He was in the ballerina's body once again. "One last time," he whispered.

Billy lunged into the water without hesitation and flew into that same quiet Little Italy alley. The same restaurant worker he'd seen the first time he came out in this alley stared at him.

"What the...where'd you just come from?" The man smiled at Billy, recognizing him. "Why are you always in this alley anyway? You hungry? Why not come in the restaurant. Lunch is on me today, okay, kid?"

As the questions were asked, Billy just smiled and walked on by. "Thank you, but I'm doing just fine."

He heard the man mumble the same sentiment as before, "strange kid," and Billy was gone.

The next block brought about the digital billboard of a popular fast-food place, and Billy stared up.

"Hey, kid. This delivery guy, we have eyes on him now. Rumor has it he always does the same route. Looks like he's headed down to three different spots. He's got to drop off a package at a sex toy shop, a skyscraper, and finally a car dealership. It was my mistake sending you back to Little Italy through the pond. Sorry about that."

"It's fine Frank. How soon before he's at the sex toy shop then?" Billy quickly thought the better of himself, realizing he was back in a child's body. "Never mind, Frank. What about the car dealership?"

"It's by the Distillery District. You've got a good twenty minutes to get comfortable, I'd say. We have eyes on him right now."

Billy ran off for cover, and when he snuck behind to the garbage dump area of the fast-food restaurant, he closed two wooden doors behind him. Then, with the flick of his wrist and the slice of his blade, he was off and running through the garden. Billy hovered over the water, waiting, watching. Then when the time was right, he jumped into the pond and came out exactly where he desired: the bathroom stall of an expensive sports car dealership.

He would look suspicious being a little girl in such a place. If anyone asked, he thought, he was waiting for his dad to get off work. Billy tucked his purple hoodie overtop his little head and went to work. He thought about Tina and how happy she'd looked. He thought about how much he needed her, how much he still loved her, and how much he wanted to hold her and breathe her in once again. Then, even though he'd told Frank he'd made peace with all this, he couldn't help but grow angry that another demon had somehow infiltrated his life, and he'd only just now found out. He would rid Toronto of its last possession as one last favor to Frank and the city he loved.

Billy watched as a brown delivery van pulled up beside the dealership and put its four-ways on. The deliveryman, around thirty-something, stepped out, and Billy recognized him immediately. To his surprise, though, no flashes or trauma from the day he'd fallen apart haunted him now. He just felt — nothing. The relief of seeing Tina at peace had eased him. Billy walked over to the front entrance of the business, slowing his pace just a little.

He eyed the deliveryman from the service waiting area.

"Little girl, can I help you?" asked a worker.

"I'm waiting for my dad, thanks."

The worker smiled and walked over to the service desk.

When the deliveryman came in with a cart of boxes, Billy moved in cautiously. The door was propped open, and the deliveryman fiddled with his flatbed cart. He bent down to adjust something, and Billy's pace and stride increased. The demon in the man seemed to pause. He sniffed the air as Billy was mere feet away, but it was too late. Billy had slid by and slammed his righteous blade effortlessly into the deliveryman's chest. He'd done it as quickly as he'd called it forth. Billy's stride never slowed after that. He didn't turn until he'd crossed the car lot. Then and only then did he take in his handiwork.

He watched the demon trembling in agony, consumed by righteous light and smoking into oblivion. Mortals surrounded the convulsing body, but they didn't know what had truly happened. When just the vessel lay bare at the dealership storefront, Billy recalled his scythe and left Toronto for the final time.

—

Frank sat with a smile on his favorite bench by the pond's edge, and Billy greeted him.

"Did you see that then?"

"Yeah, I saw."

"Why couldn't the others have been that easy?" Billy asked sarcastically.

"Hah, come on. One outta three ain't bad, kid. You really took him by surprise."

Billy smiled and sat down beside Frank. "That was the goal."

"You've really gotten good at this demon hunter thing. You sure I can't convince you to hunt down just one more? It's an interesting one this time, you know..."

"Thank you, Frank, but after seeing Tina and knowing what I know about it all, I just want peace at her side."

Frank stood up and stared down into the calm pond water. "We thought you might say that," he said with a grin. "That's okay. You did everything and more than we'd ever hoped. You're totally redeemed now. You can pass through those gates, even."

Billy looked down and saw Batariel at the gates. He stood up and looked at Frank. "Thank you for this second chance. Thank you for all of this, Frank."

"Thank you, kid, for giving me hope and strength in times of doubt and for reminding me that faith has power."

"Will I see you again?"

"One day, when my work is done."

Frank put a hand on Billy's shoulder, and together they looked into the pond one last time.

"Goodbye, my friend."

"Goodbye, Billy Walker. You're a man of righteousness. Remember to walk uprightly."

Billy stepped into the pond for the last time, and Frank smiled. He sat down at the pond edge and leaned his back against a large amethyst, watching Billy embrace Tina. They held hands, walking through the shimmer of a rainbow and through the whitest of clouds into the wonders beyond.

After the pair faded into the distance, Frank pulled out some deflated balloons from his jacket. He whistled a little tune and let the holy waters of the garden fill each of them. He would be going to see about a woman who had been wrongfully dragged to Hell's Gate by a horde of Dreadlings. He already had a body picked out for his new hunter, and he already had a target. A demon had cast down the soul of a daredevil billionaire and jumped into the body when it was revived from a heart attack...

Epilogue

Celia looked down at her hands. She looked as she had before all of this. She felt her forehead now — no horns. She questioned; was she a mortal? The overwhelming smell of rot rising from below terrified her, unlike it used to. She was in a line-up of some kind. Quivering mortals all around her stood amidst yellow ash and smoke. The brimstone landscape led to the edge of a cliff where she saw — him. The Mirror Man stood in wait, and when she turned in fear to flee, he looked at her from a distance, and now she couldn't move. That shimmering, mirrored face drew her in. She tried to move, she tried to fight it, but it was inevitable.

"You deserve to be here!" the Mirror Man accused.

"I work here!" she cried out.

"Not anymore," he replied. Then, with the flick of his index finger, Celia was cast into the air to fall into the pit of despair.

Time was of no purpose now. Celia tried to close her eyes and failed while falling for what seemed like an eternity. She knew the fall wasn't over until her heart sank in sadness, and my how it did sink. When she finally hit the ground, the stench of it all grew even worse. Dreadlings hissed at her, and she saw the fiery gates she'd gone through so many times before in the distance. The horde closed in, and out of habit she flicked her wrist. Nothing appeared. She was without hope and stripped of it all. The red arachnid eyes, the darkness of the horde smothering her, it was all-encompassing. Celia felt the pierce of their searing claws.

Her wounded carcass was thrown down in front of a familiar face. It was Vilkaris the foul, keeper of Theodore. She tried to get up, she tried to speak, but her voice was gone.

Vilkaris grinned, leaning over Celia with glowing green antenna in the darkness. "Fresh meat," he said.

He grabbed Celia by the hair and lifted her off the ground. She knew what was next. Just as she'd foreseen, Vilkaris's other palm, festering with maggots, was driven down into her face, and the wriggling of the tiny white parasites infested her. Vilkaris stood her up in front of a large, familiar cave: Theodore's cave. Celia barely stood, coughing, with a stomach full of maggots, at the cave's mouth. She thought Billy Walker had slain the beast, and then she thought better of herself. The rotting thirty-foot remains of Theodore appeared and shook the ground. The gaping wound that Billy had cut out of his guts was indeed closed, but with a festering scar. The beast had respawned in the depths of Hell.

Celia waved her hands. She tried to plead but couldn't speak. When she gathered enough strength to try to run, the slug-man caught her by the arm and tossed her in the air as though she was weightless. The stickiness of Theodore's warm tongue pressed against her, and she was snapped into his cavernous mouth. The warmth of the beast's esophagus disgusted her as digestive muscles swelled.

Celia thought about Theodore's constipation. She was not about to get stuck in his colon, or anywhere farther down, for that matter. She waited until she felt her feet dangling, and then when she fell, she kept herself afloat treading about in his stomach. She swam over to the side and clutched one of his rotting ulcers.

Celia looked across the rising tides of the beast's innards and saw the smirking face of a white-haired man who twirled his mustache at each end. Stunned, she now knew what had happened to her boss. Apparently, Malgore the reaper keeper had been stripped of his position and status altogether.

He spoke calmly. "Well, hello, Celia. I'd recognize those pretty eyes even without that demonic fire in them."

Celia did not respond; she could not. Instead, she kept her eyes locked on Malgore.

"Ah, they've taken your voice, have they? I've seen that before..." Malgore flashed a sinister grin and kept floating.

As she treaded acid, Celia knew she was about to fight for space in Theodore's stomach. My, how she shouted lamentations about her choices. Then, as clear as he had said it the first time, she heard *his* voice in her mind.

"You shall be as the mortals."

Manufactured by Amazon.ca
Bolton, ON

33666816R00146